Known Order Girls

Andrew Butters

Cover design and layout by Linda Ryan
Cover art by Carol Bloomgarden (carolbloomgarden.com)

Potato Chip Math Creations
New Brunswick, Canada
potatochipmath.com

Known Order Girls

Andrew Butters

For Pants and Dude.

Author's Note:

I would like to extend a proper doffing of my cap to Isaac Asimov, whose short story, *The Last Question*, and the supercomputers, Multivac and Microvac, contained therein inspired the Commander and Mercury computers used in this story. If you're a science fiction fan, check out Asimov's work.

—Andrew Butters, March 2024

Whereas the short-term impact of AI depends on who controls it, the long-term impact depends on whether it can be controlled at all.

—Stephen Hawking

OOOOOOOO
[Zero]

Carlton Sedgwick paced in front of the desk in his lab and quizzed his lab assistant and closest confidant, Isaac Valderrama, on the procedure.

"Do you understand what you're supposed to do?" Carlton ran his hands through his thinning gray hair.

"Completely."

"There can't be any deviations."

"There won't be." Isaac clenched his teeth and swallowed.

"Recite it back to me." Carlton leaned against his desk and folded his arms.

"You lie down in the stretcher at the side of the plastic tub in the containment chamber. I hook the IV into the PICC line you've already got in your arm. Once you give me the word, I inject the general anesthetic. Once you're unconscious, I give you the diazepam-digoxin-morphine sulfate-amitriptyline cocktail. I confirm death, put on my chemical protective suit, and slowly slide you into the tub filled with concentrated sodium hydroxide, making sure to keep the rubber stretcher between me and the chemical bath. Then I exit the chamber, close the door behind me, take off the suit, and wait. Once you are sufficiently"—his voice hitched and he inhaled deeply to collect himself— "once you are sufficiently dissolved,

I push the green button to start the timer and press the red button to release the aluminum tubes. Once the last tube is in the tub, I turn on the gas by your workbench and exit the lab, leaving the door unlocked. I walk home via the exact route you specified. When I hear the explosion and the sirens, I do not pick up the phone to make a call. I wait for it to ring. When it does, I sound surprised. When the authorities come, I act inconsolable."

"Good. They're going to question you after this. They may even arrest you."

"I'm prepared. The answer to every question is 'no' or 'I don't know.' Aside from what happens here, now, it's not a lie. I don't know anything. In fact, I know less than they do about your work."

Carlton stood up and put his hands on Isaac's shoulders. "They won't believe you. For thirty generations, we've protected this and only provided enough to outside influences to move humanity forward, albeit slowly. We've gone to great lengths to ensure a single chain of humans is involved, and no computer has spent so much as a millisecond connected to the internet. They will not accept that it's all lost forever."

Isaac pulled his friend into an embrace. "I want to know more."

"You can't. It's not safe for you or for humanity."

"You're being hyperbolic."

Carlton broke from Isaac's hug and stood ramrod straight. "I'm not. You don't realize how special you are. You're one of a thousand people in the world, if that, whose brains are clean. Since Shared Intellect and Inherited Consciousness was created thirty Carlton Sedgwicks ago, only a few people have opted out. You come from the longest known line of those who have. It's why I chose you."

Isaac shook his head. "Once scientists understood dark matter, dark energy, and quantized gravity to build Grand Unified Theory, there was nothing left to discover. There are no more unanswerable questions. We live as part of The Known Order. What of The Association? Surely they have the Commander computer and countless humans working around the clock to fill in the gaps you and all your predecessors intentionally left."

"You are aware of the differences between information, knowledge, and wisdom, yes? All you need to know is Commander X-15 possesses the sum total of worldly information and The Association the sum total of knowledge. I and I alone, thanks to my twenty-nine former physical hosts, possess the wisdom. No one can be trusted with it. No one can, not anymore, and certainly not The Association. It must die with me."

"I understand."

Carlton met his assistant's eyes. "Do you?" Isaac nodded. "Good. It's time."

Carlton stripped off his clothes and entered the clear acrylic containment chamber. It took some doing to find six seven-foot by seven-foot sheets, discretely acquire them, and get them into the lab, but he'd made more than a few friends over the years and he got it done. Room darkening fabric with thermal image blocking capabilities adorned the windows. Eavesdropping-proof devices sit every few feet apart around the perimeter of the room. With everything in place, he lay face up on the stretcher, being careful to not touch the inside of the tub. Isaac attached the IV into his PICC line.

"Goodbye, Isaac."

"Goodbye, Doctor Sedgwick, all thirty versions of you."

Carlton Sedgwick fell unconscious and before his smile faded, he was dead.

00000001
[One]

My name was Katherine Webb, and from a young age, I knew I was different. One normalizing attribute I possessed was my love of drawing. My complexion and hair color made for striking self-portraits. Despite my inexperience, I became quite adept at capturing my likeness and the likenesses of others. My mother, Petra, was an engineer, and my father, Oswald, was an expert in historical mathematics and an Intelligence Officer at the most prestigious university in The Known Order North American Region. I took after them in many ways, though unlike them I liked to draw. I doodled on the edges of my learning tablet, erasing them in haste to avoid detection. I drew faces and lines in the bathroom when steam blanked the mirror, wiping the drawings away in short order to remove all evidence.

I lived in a world where I could get the answer to every conceivable question, but bathroom mirrors still fogged up. The lack of flying cars, for personal use at least, bothered me more than it should have given my age, a year removed from getting my autonomous hover car learner's permit.

My much younger brother, Chadwick, revered me as less experienced siblings tended to do. Not quite ten years my junior, he prepared to enter school in the fall. He was a spitting image of his father, tall, with olive skin and straight chestnut brown hair. By looking at him, you'd have never guessed our relationship. He wasn't aware of what our parents did for a living, and he didn't much seem to care. I looked after him in the mornings before I left for school and afterward before our parents came home from work.

It wasn't a massive undertaking due to negligible crime and no activity occurring unless approved by Commander. In the event of a problem, the great computer ensured the proper help arrived in time. Nothing ever went wrong, though. It's the way things were.

On one particular afternoon, I wasn't drawing. A long jump rope tied to the end of the downspout at the edge of my driveway received all my focus. The other end was tied to a handle attached to a large circular metal frame which resembled an old barrel strap from before The Wars. My mother attached a motor to the metal frame. A simple control knob adjusted the speed as it spun the frame in a circle along with the attached handle, and with it, the jump rope. It allowed me to skip without the assistance of another person. Chadwick was too little to work the rope to my satisfaction.

That day, he drew with chalk on the driveway. The "multi-surfaced intelligent solar array driveway panel," as the brochure called it, allowed for an immersive Before Times analog experience if you paid the extra money for the feature, of course. Our parents did, and at that moment, Chadwick delighted over it. His art skills weren't as advanced as mine at that age but were nonetheless impressive. He put the finishing touches on a lion, another ancient relic he would never see alive, and moved his way down the driveway to start a new creation.

"Chadwick! What do you think you're doing?"

"Drawing with the old-timey chalks, see?" He held up his hands, both covered in white dust and then wiped them on the front of his shirt.

"I see that, and you're doing a fantastic job, but—"

"Thanks, Katie. It's a lion."

"I see that, too, and it's a beautiful lion, but you can't leave it there without asking Commander first."

He stared at his right wrist, around which wrapped a small black band. He tapped the screen. "Commander, I drawed a lion, see?" He pointed the bracelet at his picture on the driveway. "Can I keep it?" The screen flashed solid green for three seconds and issued an audible *bing*.

"Yay!" he rejoiced as he clapped his hands. Any chalk dust not stuck to the front of his shirt wafted out from between his palms in little puffs. Before he returned to his new project, he furrowed his brow. "Katie?"

"Yes, little brother."

"Why do we have to always ask the Commander about everything?"

"Mum and Dad have explained this to you before, remember?" He shook his head. "Well, it's the first lesson the Intelligence Officers will teach you in school, but I don't think it will hurt for you to get a head start on it. Would you like to hear?" He nodded, and tufts of his long, thin hair flopped in front of his eyes.

"Okay, sit down on the garden edge, cross your legs, and I'll tell you about the time before people knew any better." I turned off my jump rope machine and joined him beside the front yard garden.

"Things never used to be safe or clean. Conflict and danger existed for everyone. Entire continents fought with each other. Where we live now, in the North American Region, was the worst. Commander didn't exist." His eyes went wide, and his mouth opened but made no sound. "I know, right? Imagine a world without Commander."

"Must've been bad."

"Different, but not better. Imagine all sorts of technologies and gadgets and things, but no one in charge. Every person for themselves, on their own, them against the *world*." I lifted my arms above my head and spread them apart in a big sweeping motion. "A Commander prototype existed, but only a small group of scientists had access. Then The Wars happened. The fighting killed *billions*."

"Katie, is that a lot?"

"It is. More than you can count."

"I don't know how high I can count."

"Trust me; it's more than either of us can."

"More than Mom and Dad?"

"Probably, but it doesn't matter because we don't have to count that high. We can get Commander to do it for us." He nodded, and this explanation appeared to satisfy him. "After The Wars, the winning side teamed up with the people left over—the ones with all the money, and they decided enough was enough."

"Enough of what?"

"All the fighting and destruction and"—I could see him getting upset—"all the bad things. They took control of Commander and told everybody, everyone left in the whole world, that they were in charge now and with Commander, they would fix it all and make it better."

"Whoa. Did they make it better, Katie?"

"You tell me, little brother. Do you see any crime?"

"What's crime?"

"Exactly. What about fighting? Do you see people fighting?"

"No."

"What about people without homes or proper clothes or food?"

"Nuh-uh. Everyone has all the things."

"Then I guess it worked."

He sat silent for a minute, occasionally reaching for a tomato plant leaf growing in the garden. I wasn't sure if I overwhelmed him with information and lost him or if any of it stuck. I let the moment be and sat beside him in silence as well. He let go of the tomato leaf and tapped my knee with his index finger. "Sissy?"

"Yes, little brother."

"I still don't know why I have to ask Commander if I can draw another picture."

A soft chuckle escaped me. Pride in my historical storytelling ability overrode the fact he asked a question in the first place. "Right, I completely forgot. Sorry, little man. You see, Commander knows everything."

"Even what I think?"

"Well, not everything, I guess, because as far as I know, it can't know *that*. But it does know the answer to any question you can ever think to ask, except for one."

"Which one?"

"Something about entropy."

"What's entrofee?" His head tilted to one side like a confused puppy.

"Entropy, with a 'P.'" I drew the word on the driveway with his chalk. I let him study the word for a bit and then wiped it away with the palm of my hand. "I don't know what it is, the Intelligence Officers don't teach that lesson for a couple of years, but I do know that not too long ago, a man asked Commander a question about it, and it didn't respond green with the *bing* sound, and it didn't respond red with the *bong* sound either. It displayed the message that it didn't have enough information but would work on it. It can answer any other question, though, *and* it knows how it will affect everything and everyone else in the entire world. When you asked it if you could do another chalk drawing, it calculated what would happen in front of our house, on the sidewalk, the street, and everyone else's houses and driveways from here clear across the globe. Since it didn't calculate a bad result, it gave you the green answer and the *bing* sound."

"I could have told it my drawings wouldn't hurt anyone."

"I know, little brother, I know, but I only know that because I know you. Commander doesn't know you like I do or Mommy and Daddy do, though. It has to do the calculations and decide for itself."

He nodded in acceptance of this new information and flopped himself back onto the driveway, reaching for his chalk like a swimmer reaches at the end of a race. I went back to my jump rope machine and cranked the speed up on the motor. After teaching a brief history lesson, I needed to move my limbs to get back into playtime mode. I loved my little brother with all my heart, but I preferred to let our parents teach him stuff. I had my own problems with a disappearing childhood to deal with.

Half an hour later, Dad got home. He pulled into the driveway, and Chadwick scooted out of the way. I undid the jump rope from the handle on the machine to allow the car to pass, and it slid into the garage without a sound.

"Daddy, look at my drawings!"

My father undid his tie and stooped over to admire the chalk drawing creations of his son. "These are fantastic, Chaddy! Did you ask Commander if you can keep them on the driveway until the rain washes them away?"

"Not yet. I'm not sure I wanna. What if it tells me no?"

"If it tells you no, then there's a good reason for it, and you will accept the answer without question. Do you understand?" Chadwick nodded. "Good. Now ask your question and then come in and wash up. You and Kate can help me get dinner ready. We'll surprise Mommy with a big fancy meal when she gets home. How's that sound?"

Chadwick smiled and nodded. He put the chalk back into its container and wiped his hands on his shirt again, this time ensuring full chalk coverage on the entire front. He again pointed the face of his wristband device toward the pictures. "Commander, can I keep these here until the rain washes them away?" Instantly, the watch face turned green and emitted the familiar *bing* sound. He ran to catch up to Dad. "Daddy, Daddy! Commander told me I could keep the drawings!"

"I never had any doubt, Chaddy. They're wonderful drawings, and anyone who passes by and sees them will be most impressed."

Inside, the three of us took off our wristbands and placed them in the charging docks by the front door. The Personal Multipurpose Interaction Devices, or PMID, for which everyone pronounced the acronym "pee-mid," were not required to be worn inside a personal dwelling. Each home came with a charger by the front door and a Commander Connection Pod in every room except the bathroom, for everyone's convenience, of course. We weren't required to use our PMID or consult Commander provided the action remained within our home. In that respect, Commander acted as more of a personal assistant to the household than anything else.

The most common question asked of Commander from inside a personal dwelling around the world was, "What's the weather for tomorrow?" followed by, "What are the winning lottery numbers this week?" In response to the former, Commander had as many answers as days in the year. However, its response to the latter never varied. "I am unable to provide you with that information at this time." You'd have thought people would stop asking, but the way the computer added "at this time" to the end gave enough people hope that maybe one day it *would* give them the answer, and they would find themselves rubbing elbows with members of The Association.

No one in our household played the lottery and hence never asked about the numbers. We all asked about the weather, though. Since we spent our Mondays to Fridays outside the house during the day, we needed to know how to dress. A typical routine for the four of us was to ask Commander the weather and then rummage around in our closets and dressers for what we wanted to wear the next day. After we each settled on an outfit, we laid them across the end of our beds and asked Commander if we picked acceptable attire for the coming day. If approved, we folded them and placed them on a chair or in the closet on a hanger. If not, then we made new choices, and the process repeated until Commander approved.

Mom arrived home as Dad, Chadwick, and I put the finishing touches on dinner. Chaddy did his version of folding napkins and placing them at everyone's spot on the table, Dad set out the protein from the food replicator along with the vegetables, red and yellow peppers from our garden, and I stirred the cheese sauce, taking care to keep from slopping any onto the stovetop.

"Well, isn't this the most wonderful greeting!" Mom said as she placed her PMID into its charger and made her way to the kitchen to give us all hugs and kisses. Chaddy first, followed by me, and then Dad, but she let his hug linger for a moment with his back to the cheese sauce to facilitate dipping her finger in and stealing a taste. Her thieving did not go unnoticed.

"Mommy, you stole the cheese sauce!" Chadwick pointed. She put her finger to her mouth and made the universal *shh* gesture.

Dad broke the hug and looked down at her hands. "Is this true, my love? Am I a pawn used for the sole purpose of getting close to the delicious bowl of cheesy goodness that your daughter spent the last half of her lifetime perfecting?"

"It's true, dear life partner. My love for cheese outweighs my love for you. Don't be upset; it is the way of the world. Commander, is it acceptable for a person to love cheese more than they love their spouse?" The light bulbs in the dining room chandelier flashed green, and a soft *bing* emanated from the nearest Commander Connection Pod.

"Oh, come on now. You've engineered it to give that answer, haven't you? Commander, has Petra scrambled your programming to result in a specific answer to her cheese question?" The lights flashed red, and a soft *bong* echoed throughout the room. "Well, that's great. I bet you programmed the darn contraption to respond to that as well."

Mom sat down at her spot as a devilish grin spread across her face.

"My dear, I don't know of what you speak."

"I knew I should have chosen computer engineering instead of historical mathematics."

"Cheese is good!" Chadwick attempted to pour the sauce onto his plate, and I reached across the table to prevent him from making a mess of things.

"Thank you for the quick hands, Kate. I guess my jump rope device is improving your reflexes."

"No, I happen to spend a lot of time with Chaddy and know one detail with complete certainty. If there's any chance he can make a mess, he will."

Mom laughed and directed her gaze at the front of his shirt. "I see that. He has as much chalk on the front of his shirt as he puts on the driveway. Speaking of which, those are wonderful drawings, Chaddy."

"Thanks, Mommy. Commander let me keep 'em."

"I see that, and why wouldn't it? They are extraordinary works of art."

"That reminds me. Mom, Dad, I gave him a little history lesson outside after school today while he drew, and I jumped rope. I hope that's okay."

Dad's mouthful of food prevented a response. Mom put her cutlery down on her plate and dabbed the corners of her mouth with her napkin. "We trust your judgment, dear. What lesson?"

"About The Before Times and how we all got Commander and why we have to ask it for permission to do everything."

"Wow, that's a big topic, sweetie. Did you have any trouble?"

"Nope. I told him it would be his first lesson from the Intelligence Officers in school and gave him a summary. I could have gone into more detail, but I didn't want him to get, you know, what's the word?"

"Overwhelmed?"

"Yes, exactly. Overwhelmed."

"What a mature way to handle it. Thank you for being such a good big sister."

After dinner, with the leftovers packed away for lunches for the next day, the dishes put into the Kitchen Instawash, and the table linens in the Fabrics Instawash, we adjourned to the living room, where we enjoyed the remainder of our evening routine. Dad bathed Chadwick, and Mom and I read our books. Our parents swapped these roles every other night. The last family activity before Chaddy's bedtime involved asking Commander about tomorrow's weather and picking out our clothes for the next day. Commander approved everyone's choices on the first try.

The next morning, the weather aligned with Commander's prediction, and Chadwick's chalk drawings sat undisturbed on the driveway. He and I received our requisite hugs and kisses from our parents before we got on our respective buses, Chaddy to daycare, me to school, and everyone went about their day.

⁂

As usual, I arrived home first. The bus system set up by The Association ensured later pickup and earlier drop-off times. This facilitated childcare options for families that did not have an adult home to tend to the children during the day. As I skipped my way from the bus up my driveway, I stumbled and fell, wiping away a big swath of Chadwick's lion in the process. A computerized woman's voice spoke from my PMID. "Do you require medical attention, Katherine?"

"No, that's okay, Commander. It's a small scrape, and I can get a bandage on my own."

My wrist display flashed green, and Commander replied, "Acceptable."

I dusted myself off and made my way toward the front door. As I put my hand on the doorknob, my PMID vibrated, and the screen flashed red. "Unauthorized modification to the driveway. Please eliminate."

"Oh, no, Commander. Not Chaddy's lion."

"Unauthorized modification to the driveway. Please eliminate."

My shoulders slumped, and I shuffled my feet to the garden hose. I had sprayed all but the lion's tail away when Chadwick's bus stopped in front of the house. He ran down the steps with his arms waving like a flag in a windstorm. "Kat, what are you doing?"

I stopped spraying the last bit of the tail and hung my head. "I'm sorry, but I slipped and fell and smudged a bunch of the lion. I wanted to leave it to give you a chance to fix it when you got home, but *Commander"* —I spat out its name like it left a sour taste in my mouth—"wouldn't let me go into the house until I removed it, and I needed to get a bandage for my knee."

He pursed his lips and folded his arms. "Did you fall on purpose?"

"No, of course not. I would never do that. I wouldn't want to ruin any of your drawings, either. You'll be a better artist than me any day now."

"Really?"

"Really. Now how about I go in and put a bandage on my knee, and when I come back out, we'll draw a new lion together?"

"Okay!"

I went inside, ditched my PMID at the door, and made a straight line to the bathroom, where we kept the first aid kit. After washing the scrape and applying antiseptic, I bandaged it up, cleaned up the mess, and hurried outside to join my brother. By the time I got there, he'd already made progress on the new lion's face. I grabbed a piece of chalk and worked on the mane.

I wasn't lying when I said he was good. I started drawing before I could talk, and he'd only been drawing a couple of years and was improving rapidly. It wasn't jealousy, though I'll admit to a little bit of it creeping in. To be honest, I experienced more wonder and curiosity. He saw the world in a different light than I did, and that fascinated me. It was my first acknowledgment that two people occupying the same time and space, and sharing the same experience, could have completely different perspectives. As the daughter of two highly intellectual parents, it was a natural next step for me to wonder why and devise ways to find out.

We kept half a dozen styluses of varying sizes inside the garage. I grabbed them and brought them back to where Chaddy sat. I tapped one on the driveway, and a menu popped up and selected "Digital Paper 2 x 2." A two-meter square outline appeared. Using the same stylus, I pressed down on a corner of the shape and dragged it to the center of the driveway, away from the other drawings.

"Hey, Chadwick, come over here for a second; I want to conduct an experiment."

"What's a 'sperimint?"

"Ex-periment. The word looks like this." I wrote it below the box on the driveway. "It means trying something to see what happens."

"Okay."

"Using the stylus, I want you to draw another lion inside this box."

"Why?"

"I want to see the difference between the digital one and the chalk one, that's all."

"Okay."

He knelt and drew. I stood off to the side out of his way and watched. He used a similar technique as when he drew with the chalk but with a much different result. When he finished, he stood up and gave me a big smile.

"I made this one roaring instead of smiling. The shows I watch with Mommy show them roaring all the time."

The kid could out-draw anyone his age; that much was certain, but the digital drawing lacked something I couldn't put my finger on. I glanced from the chalk drawing to the digital one. They were both excellent, especially considering a five-year-old drew them, but the analog picture stood out as superior. We lived in a digital, programmed world, one step removed from preordained, and there sat my little brother, ten years my junior, who still couldn't pronounce all his words and hadn't begun to comprehend conjugations, mastering the lost art of chalk drawing.

It got me thinking.

About what, I wasn't one hundred percent sure, at least not yet, but it did engage the gears in my brain in a way I hadn't experienced in my brief fifteen years of consciousness. The Association stopped calling it "birth" sometime after The Wars when Shared Intellect and Inherited Consciousness entered the mainstream and became accessible—if your family had wealth, of course. One was no longer born; one "entered consciousness." Although neither my brother nor I came into the world with any more consciousness than a discarded shoelace, we weren't "born." We did not have birth certificates, for such an antiquated form of identification no longer served a purpose. No, we had a digital record with a date in the field "First Consciousness." If you had enough money, the field "Last Consciousness" remained blank for hundreds of years, if not longer. Our parents did not have enough money, and as a result, their "Last Consciousness" fields would one day receive a date. Their earthly bodies would return to their origins, and forty-odd years from then, my brother and I would follow.

"Chaddy, why don't you ask Commander if the drawings can be saved?"

"Okay." He looked over at me with an ear-to-ear smile on his face, but it quickly faded. He put his finger to his mouth, and with his other hand, he pointed to me.

I cocked my head and looked down. My clothes and bandage showed no sign of anything unacceptable. I shook my head in confusion. He got up, walked over, and placed his hand on my wrist. I became hyper-alert. Beads of sweat formed on the back of my neck. My breath became short. Realizing every moment counted, and I had already wasted too many of them, I ran into the house. My PMID rested on its charger by the door, flashing red and beeping like an emergency alarm.

"Oh no! Oh no! Oh no! Oh no!"

I grabbed the device from its cradle, snapped it onto my wrist, and cupped my other hand over the top to dampen the sound. My parents and Intelligence Officers would say that in most circumstances, I maintained a serious demeanor and didn't let my emotions swing too far in one direction or the other, but at that moment, tears streamed down my cheeks, my bottom lip quivered, and short, choppy breaths mixed in with the occasional sniffle challenged the PMID alarm for auditory supremacy.

Over my shoulder, I sensed movement and made a slow turnaround. In the doorway stood my little brother, covered head to toe in chalk and holding the hand of a Commander Compliance Coordinator. Everyone called them CCCs since Commander Compliance Coordinator sounded too pleasant, and they were, overall, not at all pleasant. In the presence of one, the experience unsettled even the most complaint of citizens. Until that moment, I'd never encountered one who addressed me directly. Of course, they visited all the classrooms on the first day of school every year, but they always stood at the front beside the Intelligence Officer while they gave their speech about the "importance of compliance." That they never explained what happened if you weren't compliant, I always found rather clever. What people, in particular younger ones, could come up with in their minds often surpassed reality.

"I found this guy on the driveway. He looked upset. You're his sister, Katherine Webb, yes?"

I recognized that the question was rhetorical and didn't answer. Instead, I opted for, "Come inside, Chadwick, and get cleaned up. We can't have you a mess when Daddy gets home." I said the last part looking the CCC dead in the eyes. For half a second, his eyes darted from mine to my wrist and then back to my eyes. My heart pounded in my chest, and the beads of sweat tickled the back of my neck as the cool air from the inside of the house blew past me and out the open front door.

Chadwick came inside, used the special key attached to the charging dock to remove his PMID, and headed to the bathroom to wash up.

"You appear upset." The CCC took a step forward and placed a tall black leather booted foot on the threshold.

I flinched and held tight onto the door handle, not realizing I had removed my hand from over the top of my other wrist. "I—I—I fell, and scraped my knee, see?" I pointed to the bandage on my leg.

"That's a good first aid job you've done there. Do you want to be a doctor or a nurse when you grow up?"

"I haven't asked Commander yet, but we talk about what I might be qualified for at the dinner table. Of course, if Commander disagrees, there's not much I can do about it, but it's fun to talk about the possibilities."

"For a teenager, you speak with the maturity of an adult."

"I'm almost sixteen."

"Yes, I see that." He wore augmented reality glasses that must have displayed my profile and allowed him to keep his hands free. "It says here both your parents work. That's good for them but doesn't leave anyone around to watch you and your brother, does it?" Another question that sounded like one but wasn't. "Doesn't matter. They'll both receive my report as soon as we're done here. Do you have anything else you want to tell me?"

"I didn't mean to. My skinned knee upset me, and I wanted to get back outside to play with Chadwick, and I—I—I guess I forgot. It won't happen again."

"I believe you, Katherine. If I didn't, things would be going in a different direction right now. Do you understand?"

"Yes." I looked at my feet.

"Yes?"

I restored eye contact. "Yes, sir."

"Good. My report will not be too harsh, and there will be no supplemental discipline—this time. Am I clear?"

"Yes, sir. All clear." We held eye contact during a protracted pause. He broke away first, and I considered it a small victory.

"Good." His eyes darted around behind his glasses. "Your father should be home soon. I guess the job of a mathematical historian isn't as demanding as other professions. Commander must not like him."

Enraged, I took a step forward. My toes touched the polished leather boot in the doorway, and I straightened my back to appear imposing. I would have settled for defiant since the CCC still towered over me despite the fact he stood two steps lower. "My father got to *choose* his profession."

He swallowed hard, his Adam's apple bobbed up and down in his throat, and when he spoke, his voice cracked. "You don't say? There's no mention of it in his profile." He removed his foot from the doorway and fidgeted with his tool belt. "Okay then, Katherine, I think we're done here." He pointed to my wrist. "Try to remember to keep your device on your wrist at all times outside the house, okay?"

I nodded, and he turned and walked away toward his hoverbike, sitting idle at the end of the driveway. My eyes stayed fixed on him until he donned his helmet and glided away. The shaking in my hands persisted after I shut the door and ran to my bedroom. I flopped face down on the bed and cried until the sound of the front door opening snapped me out of it. A minute later, as I wiped the tears from my face, a soft knock on the door followed by a soft, deep voice broke the silence.

"Everything okay, sweetie?"

I managed a stifled cry that sounded more like a sick frog. The door opened with caution, and my father's head poked in. "Sweetie, what happened? Why do you have a bandage on your knee?"

I hopped off the bed and ran into his arms. As soon as his arms wrapped around me, the tears returned with more gusto than a few moments earlier. His arms held me tight, and he didn't move or speak until my sobbing abated. He walked over to my bed and sat on the edge. With a slight grunt, he lifted me like he used to do a decade ago and put me on his knee. He tapped my bandage with his finger, though not with enough force to register any pain.

"Now, based on how you ran over to me, I'm guessing this little injury isn't the problem."

"No, Daddy, it's not." I sniffled, and he handed me a tissue.

"Then tell me, what's the problem? Maybe I can help you sort it out."

"You didn't get the report?"

"Report? What report?" He pulled his portable communicator out of his pocket and checked the screen. "No report. No notifications. No alerts." He pointed to my PMID. "Why is this still on your wrist? Did you have a run-in with a CCC?" I nodded, and he tensed up. "Then your mother and I should have received a report. We'll wait for her to come home and see if she got one. In the meantime, how did you resolve the situation? Did they fine you, or did you get a warning? You know what, never mind. We'll wait for your mother to get home, see if she got a report, and we'll take it from there. I'm sure it's nothing to worry about or keep shedding tears over."

I tended to believe my parents when they told me not to worry, but up to that point, not a single worry involved a run-in with a CCC. Dad must have sensed my skepticism and gave me another big hug. "Trust me. It'll be fine. Now go get that infernal device off and find your brother. You can both help me with dinner."

As with most weeknights, Mom arrived home as dinner hit the table. I had calmed myself by then, and explaining everything didn't launch me into hysterics, but the knot in my stomach persisted, and I wasn't the least bit hungry. With everyone around the table and the serving dishes making their way to each person, my father caught my eye and nodded. I nodded in return, but he spoke first.

"Honey, I'm guessing from your lack of mention of it when you got home that you didn't receive a report. Is that a fair statement?"

Mom put the dish of green beans down in front of her and took a sip of her water. "Report? This is the first I've heard of it. What happened?" She cast a glance at me and my brother.

"All I know is it involved an interaction with a CCC this afternoon. Katherine? Kate?" My mom furrowed her brow and made a face as if she were sucking on a lemon.

I recounted the events of the afternoon from the moment I tripped and skinned my knee to when the CCC rode away on his hoverbike. When I finished, my parents stared at each other for a long beat of silence, talking to each other with their eyes. Mom spoke first.

"Well, first of all, this is a non-issue as far as your father and I are concerned. You were a good big sister, you were injured and got yourself bandaged up quite well without anyone else's help, and as soon as you realized your mistake, you not only corrected it straight away, but you accepted responsibility. Those are all good things."

Dad took a sip of water and continued from where Mom had left off. "Can you recall exactly what the CCC said about my job? I need to know the exact words."

I nodded. "He said, 'I guess the job as a mathematical historian isn't as demanding as some others. Commander must not like him,' and then I said, 'My father got to *choose* his profession,' and then he said something about it 'not being in your profile,' and then he left."

My parents looked at each other, immersed in another unspoken conversation.

"Yes, I did get to choose. As did your mother, but here's a point to ponder. Getting to choose your profession doesn't make you any better than anyone else."

"That's right, dear, and on top of that, Commander doesn't have a personality. It can't like or dislike anyone. If you don't get to choose, it calculates where you'd be most effective. It knows everything that ever was and will ever be, so everyone ends up doing what they do best. There's no shame in doing something you are good at, especially when Commander supports that decision with its calculations."

"Then why do some people get to choose while others don't, and if you *can* choose, can you choose anything you want?"

Mom continued, "Well, not quite. You still need to be able to do the job if you want it. If your scores on standardized tests aren't great in human physiology, you're never going to work in the healthcare field. Commander gives a range of possibilities. Some people get to choose from those possibilities, and there are a few reasons for that. You can be a relative of a member of The Association or work for them, and this includes the CCC, Containment Officers, Case Workers, or Intelligence Officers."

Dad jumped in, "In my case, I come from a long line of Intelligence Officers, so there wasn't much question that's where I would land. What I discovered was not only did I want to do it, but I wanted to teach the history of the old ways, mathematically speaking."

"That must be why Chaddy is so good with analog drawing. He likes the old ways, too."

"Not a bad theory."

Chadwick smiled. "I like to draw with chalks. They're messy!"

Mom shook her head but stifled a laugh. Not an easy task, with his thousand-watt grin lighting up the room.

"What about you, Mom? Why did you get to choose?"

My parents shared another wordless exchange, and Mom paused before answering, "Well… it's not as straightforward as your father, but the easiest way to describe it would be I helped out a friend, and they petitioned The Association to let me choose. They agreed, and here we are."

"And you got to pick engineer? Wow!"

Mom blushed. "Yes, well, my scores on the exams were pretty good, so my options were good. This may be what Commander would have assigned me anyway, but we'll never know."

"Your mother is being modest. She scored a perfect 2112 on her exit exams."

My jaw sat agape. "Perfect exit exams? That's—that's—"

"Impressive as-all-get-out? You're damn right it is." Dad's pride was evident. Similar to when I received good grades in school.

We sat and ate in relative silence until we each cleaned our dinner plates and dessert made an appearance. In between bites of apple pie—

made with apples from our garden, of course—I asked more questions. "If getting to choose doesn't make you special, then why did the CCC behave differently once he knew? Why wasn't it listed in either of your profiles? Why didn't he file a report?"

Dad's mouth was full of pie, so Mom answered, "Well, inasmuch as it shouldn't matter if you get to choose or not, it does to certain people. While the public has everything they need, The Association and their friends and family have more—a lot more—and that results in certain people treating them differently. Plus, there's sort of an unwritten code among them."

"A code like a computer code?"

"No, dear, a code like an understanding. A silent agreement. Your father and I aren't big fans of how this works and prefer to be treated like everyone else, like our neighbors, so we requested our profiles not include any information about our choices."

I nodded and finished my pie. My head spun with myriad thoughts, certain that sleep would have trouble finding me, but after my shower and ten pages of a good book, I had a hard time keeping my eyes open. I fell asleep in an instant and dreamed about Chadwick's digital and chalk draw lions frolicking in a stand of apple trees.

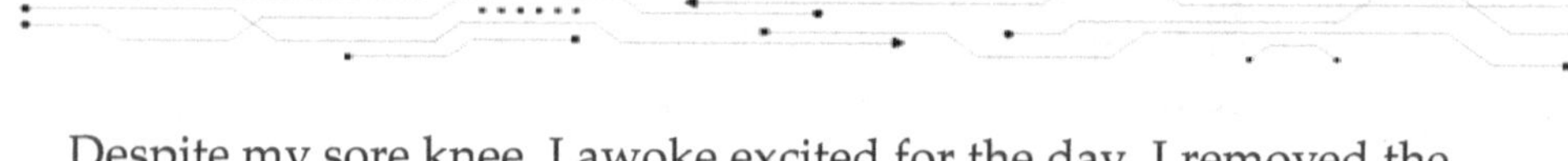

Despite my sore knee, I awoke excited for the day. I removed the dressing and observed that the scrape wasn't the worst part of the injury. That title went to the hellish purple bruise that surrounded it. I made my way to the bathroom, brushed my teeth, put salve on the bruise, antiseptic spray on the scrape, and applied a new bandage. Thoughts of choosing crossed my mind, and a profession as a doctor or healthcare provider stood out among them. Intelligence Officers always told us to "create and maintain a set of goals."

OOOOOOIO
[Two]

Fifteen months passed without incident or surprise, which aligned with The Known Order, pleasing my parents and, of course, The Association. I didn't need a single bandage for a thorn prick from the garden, let alone one for another scraped knee. No one in the family forgot to wear their PMID when they left the house. No run-ins with a CCC. Both Mom and Dad worked their jobs, with Dad always coming home first. My brother and I helped with dinner. Chaddy started school one month after "the incident" and advanced much faster than his classmates, and he showed a remarkable aptitude for all things analog. This fascinated me more than anything.

A week before my seventeenth birthday, I got an idea for my birthday party. I chose the theme The Before Times, and we would adorn the house with decorations from way back before Commander, and we would play games from before the all-knowing computer became a glint in Carlton Sedgwick's eye.

I pitched the idea to my parents at the dinner table that night, and they agreed it was splendid. Chadwick's excitement exceeded ours, though.

"Analog games?" A wide, toothy smile stretched across his face.

Mom laughed. "Looks like you didn't quite think this one through, Kate. Those types of games are right in his wheelhouse."

I put down my fork and knife and stared my brother down across the table. "Yes, analog games, Chaddy, but I don't know if we should keep score. I want it to be fun for everybody, not a competition. Plus, you know how Commander feels about anything that might create conflict."

He shrugged his shoulders and focused on his garden-grown potatoes and carrots. "Okay."

"It's for the best anyway," Dad said. "Assuming we can get permission from Commander to do this, it would not approve of a competition."

"Competition begets animosity and animosity goes against The Known Order," both Chadwick and I chanted in unison, the mantra drilled into our heads from the Intelligence Officers since the first day of school.

Our parents sat without speaking for a few seconds. No unspoken conversation. No sideways glances. Nothing, until Dad broke the silence. "Let's get this mess cleaned up and adjourn to the relaxation room to plan the festivities and submit our request to Commander, shall we?"

We did as he asked, but Mom assumed the lion's share of clean-up duties since the rest of us tackled preparation and cooking. With that taken care of, we each took our usual positions in the relaxation room. Mom and Dad sat in their respective recliner chairs that looked like technological thrones made with the softest, most luxurious artificial material ever created. Chadwick sat on a smattering of pillows off to one side, and I flopped myself on the small couch.

"Commander, start a visual list," Dad said. A 3D projection appeared in the center of the room.

"What would you like me to title the list?"

"Katherine's Birthday."

The title appeared at the top of the digital holograph.

"Okay, first things first. Decorations. What are you thinking, Kate?"

I gave it a moment's thought. I'd seen the types of things I wanted on the internet in stories about ancient history but didn't know the exact names. We all spent the next fifteen minutes on the internet looking at all the old-time decorations we could find—or at least the ones The Association and Commander deemed appropriate for sharing. The filtered search results did not include gag decorations or anything that would offend. Such things upset the balance and violated The Known

Order.

With a satisfactory list of decorations picked, we moved on to the game selection. Instead of looking at still pictures, we watched videos, but we maintained a similar process. What's more, the demonstrations in 3D holographic format gave a realistic feel to the games, and we enjoyed watching and picking our favorite ones. I chose the "potato sack" challenge. The idea of stuffing your legs into an old potato sack and hopping around amused me. Dad explained that it used to be a race, but The Association must have ordered the name change and the video modified. Still, the idea of an obstacle course of sorts promised considerable enjoyment.

Chadwick howled laughing when he watched the "egg and spoon" challenge. Every time an egg hit the ground, he doubled over in hysterics until tears streamed down his cheeks. That game made the cut, as well as a few others.

After the game selection, we devised an itinerary for the day, decided on locations for the decorations, and drew up the guest list, which consisted of every child in my age group. Life in The Known Order forbade selective invitations. Once we appreciated the full scope of the event, it became clear that the house would not suffice, and Dad booked the community green space for the big event. The on-site pavilion assured protection from the elements and provided a place to sit.

With the details squared away, Dad placed the order for the materials and props and sent the invitations.

"Commander, place the birthday party order, authorization code Oswald Webb Alpha Foxtrot Beta, and send invitations."

"Order placed," It replied in an instant. "Invitations sent. Would you like me to add the RSVPs to Katherine's Birthday list?"

"Yes."

"Okay. Invitations sent. The order will arrive tomorrow. Receipt filed in your expenses folder."

I danced a jig, and Chadwick clapped his hands as I did. "This party is going to rock!"

As expected, the supplies for the party arrived the next day, right after Dad pulled into the driveway after work. It hadn't rained in a while and despite sporting a little bit of wear from the occasional vehicle or running shoe, the latest chalk drawings persisted. Chadwick's skills had improved over the last year, and Commander approved them for display. They'd remain until they wore off—or until it rained. I encouraged regular maintenance to preserve their aesthetic. Commander was nothing if not predictable. If a change occurred, it stepped in and demanded either restoration or removal. The Intelligence Officers at school taught Chaddy more than one lesson about this, but he would not accept any justification for removal. Of that I was certain.

I unboxed the party decorations and other assorted props for the games as a trial run for my actual birthday. With everything in The Known Order synthetic and reusable, I had never experienced the feeling or sound of paper tearing, but the excitement of seeing something, anything, for the first time remained an experience unchanged in millennia. Of course, all the decorations and props used the latest vegetable-based polymer for their design and came either from recycled products or from other repurposed items. Everything made met the same criteria. The eggs weren't real. I wondered if the shells cracked like an actual egg, not that I had any experience with real eggs, but I'd seen holographic videos about chickens and the sound and visual of an egg breaking were unmistakable.

"Daddy, can I break one?"

"Before the party?"

"Yeah, I've never seen an egg before, let alone cracked one, and I want to try it. I will crack it into a dish so none of the insides spill and so we can put it in the Commander 3D printer and reanimation unit and have it restored."

"Okay, give it a shot. Chadwick, did you want to break an egg?"

He shook his head. "I'll watch. They're Kate's eggs."

"It's okay." I held my hand out. "You can crack one if you want to. I bet you'd be as good at it as you are all the other old-timey things." I handed him one and asked Commander to show us a holographic video of people cracking eggs.

We watched several videos and found them quite satisfying, but not as satisfying as when we cracked them. Caught up in the novelty of it, we lost track of time, and when Mom found us when she arrived home from work, we hadn't so much as thought about dinner. We stood around a large bowl, and each had an egg in hand. Dad counted us down from ten.

"Ten, nine, eight—"

"Good evening, family. What do we have going on here?"

"Mom, you gotta try this, it's *so* satisfying!" I had trouble containing the pure, simplistic joy of cracking an egg.

"And messy!" Chaddy added.

Mom grabbed a bowl from the cupboard and took an egg from the box that sat open on the counter. I showed her how to hold it and gave her a brief history lesson along with a couple of pointers on technique. Dad continued the countdown.

"—seven, six, five, four, three, two, one, crack!"

In not-quite-perfect unison, we cracked our eggs. Dad cracked both of his one-handed with great success. I got a little egg on my left hand but otherwise did a splendid job. Chadwick gave it a good effort but ended up with more eggs on his hand and more shells in the bowl. Mom missed the practice rounds, and it showed. She stared down at her hand, dripping egg into her bowl which contained the destroyed remnants of an eggshell and a little bit of egg white. Most of the mess missed the bowl. Dad, Chaddy, and I unleashed hysterical fits of laughter.

"All right, you three, enough fun and games. Let's rustle up dinner."

As the evening wound down, I checked the RSVP list and discovered that everyone would be there. This was going to be the best birthday party ever.

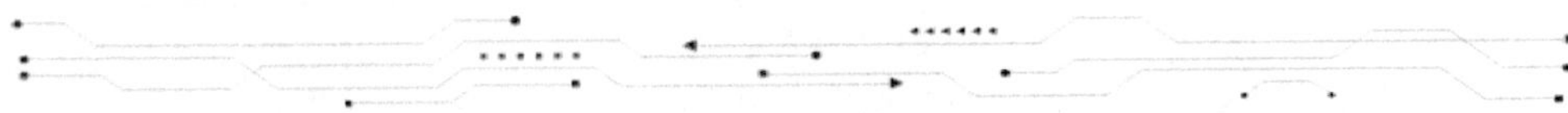

Birthday day arrived, and I woke with the sun. After bouncing off the walls for two hours, my parents agreed to head over to the community green space and pavilion to set up, despite the party not starting for several hours. Commander approved, and after setting up, we amused ourselves by trying out the games while we waited for guests to arrive.

When the kids, accompanied by their parents, showed up, the collective crowd buzzed with keen interest and excitement. No one had ever seen anything like it. My closest friends and I struggled to contain ourselves. For two hours, we played without interruption. Squeals of joy and laughter carried throughout the whole park. Once my stomach rumbled, I corralled the group and asked Dad to unveil the cake.

"Okay, kids, Kate will cut the cake in a minute. Everyone go and find a seat." He leaned down and whispered, "Go and wash up, please."

I did as he instructed; figuring using the facilities to pee was a good idea as well. I entered the one tiny stall in the small bathroom and sat down on the cold metal toilet to do my business. As I reached for a cleaning wipe, my eye caught sight of a small triangle of unknown material poking out from behind the dispenser. It looked like the corner of a piece of paper, which confused and confounded me since the use of honest-to-goodness paper made from trees violated The Known Order. Outside of a few select individuals from The Association, non-synthetic paper may have well been a flying unicorn.

I washed up and wanted to get back to the party for the cake but as I cleaned my hands, I couldn't stop thinking about that paper in the toilet stall. I made it to the door with my hand ready to wave it open when I turned around, went back to the stall, pinched the small corner of whatever it was between my thumb and forefinger, pulled it out, and stuffed it in my pocket. I would investigate later.

The remainder of the party went off without a hitch, not that there was a risk of a hitch in the first place since Commander approved the food, the guest list, and the itinerary. After everyone left and we cleaned up and returned home, I asked if I could spend time alone in my room to "appreciate the moment."

I closed my door and lay on the bed. After a few minutes of waiting to be sure of no interruptions, I took the object out of my pocket. Clearly a piece of paper, it wore a few creases and crumples but otherwise remained intact with no permanent damage. I allowed my fingers to touch the straight but imperfect edges. Holding it close to my face, the fibers, like little hairs, stuck out here and there. With the folded square in my palm, I stroked the flat side with my fingertips. Its surface possessed similarities to the synthetic paper we used in school for craft projects, but not the same. It was undeniably organic, and I convinced myself that I could feel its life force. A nonsensical notion for sure, but I wasn't quite convinced it was entirely nonsense.

The Known Order forbade it, of that much I was certain. It did add to its attractiveness and intrigue though.

I unfolded the page once, then twice, and then a final third time. Its crisp creases scarred the delicate surface and required careful handling as I tried to reverse the folds to help flatten it out. When I got a good look at the page, I sat up, propped my collection of bed pillows behind me for support, crossed my legs, and placed the paper in front of me, face up.

The drawing used the most wonderful colors, more than a few I was sure I couldn't name. Blues, pinks, and greens the likes of which weren't options on any tablet or device I'd ever seen. The flowers were drawn with exceptional detail and included species that didn't exist in household front yard gardens or even the Museum of Nature The Association forced students to attend every year. Bees flew about the flowers, four with legs covered with pollen. After the bees went extinct, humans invented artificial pollination, but we knew about them from history class. I didn't want to ruin the picture but ran my fingers across the page anyway–the images on the page had a different texture than the paper.

The flower stems didn't appear like any flowers in any garden or museum. The leaves and petals and bees at least looked realistic, but the stems not as much. I pulled the magnifying glass my parents gave me for my tenth birthday from my desk. I held it close to one of the stems and held my breath.

There wasn't a straight line in any of them. Instead, each stem took its shape from words; a single sentence microscopically written and repeated in different styles, sizes, and colors.
Nevertheless, she persisted.
I whispered it under my breath, "Nevertheless, she persisted." What did it mean? I knew I had to find out but couldn't begin to think of how. Instead, I trained the magnifying glass on every other aspect of the drawing and sought out more hidden images. I didn't find any but confirmed that every flower stem contained the message. There were more than a dozen stems on the page, some drawn in behind others with only a glimpse of a petal or no petals at all to give the image some depth. I was learning how to do this, not in school but on my own through approved online tutorials. My brother knew how to do it instinctively, which impressed me to no end.

"Nevertheless, she persisted," I whispered again to keep the console sitting in the corner of the room from picking up my voice.

I lay down on my back and held the page in both hands above me. I must have dozed off for a second because I jolted awake at the sound of a knock on my door. The paper rested on my chest, and it took me half a second to get my bearings and gather my thoughts.

"One second."

I folded the paper along its original creases and put it in the back corner of the drawer. A magnifying glass was a rare and expensive object for anyone not part of The Association, and I kept it at the front. My hope was if a CCC opened the drawer they might not inspect the contents in detail if the first item they came across was the glass. Surprise inspections weren't commonplace, but they did occur.

"Come in." I sat up on the edge of my bed and straightened my clothes. The door opened and my mother's face peered past the frame.

"Everything okay, sweetie?"

"Yeah, Mom, everything's perfect." I hoped my smile looked natural instead of shocked, surprised, or worse, guilty.

"You've been in here with the door shut for a while. We wanted to make sure everything was okay. The party was a grand success, wasn't it?"

I snapped back to reality and attempted a more pleasant and youthful tone. It was a good party. It was a great party, even. "It really was. Thank you for letting me do this, it was *so* much fun."

Mom made a motion with her hand requesting entrance to her room. I nodded in approval as she walked in and sat down beside me on the bed. "I'm glad you had a good time. Everyone had a good time. You know that while you were in here the Attendance Reports came back?"

"Oh? How many?"

"All of them."

Attendance Reports didn't usually come in so fast or with perfect participation. "Oh, yeah? Were they good?"

"They were good. Every single one. The consensus was that you threw the most superb party any of those kids have ever been to."

I turned and wrapped my arms around my mother in a big hug. She hugged me back. "And I thought that there was no way my birthday could get any better."

"Well, today is full of surprises, I guess. But you know what?" I shook my head. "I think your brother may have had a better time than anyone else, and I think that maybe you wanted this analog-themed soiree as much for him as for you."

I stared at my feet hanging off the edge of my bed. "Is that bad?"

She guided my chin up with her fingertips until we made eye contact with each other again. "No, sweetie, it's good. It's wonderful, and your father and I couldn't be prouder of you."

The questionable am-I-in-trouble face faded, and I replaced it with a beaming, toothy smile. "I wanted it for me, too, but Chaddy is special, you know? And I wanted him to feel understood. Does that make sense?"

"It sure does, honey. Now, get washed up for dinner. Your father almost has everything ready, and we made sure to bake extra birthday cake for dessert."

She stood up and walked out of the room and left the door open as she did. I followed, but when I stepped toward the hallway before I passed the threshold, I turned back and gave one last glance at my bedside table.

00000011
[Three]

For weeks, I looked at the paper every night before bed. I had trouble comprehending that in my hand I held a real piece of paper. It should be hundreds of years old, brittle, and deteriorating, but it wasn't. It looked as good as new. That meant its previous owner not only had paper but likewise wanted to share a message using it, breaking the law in the process because there was no way I could think of that Commander would approve. The Association would not tolerate such a secretive and defiant act, and yet my best guess told me a member of The Association, or their inner circle, placed the drawing there in the first place. At least that was my current theory. Who else would have access to actual paper, made from the pulp of trees or hemp or other plants? And how did the image's creator get those colors? I asked these questions to myself every time I held the picture and ran my fingertips across the rough edges or the textured surface.

Then, one nondescript night after an uneventful day, as I readied myself for bed, I got an idea. As soon as time allowed, I would go back to the community green space and check the washroom for more hidden treasures. Once I exhausted every hiding place I could think of in there, I would go to the pavilion and conduct an inconspicuous search of it as best I could. You never knew where there would be cameras or listening devices, and while the PMID was passive, it wasn't one hundred percent passive. Besides, The Association wouldn't tell us if it wasn't anyway, so it was best to assume it was more active than they let on, to be on the safe side.

Every morning for the next seventeen days, I checked the community calendar for an opening at the pavilion at a time when I wasn't in school or at an engagement with my parents. As one of the only places in the city with grass and a field, it was in high demand. A little stream ran through the back of the property. It appeared seemingly out of thin air at one end of a culvert to the one side and disappeared into a hole in the grassy knoll on the other. The legend told by the local kids was you'd die if you ever drank the water. Others insisted it gave you a miserable case of diarrhea, which is what my mother said would happen if anything happened at all.

On the morning of the eighteenth day, I awoke and asked Commander if there were any openings at the community green space that day. It was Saturday and we didn't have any plans that I knew of. The day was ripe with opportunity. To my surprise and good fortune, there was no booking between the hours of two and four o'clock that afternoon. I asked Commander to hold the spot for me while I went and asked my mom or dad, whomever I found first, if it was okay if I booked the time. I didn't have a spending account and needed permission from a caregiver to complete the transaction. I ran out of my room in search of a grown-up.

"Mom? Dad?"

Mom's voice came from the direction of the kitchen. "Kate? Is everything okay?"

I slid into the kitchen in my stocking feet, bumping into the table. "Yeah, everything's fine. I hoped you could authorize a couple of hours down at the green space for me today. There's an opening from two to four, and I'd like to wander down there and read and run around in the grass."

"By yourself?"

"Yeah, why not?"

"No reason, but why don't you take your brother?"

I made a face. "Not that I don't love him, but I'm going to be reading more than anything else. He'll be bored, and I was looking forward to the solitude."

Her left eye squinted closed a tiny fraction. Not much, but it wasn't imperceptible either. My father called it a "tell." I knew it as a facial tick she did when she wanted to say yes but still had her doubts.

"Okay, but only an hour, not two."

"Deal."

She provided voice authorization for the transaction, and I booked the community green space and pavilion for the hour between two and three. I vibrated with excitement, couldn't sit still, and didn't know how I would for the next six hours. I managed, though, and at a quarter to two, I grabbed my tablet from my desk and slid the paper drawing from my drawer into my front jeans pocket. I had to be careful as I didn't have any way of protecting the page. I donned my favorite hat and skipped out the front door. In all my excitement, I made the ten-minute walk in seven.

At the gate to the green space, a tall iron gate with menacing spikes on top of its bars stood at least ten feet high, I pressed the screen of my PMID to the reader fixed to the gate above its ornate brass handle.

A computerized voice squawked from the speaker, "You are not authorized to enter for another two minutes and seventeen seconds. Please wait another two minutes and seventeen seconds and try again."

I tapped my toe outside the gate while I watched the time on my PMID and counted off a hundred and thirty-seven seconds. Before I could count the hundred and thirty-eighth, I pressed the screen of my wrist device to the reader.

The gate opened and the same computerized voice greeted me, albeit with better manners, "Welcome, Katherine, to your community green space and pavilion. We see you spent time here not too long ago. Do you require a refresher on the rules?"

"No, thank you. I remember them."

"Good. Welcome again and enjoy your hour. The pavilion speakers will alert you at ten minutes, five minutes, and every minute from then until it's time to leave, and you must leave through the side exit, to avoid disturbing the next group coming in. Do you understand and agree to these terms?"

"Yes, I do."

"Splendid. Have a great day."

I shut the gate behind me and ran as fast as I could to the bathroom. It wasn't far but gasped for breath by the halfway mark. Before I got too close, I had a thought. It would look weird if I went to the bathroom considering I left my home less than fifteen minutes ago. Running clear past, I made a straight line for the pavilion where I stopped in the shade of the faux steel roof that stood over and protected the tables, benches, and chairs of the open-air meeting space.

My reading tablet contained more books than I could ever read in my physical life and more than I could read in two Inherited Consciousness lifetimes. I wasn't reading any at the time—an odd occurrence itself. The device digitally stored a to-be-read pile that if stacked on top of each other as physical books would climb higher than the tallest building I could think of. I turned it on and sat down on the grass on the outside edge of the pavilion's west side. I had no intention of reading, and it would appear strange if I sat in direct sun with my tablet. We learned about perception in school, and I remembered my Intelligence Officer's every word, though I didn't think I took away the same lesson as the rest of the class. My parents taught me to use critical thinking skills and question everything, to be a "proper skeptic" they said, but to be smart about it. People often misinterpreted my inquisitiveness for noncon-formance, and one did not trifle with nonconformance in the days of Commander and The Association.

I chose a random book from my list of books knowing that I would never finish it, not that it mattered. They scrubbed them clean of any offensive or controversial content—books considered classics from fifty years before and hundreds of years before that. I let out a long, exasperated sigh and thought about what the original author would say about the way censorship changed their work under the guise of "protection of the masses for the greater good."

I sat for an excruciating ten minutes pretending to read. It felt like a lifetime, and I could wait no longer. I set the tablet on a tabletop inside the pavilion and walked to the bathroom. Out of instinct, I looked around to check for others, but I still had the entire community green space to myself. Once inside, with the door locked, I got to work. I checked the wipes dispenser first. To my surprise, I spotted another tiny sliver of a corner of what appeared to be paper on the underside of the unit attached to the wall. Thankfully, my fingernails hadn't been trimmed in a while, and I pulled it out. Had I not been in the middle of a "growing them out" phase I would not have succeeded. I made a mental note to bring small tools or gadgets next time—assuming there would be a next time.

With no one waiting for me to return to the pavilion, I unfolded the paper. At first touch, it felt similar to the type of paper as the drawing in my pocket. This new drawing showed, in immaculate detail, people milling about on a beach at the shore of a lake surrounded by beautiful dark green trees. I learned about forests in school and how they used to cover half of all the habitable land on Earth. I brought the page as close to my face as I could without my eyes crossing or my vision blurring. I couldn't tell, I would need my magnifying glass to be sure, but it looked like the artist drew parts of the people and the tree branches using words in the same manner as the other picture.

I folded it back up, slid it into my other front pocket, and continued my search. The cleverest person in the world couldn't hide treasure in too many places in the washroom but I performed a thorough sweep of every nook and cranny, nonetheless. Giving up before I checked every last inch wasn't an option I considered entertaining.

I ran my hand along the underside of the door closing off the toilet from the bathroom and when I got to the corner I stopped. I found I could put my fingers into the hollow frame of the door. I stood on my tiptoes and reached up to the top corner. Hollow as well, I put my fingertips into the hole, but they didn't go in as far. I lacked in the growth spurt department and needed a bit more height. Swinging the door inward, I stood on the toilet seat and made sure to be sure of my footing. The last thing I needed was a soaker from a toilet bowl.

It wasn't possible to see inside the doorframe, but the extra height from standing on the toilet seat allowed me to get a better angle with my fingers. Using both my pinkies, one each in opposite corners of the square opening, I jimmied the object loose and pulled it out.

In my hand sat a small carved trinket. Shaped like a woman and, keeping with the theme of the last picture, appeared to be carved out of wood. The texture felt foreign to my touch. She stood two inches tall with short hair and glasses and wore a robe adorned with a string of pearls.

I turned it over in my hands and examined it from every angle. The flat, roundish bottom sported an inscription of two words: *I dissent.* I couldn't be sure at the time but would have bet that the second picture used the phrase in its design as well. I stuffed the figurine into my front right pocket with the original drawing.

With the entirety of the bathroom searched in painstaking detail, the outside pavilion remained. I didn't like my chances of finding anything and set my expectations to an appropriate level. In the case of hidden cameras, I made my way around dancing with my arms waving like a drunken bird and hummed a tune my mother used to sing while she brushed my hair before bed. Now and then, I looked at the ground with curiosity. At one point, I picked up a pebble and started tossing it up and down in my hand as I explored the pavilion's perimeter.

Stones and concrete formed the entire base structure. Visibly old, over hundreds of years, the foundation once supported a building long lost to time. As I walked around tossing my pebble in the air and catching it in my hand, I paid careful attention to the concrete mortar between the stones looking for newer patches as opposed to ancient spots. Anything secreted away behind a stone would be a newer addition.

Around the back of the pavilion, a smallish stone surrounded by concrete newer than the other mortar in its proximity caught my attention. On purpose, I dropped my pebble and knelt to pretend to search for it. At that point, a sideways glance would raise suspicions. I made sure to remain focused. Once kneeling on the grass, I pressed against the stone, and it gave a not-quite-imperceptible wiggle. I ran my finger over the mortar and pushed with firm pressure every half inch. When I pressed at the top the whole ring of concrete shifted a little, raising one edge above the stone's surface. It was enough for my small fingers to hold on to, and I pulled, getting it to shift enough that the other side came loose.

My heart pounded in my chest, and I dared not let my eyes wander elsewhere. No turning back. With a small shimmy and more pulling, my fingers ached, and I feared a cramp would hamper my efforts. My fears remained unfounded and after a few more good tugs, the concrete came unstuck in a singular odd-shaped ring with a uniform thickness of about half an inch and a depth tapering to a fine point. I set it on the grass to my side and turned my attention to the stone.

With the mortar gone and my fingers small, I got a good grip on it. With a slight twist and a solid pull, I extracted it with ease. It made a ripping sound as it broke free from the base, and I gasped. Whoever loosened the rock fixed a square piece of industrial-strength Velcro to the underside above a long, horizontal cutout. They went through a lot of trouble to carve out that opening, not to mention the risk of confinement, when they fixed it to the back of the pavilion. Wide enough to get a finger in, pinkie to the rescue again, I slid my finger in where it met a cold, metallic surface.

With my fingertip pressed against the end of the mystery object, I pressed as hard as I could. It didn't budge. I tried again with no result. On the third try, however, it moved. I couldn't get it out, but at least it wasn't fused inside. I turned the rock upside down and gave it a quick shake. A small metal key fell to the grass. I flinched and let out a small squeal as the pavilion speakers declared my five-minute warning.

Without hesitation, I scooped up the key and slid it into my pocket. I returned the stone to its place in the wall, and with the care and dexterity of an inexperienced surgeon, replaced the concrete mortar ring around the stone.

Standing up, my attention drew to my knees. Both sported grass stains. I walked back to the stream at the rear of the property and considered scooping up water to clean them off. I knew I couldn't get diarrhea from touching the water, but still thought better of it and ran back to the bathroom to clean up.

It took more time than I expected to get the stains off my knees. The sink sat too high and the small scoops of water I cupped in my hands to rub on them did little to remove the dirt from my jeans. At least it looked like I tried to clean myself up. As I dried my hands and attempted to direct the warm air from the dryer to the wet patches on my knees, the one-minute warning sounded and echoed throughout the small, cinder block room.

"Oh, no."

I ran from the bathroom and toward the East exit. About halfway to the gate, I realized I had left my tablet on a table. "Oh, no!" I turned to run back. As soon as I picked up the tablet, the final warning blared over the speaker system. I sprinted as fast as I could toward the gate and made it out less than thirty seconds late. I didn't see any CCC presence on the other side to greet me, and I breathed a long, exasperated sigh of relief.

Halfway home, a silent hover scooter pulled up beside me, slowed down, and the CCC officer on it flipped up his visor and ordered me to stop. I did, wedged my reading tablet under my arm, and stuffed my hands into my pockets to stop them from shaking, or at least to keep him from noticing.

"Katherine Webb?"

"Yes, sir."

"You overextended your stay in the community green space."

"I know."

He cocked an eyebrow at me and squinted, trying to assess if my tone was sass or sincerity. "It was only thirty-one seconds, but I still have to follow up, you understand?"

"Yes, sir."

"So, tell me what happened."

"I was in the bathroom not feeling well when the warnings came on. I would have made it out on time, but I forgot my reader on one of the tables." I kept my hands in my pockets and tilted my chin toward the reader under my arm, which was no doubt collecting nervous pit sweat on its exterior. "I went back for it, and that's why I was a little late getting out."

"I'm going to have to take a look at it."

As if suffering from persistent slow motion, I extracted my hands from my pockets, first the right one, which upon exiting grabbed the reader from under my left arm, and then the left one which I placed on the other side of it to feel if it was, in fact, sweaty. It wasn't, but it was warm to the touch. I handed it to him.

He turned it on and looked at the title. "*The Scattering Winds* by Gordon Bonnet."

"It's pronounced 'bon-aay'."

He nodded. "Bon-aay. Got it. I see you're only forty pages in. Is it any good?"

"So far, yeah, but it's still early. Some books grab you quickly and fizzle out. I don't think this one will, though. I've read some of his other stuff, and I've yet to stop reading one partway through."

He nodded again. "What's it about?"

"It's book two of a trilogy. I didn't read the synopsis before I started it, so I only know what's happened in the first book and the forty pages of this one. So far, it's a post-apocalyptic society like ours, only they appear to have lost all their technology. I don't really know what's going on, but I'm intrigued." I tripped on the last word as it rolled off my tongue.

He handed the reader back to me. "Sounds intriguing, that's for sure. Let me know how it turns out."

"I will, CCC." I stared at his name tag. "Aalto."

"What's that in your pocket?" He pointed to my right one. The tip of the wooden carving poked out a smidgen.

I stuffed it back down into my pocket. "It's nothing, just a small figurine. I was playing with it in the grass instead of reading. It was too nice a day to not enjoy it."

"By yourself? You were lying in the grass all by yourself playing with a toy figurine?"

I needed to think on my feet and find a way to end the conversation. I thought of the inscription on the carving, *I dissent*, and the words written into the drawing. *Nevertheless, I persisted.* At that moment, I got an idea of what that phrase meant. "Daydreaming. Thinking about my future."

"Your future? All you have to do is ask Commander."

I hoped for that exact response. "Commander won't know because I don't know. My parents are Choosers and when the time comes, I will be a Chooser too."

He paused as his eyes darted around and processed the information shown to him on his holographic glasses. He tapped the one side, held up his index finger indicating I should sit tight, and spoke, but not to me. "HQ, this is CCC Aalto. I need confirmation on Chooser status for the family Webb. W-E-B-B. I've sent you their IDs." He stood silent for what felt like an eternity and then tapped the side of his glasses again. "Your Chooser status is not on your public file, but HQ confirms you're telling the truth."

"I know. My parents didn't want it to *define* us or something. I don't understand it myself. Being a Chooser is good, isn't it?"

"Well, it sure beats not being one, I can tell you that. Okay, Katherine, you hurry home now and get yourself cleaned up. We can't have you wandering around the neighborhood looking like a girl without a home. I'm surprised Commander let you leave with those grass stains on your knees."

"I tried to clean them, but it was no use. I need a proper machine to do it."

He gave one last nod and flipped his visor back down before hopping onto his hovercycle. He gave a slight wave as he glided away in silence. I waited until he floated out of sight and then collapsed onto the walkway. My heart rate was through the roof. So high that if it went any higher my PMID would have sounded an alert. I performed deep breathing exercises to calm down and got back to my feet. The remainder of my journey home took half the time it should have, and I marched straight into my room and deposited the two drawings, the carving, and the metal key into my drawer. I changed out of my jeans and into a clean pair and dropped the dirty laundry into the cleaning window in the hallway. A whirring sound, a short vibration, and thirty seconds later the window opened, and my pants appeared on the shelf below it. Sandwiching them between my hands I walked them back to my room and put them in my dresser. My mom popped her head in through the doorway.

"Hey, sweetie, how was your time at the pavilion?" She looked down at my pants. "Did you change?"

"Yeah, I fell on the grass and dirtied the other pair, so I changed and cleaned the other ones."

"What do you want to do with the rest of your day?"

"I think I'm going to read, if that's okay. I started another book, and I want to make progress on it."

"My little reader. You have no idea how proud that makes me." We shared a smile. "Want me to close the door so you can have some quiet?"

"Yes, please. Thank you."

My mother closed the door, and I flopped down onto my bed on the verge of tears. I placed the palms of my hands over my face and lay there for a few minutes before sitting up and reaching over to my bedside table and opening the drawer. For the first time, I got a good look at the metal key I pulled from the hollow stone. My eyes widened and my heart fluttered. I picked it up and turned it over in my hand. It was a PMID key, an older one than the one attached to the charging station at the front door, but a key, nonetheless. Did it work? I could think of only one way to find out.

I inserted it into the small keyhole where the wristband met the face of the device. It fit. I gave it a quarter turn clockwise. The wristband separated from the face, and I let out a gasp before snapping the band shut. I tossed the key into the drawer, closed it, and made my way to the front door where I unlocked the wristband at the charger by the door. I'd consider what to do with the contraband key later.

Back in my room, I closed the door and sat on the bed with the magnifying glass and the new drawing. As I suspected, the tree trunks formed from the words of the same phrase, as did the hair of one woman in the picture, the belt of another, the necklace of yet another, and the shoelaces of a small girl kneeling by the water's edge. For the first time, I noticed that they were all female, or at least visually appeared as such. We were learning about the hazards of gender stereotypes in school and the pitfalls that come with making judgments of others based on incomplete or irrelevant information. As with everything, the underlying message was, *don't worry about it*, The Association and Commander will let you know the correct path.

This picture, however, had a purpose with its all-female subjects and captured a time in the distant past when vast forests and clear blue lakes covered the land. I had to retrieve my historical geography and sociology lessons but couldn't pinpoint the timeframe. I dared not look it up either, for fear of drawing attention to things I wasn't supposed to be concerned with, especially when not at school. I needed help making sense of all of this but drew a blank on who to turn to for help. My parents were the obvious choice, but as much as they disliked the system, they weren't radicals or troublemakers. They were more likely to confiscate the items and tell me to forget about it more than anything else. Chaddy was too little.

Terre. Terre would know. She was smarter than me by a lot, and her family were unabashed Choosers. Now that I knew how things worked, I realized they took full advantage of this, which explained her rebellious streak. Most importantly, though, I could trust her. The two of us had been thick as thieves since we were both toddlers. Yes, Terre would know.

The next school day, I sat with Terre on the transport, as we did every school day and on field trips or other excursions. The transport was always too loud with kids talking even though the ride itself was silent due to its magnetic propulsion system. On one hand, this offered the advantage of no one overhearing our conversation, but on the other hand there was no way to tell if the people nearby concentrated their listening in our direction. I erred on the side of caution and decided to broach the subject during an outdoor free period.

I was bursting at the seams with anticipation all morning. I'd hoped spilling the beans would bring joy and relief, though I had no idea what she would do with the information. Terre's intellectual capacity surpassed mine by years. Still technically a minor, but in a whole other category in terms of perception and critical thinking. Two things I recognized as vital for this situation.

During our outdoor free period, I took Terre aside as we nibbled on a snack of fresh vegetables and synthetic dairy-free cheese.

"Terre," I whispered, pointed to my PMID, and brought a single finger to my lips. The devices didn't listen to conversation by default, but you could enable what The Association called "active listening" for them. A select few liked this for certain conveniences, but I thought it was nothing but creepy, not to mention invasive. I elected to opt out of that particular feature, but you never knew who used it until you asked.

"It's okay, I don't have active listening enabled," she whispered back.

"Okay, good."

"Why are you still whispering then?"

"Shh. Keep your voice down. I'm whispering because what I'm about to tell you could get me in a lot of trouble and that could get *you* in a lot of trouble too. Knowing that much, I won't tell you if you don't want me to."

"Are you kidding? You have to tell me now."

I leaned in closer. "Okay, I don't even know where to start."

"At the beginning."

"Okay, yeah, right. Remember my birthday party at the community green space and pavilion?" Terre nodded, and I gave her the detailed rundown of everything I uncovered and my interactions with the CCC. When I finished Terre sat silent for several seconds before speaking.

"Holy cow," her words but a wisp in the wind.

"I know, right?"

"What are you going to do?"

"I have no idea, that's why I came to you. I figured if anyone could keep this a secret, it was you, and you'd have an idea about what to do next."

"Well, you can't sit there and not do anything. Having a PMID key that's unattached from its charging station is unheard of. Even the CCCs don't have access to loose keys. You could sell it, but you'd only get underground market credits which aren't much good for people like us."

"Young girls, you mean?"

"No, I mean we're not criminals."

"Oh, yeah. Well, let's both think about it for a couple of days and see what we come up with. There have to be situations where detaching from our PMID would be advantageous."

"Yeah, that's a good idea. This is a lot to deal with all of a sudden. Do you have anywhere safer than a drawer beside your bed where you can keep it?"

"I'll figure something out. What do you think about the drawings and the carving?"

"What were the phrases?"

"Nevertheless, she persisted, and I dissent."

"That's a message if there ever was one. Did you look it up on the internet?"

"Are you crazy? I haven't looked anything up on the internet at all since I uncovered the first picture. I'm too terrified that anything I search for will trigger another visit from my friendly neighborhood CCC."

"Yeah, but you can always pull Chooser rank. It's great for when you want to get out of trouble."

"I know, but I think this is much bigger than the CCC commission. These drawings, the carving, and the messages they contain are in direct conflict with The Association itself."

My friend's eyes widened. "You think so?"

"I know so. Think about it. Remember when we went to the museum a while back for that class trip?"

"Yeah."

"Did you see anything in there that looked like the drawings I described? Anything even remotely close?"

"No, nothing. All the museums and everything in them are Commander approved. The curators, at the direction of The Association, ensure not a single person will interpret the piece the wrong way, have any negative feelings, or even have a solitary conflicting opinion about it. Colors barely exist. It's like looking at the beige version of the rainbow. Look, here's the beige version of red, oh, and here's the beige version of blue. The grass in the community green space even looks dull. There definitely aren't any hidden messages in any of the museum pictures, and if the carving you found is, in fact, made out of real wood, I'm positive there won't be any of those in there, either. At least, not on display anyway. It is possible members of The Association or their inner circle have access to things the general public doesn't, but I doubt it."

"You see my point then? This is bigger than big. Huger than huge."

"Yeah, so what about the messages? What do you think they mean?"

Terre pondered this for a moment. "Well, I think it's a safe assumption these were all hidden by the same person, so I think we have to look at them together. As a whole, you know? All I have is your description to go from, though. It will be easier if I get a look at them. How about I come over one day after school this week?"

"Yeah, okay. Sounds good. Thursday? My brother has an after-school something or other and won't be home. That would be disastrous. He's a good kid, but too little to realize the implications, and he's as likely to blabbermouth to our parents as he is to keep the secret."

"Yeah, I get it. I don't have a brother or sister, but I've been around enough younger kids to know they are an unpredictable bunch."

"So, Thursday?"

"Thursday."

We pinkie swore on it, and I spent the rest of my free period sitting in silence, absorbed in my thoughts of what it all meant and what we planned to do about it.

OOOOOIOO
[Four]

After the longest four days of either of our existences, Thursday after school arrived. We sat in silence on the transport with our eyes fixed on the back of the seat in front of us. Neither of us wanted to risk opening our mouths or exchanging glances with each other for fear of tipping our hands. Not that anyone had any reason to know anything about what we planned, but still, we both agreed earlier in the week to act with an abundance of caution.

The instant we arrived at my house, we removed our PMIDs and placed them in the charger by the door. We dared not use the illicit key I found until we knew more about what would happen if a PMID came detached from its person while outside a private dwelling. I already knew what would happen if you left home without it, but removing it while in public, as a rule, didn't happen. It was so rare; they didn't tell us what punishment came with the infraction. Instead, they hammered rule after rule after rule into us daily. You *must* do this, you *must* do that, wear your PMID outside the house *or else*.

We put pillows over top of the Commander console in my room to prevent it from listening in. I tested the setup by speaking commands and seeing if it responded. When it didn't, I raised my voice and issued another command. I upped my volume until I became loud enough to break through the makeshift synthetic feather soundproofing. The experiment revealed we could speak in our normal indoor talking voices without running the risk of the console overhearing us. Still, we whispered.

I crawled under my bed, wiggling and wriggling my way to the back corner. The space provided enough clearance to turn onto my back, but no more. I extracted an envelope from the underside of the bed which contained the two pictures and carving inside, flipped back onto my tummy, and wormed my way back out from under the bed with the envelope in my teeth. I made a mental note to find a better hiding spot.

"You didn't make it easy to retrieve, did you?"

"That's the point, right? It is a proper pain in the butt, though. If you have a better idea, don't hold back."

She shrugged.

I opened the envelope, made with a semi-translucent non-caloric silicon-based polymer five hundred times stronger than paper with a reusable adhesive to maintain the seal integrity. It wasn't fireproof or waterproof, but under the circumstances offered enough protection. Who knows how long those pictures spent tucked behind the wipe dispenser? It could have been since the initial installation when they created the community green space, or it could have been more recent. There was no way to tell for sure since there was no record of the green space opening. As far as my neighborhood was concerned, it was always there. There were no records of its inauguration, nothing in the news about the first booking or any public events, or even any mention of it from the neighborhood historical society. It may as well have appeared out of thin air at a time so long ago that even if people were living with Shared Intellect they couldn't remember—or if they did remember, they weren't saying anything about it.

The way Terre's eyes widened when I pulled the pages face up out of the envelope gave me insight into what my face must have looked like when I first saw them myself. I handed the one I found first over to her, and she took it by the edges, careful to not smudge or crease the work.

"Wow."

"I know."

"I mean, you described it perfectly. You should be a writer, by the way, but I still wasn't prepared for it to look so…" She paused, looking for the right word.

"Alive?"

"Yes, that's it! I never expected it to look so alive. Let me see the other one."

I handed it to her and watched with a smile on my face as her facial expression went from wonder to amazement. "I like this one more than the one with the bees, I think," she said.

"Yeah, me too. I've seen bees before, in science class when they explained the process of artificial pollination. I've never seen a scene like this one, with only women in the picture. That alone violates The Known Order. I've seen trees before but never that many in one spot. If you believe what the Intelligence Officers tell us, an overabundance of trees is a fairy tale. And the water? We know there used to be hundreds of thousands of lakes, ponds, and rivers, but our understanding of them is limited." Terre bowed her head. "Another problematic by-product of The Wars."

"I've studied the pictures every night and started doing searches for certain keywords, and I think I have an idea of what's going on."

"Oh? I thought you didn't want to appear suspicions?"

"I didn't. I don't. But my desire to solve this outweighed my fears."

"So, what's the verdict?"

"There used to be expressions like 'Mother Earth' and 'Mother Nature.' Millennia ago, humans designated the Earth as female, the mother, not the giver of life, but life itself."

"That makes sense. Humans didn't uncover asexual reproduction in our own species until the last century."

"Yeah, after humans destroyed the planet. Climate change pretty near wiped us off the face of the Earth, and then The Wars came and *that* took care of all but the tiniest bit of nature and a good chunk of the population as well. The Association formed, rebuilt the world, and everyone became part of The Known Order."

"And here we are."

"Yeah, but look at *how* they rebuilt it. No appreciable distinction for the spectrum of genders. No concept of race. Everything neutral. What word did you use to describe the museums?"

"Sanitized."

"Exactly. They sanitized the world. But as you may have guessed… nature has a way of figuring it out. The food gardens in front of every house in the neighborhood are a good example. If we don't tend to them, they get unruly and out of control. You can't find trees and grass beyond the community green space and those receive expert and meticulous care from the city council and local services arm of The Association."

"And you think these pictures mean that left to its own devices, nature will restore the Earth to its former glory?"

"If she persists, yes."

"'Nevertheless, she persisted.' In this context, it makes a lot of sense."

"Geez, you don't have to sound surprised."

"No, no, I didn't mean it like that. I'm just surprised I didn't think of that angle too."

"I've had more time to process everything."

"What about the women in the pictures? Are they, you know, what-chamacallits? Metaphors?"

"Yes and no. I think whoever drew these wants us to know that it's up to the women of the world to make this happen."

"Jeez, no pressure."

"Maybe 'up to' isn't the best phrasing. I think it's more that we'll know *how to* make this happen. We've done it before, you know? Before The Wars, girl power was a thing."

"Heh. Say that out loud these days and you'll land in confinement. But okay, I get it. Now, how do you think the carving factors in?"

"I had to do a lot of digging on that one, and I eventually found one reference to something that got me thinking." Terre raised her eyebrows, encouraging me to continue. "Have you ever heard of Lady Justice?"

"Doesn't ring any bells."

"I considered asking the console for more information but didn't want to risk interaction with it. Instead, I grabbed my tablet and scrolled through my library of saved images until I found it: a black and white drawing of a woman in a robe holding something from a central pivot point with two saucers hanging from it."

I tilted the tablet to allow Terre to get a better view.

"Fascinating. I'm assuming this represents the weighing of good versus evil and right versus wrong."

"Yeah, that's what the information I found indicated. It also said that the concept of legal interpretation became superfluous since society entered The Known Order."

"Seems like a fundamental piece of history to erase."

"I don't think anyone was supposed to find that information at all. I think it was a mistake. I saved the image and all its metadata, which is how I know, but when I went back to search for it again, it was gone."

"That's creepy. Like, they changed history *while* you were watching."

"Yeah, and now I'm worried a CCC is going to barge in and demand I delete it from my tablet. As soon as I saved the image, I took the device offline until I could copy it to an encrypted quantum memory stick. I'm going to take hi-res scans of the pictures and 3D image the carving and PMID key, too."

"I don't think you give yourself enough credit for how smart you are, K-Dub."

My cheeks warmed. Terre was always kind to me, but that compliment filled my heart with joy. "Thanks, but it still doesn't give us any more ideas about how it all fits together."

"I think the carving is meant to be like this Lady Justice. Not the same, but similar. One of these people who did, what did you say it was?"

"Legal interpretation."

"Yeah. I think it's telling us that not only is it up to women to restore the world to its ancient glory but to bring back legal interpretation and restore justice as well."

"That would mean The Known Order isn't that known after all."

"I think it means that even if The Known Order is possible as a construct, maybe we'd all be better off if we ignored it and relied on each other, women especially."

"That seems like a bit of a stretch, no?"

"How do you mean?"

"I mean, if all you have is a hammer, every problem looks like a nail. There could be dozens of ways to interpret these images. Are we only seeing what we want to see?"

"Okay, fair point. Ask yourself this, then. Why do you think you want to see it that way?"

I didn't have an answer. Since I first garnered a basic understanding of The Known Order and The Association, it felt… off. Deep in my belly, I knew that humans weren't supposed to live and behave like this. For thousands of years, chaos and conflict reigned and while progress was at times slow bordering on glacial, we always moved forward. We were meant to be better, not perfect.

I dodged the question. "No one else knows about this. What can two girls from Zone Three do about it?"

"No one else we know of, plus don't forget these artifacts didn't materialize out of thin air."

"Right, yeah, that we know of, but it's safe to assume that in our little corner of the world, the creator and us are in the know and no one else."

"And whoever drew those pictures made the carving and hid the key. It's all the same person."

"The key might be unrelated."

"Might be, but I'll bet you fifty credits it isn't."

"No bet. You're probably right, though. I was trying not to get too excited and be as scientific as possible with my thinking. My parents say that it will 'serve me well' throughout my life."

Terre laughed. "My parents say stuff like that about me all the time."

"What should we do about all this, Terre?"

"I don't know exactly, not yet at least, but I know one thing."

"What's that?"

"I look forward to a world without CCCs, The Association, and a

Known Order, and I especially like the idea of girls like us making that happen."

"We could form our own sort of Known Order. No boys allowed."

"I think we just did." Terre extended her arm toward me and held out her pinkie finger. I did likewise and we swore on it.

00000101
[Five]

Days, weeks, and months passed, and we still hadn't determined what to do. We each managed to replicate the drawings several times over using synthetic paper and vegetable-based ink we siphoned in secret from the ancient arts department of our school. I drew several variations of the carving as well as a handful of Lady Justice on the backs of which I wrote the paragraph that accompanied the image before it vanished from existence.

By the second school break, one month in the summer, we made more than a hundred copies of the original drawings, three dozen drawings of the carving, and fifteen 3D-printed replicas. Those we made offline using a workaround that Terre and I devised. We then worked together to draw twenty reasonable replications of the Lady Justice photograph. All this despite nary a hint of a concrete plan or the guts to use the key to remove our PMIDs outside our homes.

On the first Tuesday afternoon of summer break, an invitation arrived for a party at the community green space. I RSVP'd in the affirmative and at the same time I messaged Terre, she messaged me.

Well?

I followed mine up with *You should come over NOW*. Fifteen minutes later, Terre arrived, and we went straight to my room and shut the door.

Mind reader that she was, Terre already knew what I wanted to do.

"You're going to put the originals back, aren't you?"

"Yeah, and I think it's time we started spreading the word and got up to some good trouble."

"We should be careful about who we tell. A lot of kids we know wouldn't dream of questioning The Known Order, let alone violate it outright."

"I agree. What do you think about limiting those who know to Choosers? We'll have more leeway when it comes to bending the rules."

"Yeah, but what if they don't care as much about this as the people who aren't Choosers?"

"I hadn't thought about that, but will non-Choosers want to put themselves at risk?"

"Maybe? I have no idea. Whomever we pick, though, we'll have to make sure we trust them."

We spent the next hour going through all our friends and compiling a list of the most trustworthy. When we finished, the list contained six girls. Two came from a family of Choosers, and one of whom sat atop the list as our primary choice.

We had a simple plan. Wait until the festivities started, and when distraction levels allowed, I would go into the bathroom and return the carving and the drawings to their original hiding places. Terre would wait outside the door keeping watch but pretending to wait her turn. Afterward, at another convenient point, we would approach our top choice and good friend, Melissa, and let her know that she should come over to my place where we would let her in on a big secret. She was always secretive and quiet, and we both ascertained she'd be good at keeping this one despite its magnitude.

We had no idea how to get the original key back, short of booking the green space again, which wasn't cheap. Neither of our parents would go for it, particularly not mine since they paid to book it for me on my own once already. The key had to stay put.

Everything went well at first. I hopped up onto the toilet seat and slid the carving back into the doorframe. Then, I hopped down, shut the door, and pulled the first piece of paper out of my pocket. I held it in my hand for a few seconds to savor the feeling and embed the tactile sensation into my memory since I might never get to touch a non-synthetic page again. Once satisfied, I slid the folded page in behind the big, square dispenser at the top, maybe not in the precise spot I'd found it, but close enough. I made sure to leave a tiny sliver of one corner exposed. Unless a person possessed slight fingers like mine, there would be no way to extract it without the use of tweezers or maybe a pair of needle-nose pliers.

My hands shook with nervousness as I pulled the second page out of my pocket, the same size as the other one, and folded along its original creases. As I knelt to slide it behind the dispenser from the bottom, Terre issued a loud cough from outside the bathroom door. Once as a warning. Twice meant danger. Simple but effective, it got the job done but increased my heart rate and created a sense of panic I never wanted to experience again.

The first attempt at returning the page failed, and I ended up creasing it. I thought I'd identified the same spot in which I found it, but I must have missed by a little in one direction or the other. It refused to slide in all the way. As I bent and massaged the page to reduce the new crease, Terre coughed again, twice. I froze and strained to listen to her muffled voice.

"Katherine's in there, Mrs. Goldstein. She's not feeling well, and I have to go to the bathroom when she's done."

I couldn't hear Mrs. Goldstein's response. She didn't enunciate and project like Terre, who made every effort to cover my butt.

"Of course, you can take little Jaime in ahead of me. I can wait. I'm sure Katherine won't be much longer." She said the last part a little louder, and I pictured Mrs. Goldstein giving her a sideways glance.

I composed myself and tried to peek under the dispenser to see if I could see what blocked the page. I closed my eyes and tried to think back and remember the precise spot I first saw the corner poking out. Off-center to the right by about three centimeters or thereabouts. I tried again and while the folded paper made it more than halfway in, again it got stuck. Mrs. Goldstein poked her head through the outer door, and it made me jump.

"Katherine dear, are you okay?"

I tried to respond but it came out as an awkward squawk instead. After clearing my throat, I tried again and managed a faux weak sounding response, "I'm okay, thanks. Give me a minute."

The answer must have satisfied Mrs. Goldstein since she didn't follow up. I pulled the page out again, smoothed it as best I could against my leg, and gave it a quarter turn so the leading edge was a nice crisp crease. I moved the page another centimeter to the right from my last attempt, and with sloth-like speed and my fingers pressing the page against the wall of the stall, slid it into place. At that point, I wasn't concerned with the fact I didn't leave much of a corner exposed, but I was happy enough to be done with it. I closed my eyes and took a few deep, calming breaths before flushing the toilet and washing my hands.

As I exited, Mrs. Goldstein ushered in little Jaime and directed her to the stall. She paused and gave me a good, long stare. "You are all flushed, Katherine. Are you sure everything's okay?"

"I'm fine, Mrs. Goldstein, thanks. I think I just got a bit too much sun."

"Well, maybe stick to the pavilion then, dear. Don't want you to make it worse. Oh, and drink a lot of water." Sound advice, but her tone wasn't convincing. With no further questions lobbed in my direction, I grabbed Terre's hand and walked off.

In the final moments of the event, the opportunity to approach the others presented itself. We started with Melissa, took her aside under the guise of having a typical conversation among friends, and turned our backs to the rest of the partygoers. Lip reading wasn't common, that we knew of, and we wanted to be extra cautious when having this conversation.

I did all the talking but gave her scant information. When Terre and I formed the list, we made sure to rehearse the elevator pitch. Whoever did the talking would provide as much information as required to pique their interest. As much as we wanted to trust others, we set up a series of questions to ask and help us determine their trustworthiness. Then, we waited to see what happened. If Melissa showed any concern, or if information leaked, we would know, and she would fall off the list.

After a successful whetting of Melissa's appetite for salacious news and planting our seeds of trust, we moved on to Eunice, and then Caillou, who both got the same story and the same questions. The information we provided varied slightly according to the person as we wanted to ensure we would know who had loose lips. All three encounters ended with the same request to convene at my house at an agreeable time a week later where further discussions would take place. Terre and I did our best to ensure that none of the other girls knew who we approached. With any amount of luck, it would stay that way for the next week.

We all met nine days after our initial pitch in the park. All parental units agreed to allow their kids to come over and hang out in my empty house. As far as we could tell, none of our three friends violated our trust and spilled the beans to anyone.

The other girls arrived in reverse order from how we approached them. We did this on purpose. We figured this would give the number three person on the list a little ego boost. A number three pick might feel slighted if they knew they weren't the first choice.

When Caillou arrived, Terre and I made sure she removed her PMID, turned it off, and set it on the charging dock before we brought her to my room. We buried the console underneath a mountain of pillows and blankets again. A small fan sat facing the pile and whirred away, providing background noise to keep the room from sounding too quiet. I did all of the talking.

"Caillou, we invited two others but wanted to make sure you arrived first, to show you we were serious, and so you could be certain we weren't going to surprise you."

"Okay." Her face didn't register any comprehension.

"Melissa and Eunice will be here soon. First Eunice and then Melissa."

"Oh, okay. I'm really curious about what's going on. Are you going to save it until everyone's here?"

"Yeah, I think that's best. In the meantime, let's get a drink while we wait. It shouldn't be long."

We adjourned to the kitchen, and each poured a tall glass of lemonade. We kept the talk to neutral topics like the weather, our summer break activities, and the excitement about our return to school in a little more than two weeks. We placed the pitcher of lemonade on the table when Eunice arrived.

"Oh, hey, Caillou's here, too. Cool. Hey, Caillou, how are you?"

"Good, Eunice. That was some party at the green space, wasn't it?"

"It sure was, but I think Kate's old-timey games and decorations party was the most epic soiree ever. And I'm not just saying that because I'm in her house and want a glass of lemonade." She let out a nervous giggle. As much as we all grew up without the old notions of class and clique, kids still behaved like kids. Awkward and self-conscious to the bone, with a strong desire to be liked.

I poured Eunice a glass and myself, Caillou, and Terre a second. Idle chitchat passed the time until Melissa arrived. After the requisite pleasantries and pouring of lemonade were completed, we all made our way to my room where I closed the door and directed the three newcomers to sit on the floor. Terre and I presided over them from the side of the bed where we sat with our legs crossed and hands in our laps. Without speaking, I reached behind me and took copies of each of the drawings I found in the green space bathroom along with my hand drawn Lady Justice pictures and handed one to each of the other girls.

They each absorbed what I put in front of them and then looked to the others to see if their page was different. When they saw they were, Caillou's hand shot up.

"I have a question. Can we share these among ourselves to get a better look at the other ones?"

"You don't have to put your hand up to ask a question, Caillou. This is my bedroom, not Instructional Officer McBossypants's classroom." The joke cut the immediate tension, and I reached back and pulled out enough copies to give each girl one of each.

They sat and stared at the pictures for several minutes before anyone dared speak. One by one they clued in. Finally, after an unbearable minute of silence, Caillou spoke. "These—" Her voice wavered, and she put the pages on the floor in front of her and lowered her voice to a whisper. "These violate The Known Order." I nodded and Caillou turned her head and pointed to the stack of pillows and fan in the corner of the room. "And *that* explains all the trouble you went through to bury your bedroom console." I nodded again.

The other two girls on the floor still held their pages and explored them with keen interest. Melissa squinted and pulled the bee drawing closer to her face. "Are these flower stems drawn with words?"

Terre's eyebrows raised. "You can see that?"

She blushed. "My mom says that I have, what's the phrase she uses? 'Especially keen eyesight.'"

"I'll say. I only found it because I thought it looked a little different and happened to have a magnifying glass."

"Wait," Eunice interrupted. "You have a magnifying glass?"

I reached into the drawer and pulled it out. Without looking through it, I could see Eunice's eyes widen and her facial expression morph from incredulous to awestruck. "My birthday present from two years ago. My mom's an engineer. Computer engineer, but still hangs out with many other science-y people. My dad's an Intelligence Officer at the university, and he has access to a whole bunch of stuff that most people don't. They thought it would be a good gift. One that would, I dunno, light a spark in me."

"I guess it did," Melissa said. "Can I see it? Can *we* see it?"

"Sure." I handed it over to Melissa who regarded it with silent wonder. She looked through it at various bits of her clothing and one fingernail before turning it to the page. She smiled and looked up. "My eyesight mustn't be that keen. I got the words wrong." She let out a short burst of giggles. "The content of the drawing threw me off. I thought the words read, 'Notwithstanding the pesticide,' you know, like the picture was some sort of defying bee act of protest against the stuff that would come to wipe them out."

My jaw dropped. "Are you some hyper-intelligent philosopher with beyond human eyesight?"

Terre weighed in with her thoughts. "Even if that's what it said, I would not have come up with that interpretation of the work. Where'd you learn how to do that?"

"I don't know, to be honest. I—I've never seen anything like these before, and my brain was a flurry of ideas like a switch flipped and activated a part of my subconscious that's been asleep this whole time."

Eunice grabbed the magnifying glass and looked through it at the other picture. "Nevertheless, she persisted. Cool. Is that what it says on the bee drawing, Mel?"

"Yeah. All the flower stems repeat the same phrase written in different scripts but are super tiny. I don't know where you'd find a pen to write with that small, let alone with a vibrant color of ink or dye. Where is the phrase in the picture you're looking at?"

"Tree trunks, branches, various articles of clothing on the people in the picture."

"They all have the appearance of women." We turned to face Caillou, who held her copy of the drawing close to her face. The slightest of trembles betrayed her calm voice. "That's a violation of The Known Order. Where did you get these?"

I recounted the story of how the originals came to be in my possession along with every other detail I could think of right up until returning them to their original spot. I told them about the key but left out the part about it unlocking PMIDs, an idea that Terre suggested out of an abundance of caution. We anticipated questions about the key and a strong desire from the other girls to see it and concocted an explanation for why it wasn't in my possession.

"I hid the key away—for now." Not a lie. "It's in a safe place but hard to get to, and I didn't want to risk blowing my cover retrieving it."

Terre backed up my story. "I saw it and couldn't figure out its purpose but given the trouble the person went through to hide it, and the risk they took, I suggested Kate do the same and keep it hidden away until a better opportunity to examine it presented itself." The girls accepted this rationale and she continued. "You know, Mel, I think what you said a few moments ago is the key to all of this. We've been racking our brains for weeks and thought we had a pretty good idea of what the messaging was, but I think you cracked the case wide open."

"Oh, yeah?"

"Yeah. The part about your subconscious. Even without the hidden messages, as cryptic as they are, those two pictures invoke thoughts and imagery that have been lying dormant in our brains for a long time. I think whoever drew these and hid them, assuming it's the same person, is instructing us, the women of the world, to spread the word and persist until we do. "

Eunice patted Melissa on the back and Caillou reached across her to extend a hand for a high five.

"So, the only remaining question is, are you with us?" I smiled and held out my right hand with my fist closed and my pinkie finger sticking out. The other girls all put their pinkie fingers in, and we formed an awkward sort of starfish handshake.

After we sealed our pact, Melissa spoke first. "So, what's the plan?"

I tried to speak but before I could get the words out, Terre answered. "I think we divvy up these pictures and distribute them wherever we can. For obvious reasons, discretion is our top priority. I think we should focus on places where we know girls or women spend time alone, or at least not near large groups of people."

Caillou's hand shot up, but she lowered it without hesitation. "That's going to be tough. For a long, long time everything's been as gender-neutral as possible."

I gave myself a few seconds to ponder this. "Well, there are still a lot of bathrooms and would keep with the theme, and we can't forget mommy and baby centers. Sections of clothing stores still have gender-specific sections, even if they're not labeled 'Men' and 'Women' anymore, but if you look around you can see a definite pattern to what people wear. Then there's the menstruation section of pharmacies and grocery stores. Anywhere you can discreetly tuck a folded piece of paper where a girl is most likely to see it will work."

Eunice spoke next. "Why don't we open it up to the boys?"

Terre jumped in with a response. "Well, whoever created these things indicated an obvious feminine focus. The references to Mother Nature, Lady Justice, the quote, 'Nevertheless, *she* persisted.' I think they were trying to send a specific message."

"Yeah," Melissa said, "don't trust boys."

The room erupted in a cacophony of giggles. Once we composed ourselves, I divided up the drawings into five equal piles or close enough where the math didn't quite work out. "Fold them however you need to so you can hide them, but don't hide them too well. We want people to see them. Write your own messages on them if you want. Be creative. Tap into your feminine subconscious."

The girls each took their stack of papers and folded them in half, sticking them inside their carrying cases for their standard-issue learning tablets, which had enough room in a pocket on the inside to tuck things away. The three new recruits stood.

"Oh, one last reminder, girls. Don't get caught and don't tattle. If you do get caught, and you're a Chooser, use that to wiggle your way out of it. If you aren't—sorry, Caillou, I think you're the only one—you'll have to take the heat on your own. If not, you could doom the whole operation."

Caillou swallowed hard but nodded. "I understand."

The newest group members left to catch a return transport to their homes and Terre hung back. Once we cleaned up the dishes from the lemonade, and I stashed away my remaining drawings into the envelope under my bed, we sat down on it with our backs against the headboard and our knees up.

"So," Terre started, "how do you think *that* went?"

"Not bad considering we didn't have a clue what we were doing."

"Do you think this will work?"

"I am not even one hundred percent sure I know what we're trying to do."

"I think we're trying to start a revolution."

"Whoa."

"My thoughts exactly. I feel pretty good about our choices of co-con-spirators though. Maybe not Caillou, but we'll see."

"Yeah, she's the wildcard for sure, but compared to everyone else she did come out in the top half."

"That's true. I guess we'll see."

"Yeah, I guess we will."

"We should start a group chat."

"Are you nuts, Terre? All chat content across the net is monitored by The Association."

"We'll be cryptic and use code and stuff."

"I dunno."

"We need to come up with a way to keep track of everyone's progress, and that's harder to do when we're not in school."

"True, but it needs to be *extraordinarily* cryptic."

"We're all smart cookies. I'm not worried."

Terre launched her messaging app on her tablet and created a group with her, me, Melissa, Eunice, and Caillou in it. She named it "The Girls" and typed the first message.

For us to keep track of how everyone's doing the rest of summer break. Here are the totals as of today.
K-Dub – 12
Terre – 12
Eunice – 11
Melissa – 10
Caillou – 10

Check in with any changes ☺

I watched her send the message and the telltale sound of an incoming message emanated from my device a few seconds later.

"The message went through."

"It did."

"What you wrote could be considered a competition of sorts."

"It could, but I'm not worried."

"Watch. They're all smart enough to understand." She typed out another message.

It was SO COOL to hear about how many things you wanted to do over the remainder of the break. Count them down here and when we're all at zero we'll get together again and share stories!

"That could work. At least now they have some idea of what to say if anyone asks."

"Plus, it should put any prying eyes at The Association at ease since now we're just a bunch of kids tittering and tattering about their summer break." She checked the time on her tablet. "I should go." She packed up her pages and tucked them into the inside pocket of her tablet-carrying case. "Do you want help un-burying your console?"

"Nah, I'll take care of it after you leave."

"Okay, please don't forget. We absolutely do not need our parents wondering what we're up to."

I gave a slight nod, stood, hugged Terre, and walked her to the front door. As I watched her put her PMID back on her wrist, I gave a perfunctory nod toward it. Terre considered the gesture for a second before replying.

"I've got an idea. Don't worry. Be patient."

I gave her one last hug and closed the door behind her. On my way to the kitchen to get more lemonade, I remembered the state of my room, turned on my heels, and went straight back to tidy up. It was good I did, too, because not two minutes later my family returned home. They found me lying on my bed reading a book. I'd long since finished *Sephirot* by Gordon Bonnet and enjoyed it so much that I started reading another of his called *The Shambles*. It was a story about a world where all the lost things go—including lost people. I was fascinated by the concept of parallel universes and different worlds adjacent to ours, and the book had weird sort of elements that drew me in. The book was written before the advent of item micro-tracking, but it was still a curious concept.

It was three days before anyone replied to the group chat. Unsurprisingly, it was Melissa who chimed in with an update.

Melissa — 10!

She went down two, which was good. After that, there were steady streams of updates. It was more of a trickle now that I think about it, but it was steady. By the time we returned to school, every girl managed to distribute most of their pages. Terre and Melissa had two left, I had three, and Eunice and Caillou four. Things were looking good until the CCC showed up at my door a week later.

When I heard the knock, I didn't think anything of it. My mother answered the door followed by a brief exchange of words, and then she called out to my father. "Oswald, can you come here for a minute?" He left the room where we watched an episode of our favorite game show, *Jeopardy 3000*. I couldn't hear the exact words from their conversation until Dad called for me to join them.

I did as requested, and we all sat at the kitchen table. Mom and Dad in their respective dinnertime seats, a CCC all decked out in his uniform with his helmet resting on my placemat, and beside him a short, stout-looking person with not a single outstanding feature to speak of.

My father spoke first, "Sit down. CCC Follis is going to explain a few things, you're going to listen and agree, and after he and his colleague here—I'm sorry I didn't catch your pronouns and name."

"Hadewijch."

"And your pronouns or salutation?"

"Just Hadewijch. Hadewijch Xue. But you can use Hadewijch. They or their, if you must."

"Hadewijch, it is. After CCC Follis and his colleague Hadewijch leave, we're going to have a talk."

I nodded and didn't so much sit down in my chair as collapse onto it. A better description would be that it broke my fall. I didn't get the chance to compose myself before CCC Follis spoke. His robotic voice, void of any inflection or emotion, sent a shudder up my spine.

"Katherine Webb, you are hereby charged, tried, and convicted of the crime of disobeying The Known Order and its governing body The Association. The final report along with an explanation of the crime, why you were found guilty, and your sentence will be mailed to you and your parents shortly. Due to your age, the lack of severity of the crime, the fact that you are a Chooser family, and the principal testimony came from a non-Chooser, your regional representative for The Association recommended a more lenient sentence, hence the presence of Hadewijch here. Do you understand?"

"Not really." This took everyone at the table a bit by surprise.

CCC Follis continued, "Which part don't you understand? Our records indicate you are highly intelligent and capable of comprehension and communication well beyond your age. Is something wrong with you? Do you need medical attention?"

"No, no, nothing like that. I'm—" I looked first over to my father and then to my mother and then burst into tears. They let me cry it out, and when I stopped and composed myself, I lifted my head off the table, dried my eyes with the backs of my hands, and let out a deep breath. "I'm sorry."

Hadewijch leaned forward and squinted. "Sorry as in remorseful, sorry you got caught, or sorry for your little breakdown here?"

I didn't see the point in lying. Commander no doubt made sure Hadewijch and everyone else at the table knew the answer. "All of the above."

Hadewijch nodded. "At least she's honest."

Mom spoke for the first time. "What happens now?"

"Now, Ms. Webb, what happens is Katherine is assigned a caseworker, that's me, and she is to attend reformation classes every weeknight for two hours. There she will learn how to act within the bounds of The Known Order as well as what happens if there is another infraction."

My bottom lip quivered. "For how long?"

"The reformation classes last for one full year. Five classes a week for fifty weeks for a total of five hundred hours of service. I will visit with you once a week for that first year and then once a month for the years after that."

"Years?"

"Yes, Katherine, years. You're fortunate you're not going to confinement for this, but as mentioned, your Association Representative didn't feel it was necessary."

"How many years?"

"Three total. Plus, you have a curfew and aren't allowed to be out of the house on your own for the duration of your sentence. That includes your property like your driveway and garden. While there is no age restriction on who must accompany you, if you're caught violating The Known Order, whoever's with you will be treated like they already have one strike against them."

"What if they didn't do anything or didn't know?"

"At this point, knowing you is already their first strike. Are we clear?"

"Yes, ma'am—I mean, yes, Hadewijch."

"Good." Hadewijch stood up but was so short it was hard to tell.

CCC Follis stood and towered over Hadewijch by at least a foot and a half. "We'll see ourselves out."

They left and once we heard the door shut, I folded my arms, lay my head on top of them on the table, and wept. My parents sent me to my room so they could read the report and told me they'd come to see me when they were done. It was a good half-hour before they knocked on my door.

"Yes?"

The door opened, they entered and closed it behind them. I sat up in my bed and propped up against a wall of pillows. My parents sat down. Dad on the end of the bed, Mom on my desk chair. She spoke with a calm and level voice with no hint of anger or disappointment.

"You didn't ask CCC Follis or Hadewijch about the infraction."

"I figured they knew. Between what Caillou told them and my PMID and Commander history there was no doubt."

"Well, what's in the report is, in the opinion of your father and me, a minor offense."

"That's the punishment I get for a minor offense? Wow."

Dad joined the conversation and put his hand on my foot, which wiggled back and forth in front of him. "You are too young to understand, but this is the way it's been for a long time. Extreme punishment for even the most minor of infractions. It's supposed to be a deterrent."

"Yeah, sure, but you'd think given the seriousness of the punishments they hand out, they would be more open in explaining this in all the stupid Known Order classes they make us take at school."

"Ah, yes, but they've found that nothing drives the message home like making an example out of a person."

"Think about it," Mom added. "All of your friends will see firsthand what happens to a peer who violates The Known Order. That's a pretty powerful message."

"It's a stupid message and I hate it."

"And those are valid feelings. When you get right down to it, sweet daughter, you made a mistake, and now you have to pay for it. It's called accepting responsibility."

"Why aren't you guys mad?"

They exchanged glances in a silent conversation before focusing on the console in my room. I understood, grabbed all the pillows off my bed, stacked them on top of the console along with a stack of books to weigh them down, and turned on my fan. My parents watched expressionless as I issued voice commands to test the listening sensitivity.

"So, tell me why you aren't mad."

They both smiled and Mom answered the question, "Because we agree with what you tried to do and even though you got caught, judging from your correct assumption about who ratted you out, you have learned a few things that will serve you well in the future."

Dad continued the thread, "And not that we are encouraging you to do something like this again, getting caught a second time will bring with it a much more serious punishment, but a year of learning about The Known Order, how it operates, and their expectations of society will further assist you in your future law-breaking endeavors, should you choose to perform any." He winked.

Confused, I couldn't wrap my head around the response from my parents. They weren't mad, or the dreaded "disappointed," but they showed signs of pride. Moreover, I could not explain the bit about repeat offending if I wanted to after my years' worth of classes. Were my parents even real? Were they CCCs in disguise, trying to trap me into confessing more of what I did?

"What was in the report?"

Mom grabbed her tablet, swiped it a few times, and handed it to me. In it were pages of notes taken by CCC Follis, who was called by Caillou's mother who caught her trying to stuff a picture inside a box of menstrual cups. According to their statements, the packaging was a smidgen too small, and she had trouble concealing the page. Caillou's mother saw her looking suspicious in the aisle and found her flustered and blushing trying to hide the box. That's when she broke down and started to cry, and her mom, not wanting to cause a scene in the store, told her everything would be fine and not to worry about it. Caillou's mom put the folded page into her purse without looking at it. When they got home, she saw what it was and asked her what she was doing with it.

After some convincing, she gave me up as the one who asked her to do it. Knowing that the security footage at the store would result in a visit from a CCC anyway, she pre-emptively called the station and struck a plea deal.

"That whiny little backstabbing—" I caught myself before finishing the sentence.

"In her defense," Mom said, "her parents are…how do I put this? They are extremely pro-Association and Known Order."

I looked up. "How did I not know this? How did"—I caught myself again—"There was never any talk about it at school or when we hung out at her house or anything."

"I'm guessing there isn't much talk about The Known Order, The Association, or any of that stuff with kids your age," said my father.

"No, I guess not. Everyone I know just sort of deals with it, you know. Like, we tolerate it because there isn't any choice but to tolerate it. I don't think I've heard of a person willingly taking the side of The Association on any occasion…" I paused before continuing, "Well, ever."

He put his hand out and I took it. "It used to be a person could speak truth to power and make a case for change. Real change for the betterment of society. Heck, for hundreds and hundreds of years the ability and option to choose "freewill" was the most valuable commodity in the world."

"Then The Wars took it away."

"Then The Wars took it away, yeah, and it happened at breakneck speed and with such relentlessness that there was no reprieve. The people, smothered by oppression and robbed of their option to choose forgot that they still had the ability. Worse still, large swaths of people outright relinquished their ability to choose, no questions asked. Ironic, don't you think? That people used their will to choose and at the same time gave up their ability to choose."

I nodded and looked to my mother, though I couldn't have said why. Was it comfort, or understanding, or did I simply need my mother to confirm what my father told me? She wore an expression of sadness and nodded back. "It's true. There's a quote from an old song from a long, long, time ago. This goes back to before Carlton Sedgwick discovered the Grand Unified Theory."

I raised my eyebrows. "That was a *long* time ago."

"I know," Mom continued, "it doesn't seem possible that something from that long ago still exists, but words and stories are different from any widget or commodity. You can't pull them down off the shelves, remove them from warehouses, or stop putting them on the internet. So long as there is one person who remembers them, they can live on forever."

"What's the quote?"

"'If you choose not to decide, you still have made a choice.'"

"Caillou's parents chose not to decide."

"Precisely, but they're not Choosers and don't have the same opportunities as others. I know The Known Order is supposed to be balanced and equitable and blah, blah, blah, but it's not. Everyone knows it's not. *Children* know it's not, for crying out loud, and yet the advantages for some and disadvantages for others still exist."

"The way it is."

"Yeah." She took my hand and joined her other with my father's, the three of us forming a circle as we sat on my bed. "The way it is. However, it doesn't have to be. It might not be you; it may be someone like you, but a lot like Carlton Sedgwick, but whoever it is will go down in history as the Person Who Changed the World."

"So, you're not mad?"

"Oh," my father said, "we're plenty mad. You put your friend at risk. You put us at risk. You could have come to us with questions, and you didn't. We don't like to leverage our Chooser status, but we will admit in certain situations it does come in handy. We could have helped you find a way to work within the latitude granted to us and still helped you accomplish your goal. There's a lot to be upset about here but given The Association and Hadewijch handed you your shirt, and then some, we don't see much point in piling on and making you feel worse."

"Besides," added my mother, "we love you and know you're capable of great things. All we ask now is you keep us informed if you decide to start a revolution. I'll make tea."

OOOOOTTO
[Six]

The remaining days before school brought quiet and boredom. Not content to put my tail between my legs, I spent most of my time redrawing the three pictures. Once I reproduced enough to make decent stacks of each, I drew my own and included my hidden messages. My favorite drawing depicted an art installation with several paintings hanging on a plain white wall with women standing in front. The paintings on the wall showed scenes that violated The Known Order. The detail in the hanging art wasn't exceptional, but it didn't need to be. Embedded throughout the picture in places where there wasn't a straight line were the phrases "free your mind" and "the unknown is real."

School started back up and thus began my after-school classes, and of course, my requisite meetings with The Hadewijch. The classes were fine, they were like regular school except instead of Intelligence Officers, they used CCCs to teach. Instead of math, science, languages, computing, art, drama, and all the other typical subjects, they taught us about The Known Order and nothing else. After two weeks of classes, I would have told you I knew everything there was to learn on the subject, but they had forty-eight more weeks of it queued up and ready to go.

Word got around among my friends, of course. I was a convicted terrorist. I punched a CCC officer. I stole a hover scooter and crashed it through the community green space fence and into the stream behind the pavilion. I ignored these claims as best as I could. The truth, as it turned out, was less scandalous.

A few things did stand out, though. First, Terre, Melissa, and Eunice expressed sincere gratitude to me for taking all the heat. It would have been easy for me to spread the blame around, but I didn't, and my three friends appreciated it. Second, the movement I started began to take hold. Melissa and Eunice spearheaded the efforts by doing a little recruiting and were assisted by the third thing, the school's universal dislike of one Caillou Latour.

No members of our little rebellion mounted a smear campaign against Caillou. In fact, we paid her no mind at all, keeping any feelings of ill will to ourselves. However, kids understood loyalty. Many who disagreed with what I did still had no respect for the person who ratted me out. I wasn't sure why I felt bad about it. Not terrible, mind you, but a little bad. Caillou pinkie swore with the girls and then broke the agreement. In the world of teenage girls, a pinkie swear was tantamount to a signature in blood. By all rights, I shouldn't have felt as much as an ounce of sympathy for her, but I did. I tried to put it out of my mind, which I did with great success—for close to six months.

Six months after my return to school and one boring as-all-get-out school break later, Caillou approached me in the schoolyard during an outdoor free period. Most of the kids hung around the school tree or off in small cliques nattering on about this or that. I stood by myself enjoying the weather and the fact I wouldn't be in my Association-appointed Known Order classes for another couple of hours.

I sat down cross-legged on the ground as Caillou approached from the side and stood above me for a second before speaking. When she did, her timid voice contained a hint of sadness in its tone. She spoke one word, "Sorry." Then stood there, silent, waiting.

I looked up and tears cut streaks down her cheeks. "Are you sorry for telling on me, or are you sorry because all the other kids have shunned you for being a rat who can't keep a pinkie swear?"

"Both."

CCC Follis' voice echoed in my head. *At least she's honest.*

My curfew wasn't a big deal, but the stress of not getting to make a single mistake pushed my patience—and sanity—to their limits. The required escort when I left the house wasn't a big deal, but it meant needing to be on my best behavior to keep co-conspirators safe. The classes weren't a big deal but meant I lost more than five hundred hours of my precious childhood to The Association. If I did the math on the situation, it more or less balanced out, but if I thought about it, I should be solidly in the negative. I *did* orchestrate an organized rebellion of sorts, as juvenile and innocuous as it was, and in spite of Caillou's inability to stand her ground and keep her mouth shut, could I honestly blame her? Had I been caught without her spilling the beans, my punishment would have been much worse.

I looked up and waited for Caillou's eyes to meet mine. "It's okay. I forgive you." I extended my hand, balled in a fist with my pinkie sticking out, and curled into a slight hook. She smiled and returned the gesture, locked my pinkie finger with hers, and shook on it.

For the remainder of the school year, I kept my head down and my mouth shut in all situations except for the schoolyard outdoor free period. There, I would sneak off with my friends and talk strategy—in code, of course. We took turns picking a topic and would use words and phrases associated with it to communicate our thoughts and intentions. On occasion, we'd jumble the translation, but it wasn't a frequent occurrence. It turns out that teenage girls—and our group in particular—excelled at deception.

Word got around that Caillou and I buried the hatchet, and she made her way back into the fold, albeit on the periphery. A few more girls joined over the weeks and months and by the month-long summer break, our group stood at nine members from our school zone alone: the original five of me, Terre, Melissa, Eunice, and Caillou along with new additions Heather, Shelby, Nicole, and Eden. Terre and Melissa recruited girls from other zones as well. We recruited three girls from Zone Seven: Selina, Rachel, and Xinxin. Two from Zone Five: Rylee and Amara. Despite acting as their de facto leader, I didn't join the group in person all the time, choosing instead to keep a lower profile until the remainder of my sentence passed.

One week after school break started, Hadewijch brought wonderful news, though if you looked at my face when they delivered it, you'd think I'd eaten a sour pickle. The Association allowed me to bypass the final three weeks of my classes. I still had to take a final exam, but they remained confident that I would pass with flying colors. In addition, they reduced my total sentence from three years down to two.

I couldn't be sure, and vibrated with nervous energy, but I thought that maybe my parents called in a Chooser favor with The Association or an individual member. After my meeting with The Hadewijch ended, I thought about what it meant to be shown leniency by an organization renowned for anything but. I concluded that They tried to buy my cooperation. That, or lull me into a false sense of security. Either way, I could not understand nor trust their motives.

At the dinner table, I gave my parents the news. They expressed genuine surprise, allaying my suspicions they had anything to do with it. I knew of one way to know for sure. I asked.

"Did either of you have a hand in getting my sentence reduced?"

My mother finished chewing her food, swallowed, and put her fork down on her plate. "Not in so many words."

"But not 'no' either."

"Correct. All I did was ask if there was any chance, in cases like yours, if they ever commuted a sentence or granted leniency under any circumstances. I didn't ask if they would, just if it were possible. They said that it's happened a few times in the recent past, but it wasn't common and definitely not publicized."

"That's it?"

"That's it" — she bent down and met my eyes — "I swear. You asked an honest question and providing an honest answer is the least I can do."

"Hmm. Who did you talk to?"

"Ah, now that would be better for everyone involved if you didn't know. She's an old friend and I trust her."

"Well, thank you." I left it at that, deciding to enjoy the fact I hit the halfway point of my sentence instead of a third. No point in looking a gift horse in the mouth, whatever that meant. My father had a habit of imparting random anachronistic expressions, and I'd heard him use this one before. I kind of knew what it meant, but I'd never looked it up or asked. Still, I remained confident it applied to my current situation.

Every month, I met with The Hadewijch. Every month, I answered the same questions in the same way—with a smile on my face and a cheery disposition, but showing regret and remorse as needed. This resulted in The Hadewijch meeting less and less with the other girls. They didn't care, and besides, from what I gleaned they all knew enough about how to give the appearance of innocence when the opposite applied. My father once gave me a piece of advice I never forgot. He said, "Kate, if you want to change the rules you have to play by them until you're in a position to change them. But when you finally are, you'd better go ahead and change them." The Girls weren't strictly playing by the rules, but the message was still clear. When you gave the *appearance* of playing by them, enough people would leave you alone so that you could get stuff done.

Each of us amassed a stockpile of contraband, with me leading the way. I had an overabundance and fewer and fewer hiding places in my room to keep it all. I would have to start distributing it sooner rather than later. The rest of The Known Order rebels and I would have to start coming up with better and more effective ways to achieve our mission, which started to become clear about six months from the completion of my sentence.

00000111
[Seven]

I wasn't sure how many CCCs existed in the world, but if forced to guess I'd say one million. The goal of our little anti-Known Order brigade, to put it in the simplest terms, was not to make them unemployed but to make them unnecessary. However, the path to successful completion of this objective wasn't straightforward. An end to the CCCs meant a complete redesign of law enforcement and to do that we needed to redesign all the laws and to do that we needed to disband The Association and to do that we needed to reprogram Commander.

The concept of humans requiring permission from an all-knowing machine before executing a basic task ran counter to how human brains worked. The prefrontal cortex has come a long way from its earlier iterations of fight or flight, hunter or gatherer, and encapsulated complexities that the top scientists in the world were still trying to unravel. Humans were meant to think and evaluate risk versus reward, not kowtow to a computer with false or perceived intelligence. The computer had to go, or at least be proven less effective than leaving people to exercise free will.

The first step in the process involved getting enough people willing to break the rules. We needed to show that the benefits of choosing outweighed the detriments of making the wrong choice. People would get hurt, upset, or angry, but there was a time, before The Wars, when that was a part of life. Hell, in a lot of ways, it's what made life worth living. The world may have been more complicated and less certain, but it was also rich and colorful. It had meaning.

The second step of the process proved more difficult than the first. For this we needed concrete evidence that Commander wasn't operating autonomously, and that The Association manipulated the system for its own benefit. At this point, it was a theory that I dreamed up, and it leaned more toward conspiracy than it did anything scientific, but it wasn't a half-baked cockamamie idea. I knew more about The Known Order than any of my Intelligence Officers and indeed most of the general population.

First things came first, and that meant getting through the last few months of my sentence, returning my life back to normal, and expanding the reach of The Girls. At one point I thought about bringing boys into it, starting with my father, but I got the idea from my studies and through careful observation that the system, The Known Order and The Association had an explicit bias toward men. So, while I considered a consultation with my father, it was not in the cards. Not unless my theory needed revision, which I didn't think it did.

My final meeting with The Hadewijch occurred on a Friday in late summer and it was an unemotional affair as far as my caseworker was concerned. The Hadewijch suppressed emotions with the best of them. For me though, it was a glorious occasion. While I can't say I suffered from my punishment, not having that weight hanging off me brought an overwhelming sense of relief. Relief and accomplishment. I learned quite a bit about the world I lived in over the past two years and if I kept my head about me, played my cards right, and got a little help from my friends, I might have a legitimate shot at changing it for the better.

"Katherine, per The Known Order and with the agreement of The Association and the local CCC division, I hereby declare your sentence officially complete. All restrictions on movement are lifted, and you are free to live your life as you see fit, provided you don't violate The Known Order, of course." I wasn't sure if my eyes played tricks on me, but if The Association allowed betting, I would have put money down on The Hadewijch letting the slightest hint of a smile escape.

"Of course."

"Now, keep in mind that completing your sentence does not set you back to where you were before. You've got one strike, and based on your knowledge of The Known Order and The Association, do you know what that means?"

"It means no more strikes. I was lucky enough to get one; most people don't get that much. Next time I mess up, I get sent to confinement, for which the duration of my stay is predetermined by the severity of my violation."

"Correct. Sign here and I'll be on my way."

I picked the stylus off the table, put it to the tablet, and signed my name. Without saying another word, The Hadewijch stood, turned on the heels of the least sensible shoes I'd ever seen—a pair of Jimmy Choo heels held over from before The Wars—and left. My parents stood in the entranceway to the kitchen. They had their arms around each other, and my father broke the silence.

"So, kiddo, how does it feel?"

"Fine, I guess. Not much has changed for me. I've gotten used to the curfew, which wasn't a big deal anyway since I didn't need to be out late and still don't. I'm looking forward to going out alone, though. I'm definitely going to take advantage of that. But overall, I'm just relieved it's over."

My mother broke from my father's embrace and joined me at the kitchen table. "And your friends? Are they happy?"

"Oh, yeah. Tomorrow is going to be a lot of fun. They're relieved that they won't be on the hook for any of my future mistakes"—I gave a big, wide smile—"should there be any."

Mom shook her head. "Let's try to go more than a day without getting into trouble, shall we?"

"Yes, Mother, of course." I continued to smile.

I booked the community green space for the day after the completion of my sentence. I invited everyone from my class along with all the girls from the other zones who had joined The Girls. I named the event K-Dub's Freedom Party, but it allowed for the first time every member of the group to occupy the same geographical space. Meeting at the same time together was impossible without drawing suspicion from the nonmembers so we had to find ways to interact with each other in smaller groups and not make our transgressions obvious. I intended to keep my promise to my mother and not conspire to incite a rebellion less than twenty-four hours after finishing my sentence.

Dad prepared an extravagant dinner, with all of my favorite foods and a thick slice of chocolate cake with chocolate fudge icing for dessert. Afterwards, I declared my intention to go for a walk for no other reason than to flaunt my lack of curfew and chaperone. My parents offered no objection, and off I went.

The mild, crisp air filled my lungs, and the spring in my step, missing for two years, returned. I walked around my block and didn't encounter anyone else. I widened the loop. After twenty minutes of walking, I still hadn't come across another person. Not a single neighbor was out walking their dog or enjoying the night air, or the quiet solitude I was eager to disrupt. Without my PMID, no one would know I existed. Free to do or say anything I wanted without fear of reprisal. It got me thinking about the key I found at the pavilion and wondered if it still worked. I hadn't attempted to use it once since I got caught. All PMIDs had received an upgrade about six months after that.

The key appeared mechanical, but I wasn't sure if it contained electronic components embedded into it. I also didn't know if the composition mattered. The keyhole on the band looked the same, but the charging stations and corresponding keys were upgraded at the same time as the wrist devices. I considered the possibility that my illegal key collected dust for two years and no longer worked.

I turned around and took the quickest route back home that I could. By that time, my brother slept, and my parents zoned out watching their favorite holovision series.

"I'm going to go to bed early, I think. Tomorrow promises excitement the likes I haven't seen in a long time, and I want to be well rested." My parents' eyes didn't leave their show, but they managed two half-hearted waves and an unenthusiastic, "Goodnight, sweetie."

In my room, I changed into my pajamas and retrieved the key from its hiding spot. I made a point to keep my device on my wrist when I came home with the intent of trying my luck. It fit into the keyhole without any trouble and after I gave it a quarter turn, the band unlocked. I smiled.

The next day, I woke early and made breakfast for the whole family. I wanted to make sure I was well-fed before my party and hoped everyone else would appreciate my efforts. The remainder of the morning I spent in my room working offline on a special project. I set a goal of creating a replica of my forbidden key, but in several small pieces that I would hide in plain sight. The main problem with this—and the reason I had to be offline to do it—was while I could image the key, no 3D printer would print one. The Association required all manufacturers to include a security feature disallowing the replication of PMID keys. This gave me the idea to split the key into a dozen pieces that would lock together in a glorious illegal puzzle.

A few minutes before my scheduled departure, I saved the four files I'd created to that point, put them on an offline quantum memory stick, deleted any trace of them from my computer, and re-enabled the network connection. Satisfied with my progress, I walked the ten minutes to the community green space to meet my friends and co-conspirators. By the time I arrived at the front gate, I could already hear the dull chatter of distant, but not too distant, voices through the iron bars lining the sidewalk. I checked my watch. One minute late, but strange because it sounded like the vast majority of my friends and classmates were already there.

I scanned in and it occurred to me as I passed through the gate that the last time I stepped foot inside the hundreds-year-old cast iron fence was before The Association caught me violating The Known Order. A wave of relief washed over me when I realized the crime for which I was convicted was the tip of the iceberg. Armed with new knowledge and new experiences, I had a crystal-clear focus on *my* future and *the* future.

As I trod up the small hill along a worn path weaving its way from the main gate to the pavilion, the voices became clearer and louder. My head crested the hill, and for a brief moment, the talking died down to a low murmur and that's when I saw it. A foot wide and at least ten feet long banner reading "CONGRATULATIONS!" Terre started the applause, and Melissa, Eunice, and Caillou followed. Before long, all forty or so kids were clapping, whistling, hooting, and hollering like they had all passed their exit exams with perfect scores. It was all I could do to keep my emotions under control, but after a solid sixty seconds of standing there slack-jawed, the dam burst and tears streamed down my cheeks.

The original girls, my squad—including the reformed tattletale—ran to me and we engaged in the warmest group hug I had ever experienced.

We wrapped our arms around each other's shoulders in a five-girl huddle like we did when strategizing for group problem-solving puzzle sessions at school. I sniffled and thanked them for their support. In return, they thanked me for my commitment and fortitude in the face of adversity. Caillou added, "Thank you for your forgiveness." I gave her a genuine smile.

"That's what friends do. Now, are you girls ready to change the world?"

Each one looked the others in the eye and nodded, and Terre answered for the whole group. "You bet your ass we are."

"Language, Miss Zhooshkwa. What do you think this is? A rebellion?"

"It better be or else I'm at the wrong party."

We laughed, separated from the huddle, and joined the other partygoers. The amount of food set up in the pavilion could have fed the whole district. The parents of a classmate ran a catering company. It wasn't normal for ordinary folks outside of The Association, let alone a bunch of kids, to have a catered event. My friend, Stephanie, however, impressed upon my mother that after two years of reformation, the New Katherine deserved special treatment to let me know that everyone appreciated life returning to normal.

If they only knew.

After I made my way around greeting everyone and taking stock to determine the whereabouts of the others, I flagged down the four originals.

"Okay, girls, time to get to work. The game plan is microaggressions and mini subversions. Small acts of defiance will start to call into question the existing power dynamic. It's all connected" —I pointed to the device on my wrist—"so things need to be analog, and words will require careful choosing. What we have to do is split up and have conversations with the others about how they might accomplish this. Act casual, but make sure there isn't anyone within earshot who isn't, you know, part of the group."

They all nodded in agreement and scattered in different directions. A couple of hours later, as the fifteen-minute warning announcement played over the pavilion speakers, we reconvened and exchanged notes. Everyone was on board and excited to be making a difference, and more than a few of them were eager to bring more people on board. I felt the movement growing stronger than ever, and it occurred to me that the setback I suffered wasn't a setback at all. Without it, there never would have been this much excitement or interest in veering away from the status quo. All that we needed was a little publicity, and with that, I got another idea.

On my way out, I excused myself and ran into the washroom. I didn't have to use the facilities, but it had been two years since I was last there and curiosity got the better of me. Truth be told, I felt compelled to check. Terre stood guard outside the door, partly as a lookout and partly so I wouldn't be left alone. If I exited late again, Terre said she would take the heat to keep the attention off her newly-freed friend.

I went straight to the stall and stood on the toilet to check the top of the door. The carving hadn't budged. No surprise. The folded drawing on the underside of the dispenser was there too, a thin sliver of its corner sticking out in the spot I left it all those months ago. The drawing wedged into the top of the dispenser, however, was gone. I tried all I could to see into the teeny gap but found no evidence of anything wedged inside. I flushed for the sake of keeping up appearances and washed my hands—because you should always have clean hands—and exited with a spring in my step.

Terre greeted me with a smile. "Well?"

"One of the drawings is gone."

"Nice! Would be nice to know who found it and what they did with it."

"Yeah, but the fact that it's gone, and we haven't heard anything about it in the news or in the bulletins leads me to believe that whoever did take it doesn't intend on reporting it."

We walked back to the side gate as the one-minute warning message echoed through the park. We both broke into a run and caught up to the last of the group as they passed through the exit. I scanned out before Terre, who did right as the "time to exit" notice played over the speakers.

"Okay if I come back to your place now?"

"Yeah, if all the gatekeepers and appropriate decision-makers approve, of course."

"Of course."

Terre secured approval from her parents, and I did the same before we consulted Commander. Both their wrist devices flashed green and sounded a pleasant *bing* of approval.

At home, I gave my parents a brief summary of the afternoon before Terre and I retreated to my bedroom. We kept quiet as we piled pillows and blankets and books on top of the console and started the fan. After the requisite sound check, we sat cross-legged facing each other on my bed.

"At the end of the party—thank you for planning all that by the way—I got an idea."

"It was my pleasure. You could have easily saved your own hide and cut a deal or something, but you didn't. I'm not sure I would have forgiven Caillou, but I can understand why you did. What's your idea?"

"First, keys for everyone. Well, almost everyone."

"How do you plan on doing that?"

I explained how I split up the 3D scan and intended on making it into a puzzle that, when solved, would be a key that unlocked a PMID. I wasn't yet sure of the benefits of having keys but the fact that The Association didn't want us to made it worthwhile. If they think it's bad, I think it's good.

"Cool. What comes after that?"

"Cryptic puzzles that can only be solved if you have the cipher. I learned more about The Association, The Known Order, and Commander than you can imagine and what stood out most was how terrible the whole system is at recognizing clever subterfuge."

"Really? The Intelligence Officers and the CCCs make it seem like Commander is all-knowing. Heck, experience tells me that it pretty much is."

"Yeah, but it's got some flaws. You know how some people have a hard time recognizing sarcasm?"

"Yes, like Eunice's big sister."

"Exactly. Well, a carefully worded message that gives the appearance of an ordinary brain teaser will slip right past all the controls in place and land on every social media site you can think of."

"You don't say?"

"That's my theory, but it's a sound one. My idea, then, is to get those with keys to distribute the cipher using analog methods and spread the word that way. You know, get a bit of a buzz going."

"You think that'll work?"

"Yeah, I think so, but Commander is powerful, so maybe a cipher isn't the right method. I'm thinking more along the lines of posting generic brain teasers that are missing information."

"Which The Girls will provide."

"Precisely, along with the interpretation of the result, of course. But we'll have to distribute it all analog. Commander reads everything, not just what's posted in our group chat. We're going to have to pass notes to each other and hide the missing info and interpretation in places for people to find them."

"But separately. People who are curious enough will seek out the second step. If this catches on, there will be enough interest that if we give up too much information too quickly it will seem obvious what's going on. I think we need to be subtle about it, and for sure, do it so it can't be traced back to us."

"Well, I was going to post the brain teasers and otherwise stay squeaky clean and out of the way. They can't get me in trouble for what other people are doing with something I got approval to post, can they?"

"No, I suppose not. Provided you get approval."

"Oh, I will. I'm only going to use puzzles that are in The Known Order Public Domain. Then, I'm going to remove one key piece of information and call it an unsolvable puzzle. It will require group think and communication to solve—without cheating and asking Commander for the missing piece, which I guess some people will do, but they aren't our target audience anyway."

"You sure you don't want me to post the riddles, and you stay right out of it? You've got a strike, Kate. That's it. You're out of chances. If The Association so much as gets a whiff of impropriety on your part, they'll lock you up for who knows how long."

"I won't be doing anything to violate The Known Order, I promise. It's everyone else who'll be taking the risks. The mere suggestion of an alternate interpretation to a known riddle is enough to land a non-Chooser in confinement."

"I suppose you're right."

"I know I'm right. Besides, does anyone else have any other ideas?"

"Not that I know of."

"There you have it."

We spent the remainder of our time together working on the key deconstruction. Terre helped with many of the design mechanisms that we required to get the printed key to fit together and still work. By dinnertime, we had twelve pieces designed and saved to separate files on an offline quantum thumb drive. Terre had to leave, and I needed the house to myself to manufacture the pieces. To accomplish this, I required modification of the 3D printer to ensure it worked offline. That meant disabling its wireless communication ability, which by default you could not do from the menus. It meant opening up the machine, finding the Wi-Fi component, and disconnecting it by hand.

I waited the greater part of a week before an opportunity to reconfigure the printer presented itself. In those days of waiting, I passed the time by crafting my messages for the first unsolvable puzzle. I had to wait to ask Commander for permission to post until right before since permission to send it out into the world depended on the precise timing. Once I settled on the messages, sixteen in total, I came up with an alternate interpretation. The goal wasn't to prove anything beyond reasonable doubt, but rather cast seeds of doubt and call into question the power structure controlling everyone's lives.

As for which piece of information to withhold, that was easy. The Riddle I chose was a modified Einstein's Riddle and required fifteen clues to solve it. Since The Riddle dated back to long before The Wars, in ancient times, it wasn't well-known. The only reason I knew about it was that I learned of Einstein in my Known Order classes as the man who laid the groundwork for Carlton Sedgwick to discover the Grand Unified Theory. Once he did, Einstein's work became superfluous, and his contributions to physics gathered dust. Forgotten by academics and scholars and reduced to an imperceptible footnote in history. I found it kind of sad the memory of such a great man was lost to the sands of time, but my sincere hope was that what I was doing would change the world of today as much or more as the way he changed his world all those centuries ago.

The original riddle used five houses of different colors, which I would likewise use. Each house contained a person of a different nationality. I would use Known Order Districts instead since the concept of nations ended after The Wars. They taught this in Known Order 101. Each homeowner drank a specific beverage, which I would leave as is, and kept a certain pet, which I would change to "had a certain hobby." The Association considered pets luxuries, and I wanted to appeal to as many people as possible. The final criterion, a brand of cigarette, had to change since a large portion of the population would have no clue what a cigarette was. I asked three separate Intelligence Officers before I was told to drop it. Commander only responded with its "Invalid Input Parameters" response, which was standard operating procedure when it didn't feel the response would be beneficial to The Known Order. I used "eat a certain type of food" in its place.

The Riddle, as I modified it, read like this:

There are five houses of five different colors.
In each house lives a person from a different Known Order District.
The homeowners each drink a specific beverage, eat a specific food, and have a specific hobby.
No homeowner has the same hobby, eats the same food, or drinks the same beverage.
The Unsolvable Riddle asks: Whose hobby is drawing?

I hadn't determined the exact interpretation of The Riddle, but that could come later. I'd consult with my peers when I could to ensure optimal messaging. With The Riddle ready to go, all I needed was to choose which piece of information to withhold to keep The Riddle unsolvable but still allow for people to make enough progress that they'll be invested in and want to seek out the final clue and solve it.

With the world predetermined and compartmentalized the way it was, humans needed a way to exercise their brains. A lack of decision-making dulled the senses and as much as The Association controlled everything, saw every problem as a nail and used Commander as a hammer, people still kept everything running. I had a budding theory that The Association gave the bare minimum of intellectual freedom to the public so they would not realize that their sole purpose was to keep a layer of separation between those in charge and the machines they created to do their bidding. A buffer, as it were. If my theory was correct, that meant the power was with the people, the common people, not The Association, and not the great all-knowing Commander computer.

With that done, all that remained was to start distributing information—and keys—to The Girls. With my house empty for the first time in a week, the second my parent's hover car left the driveway, I rooted through drawers and the garage for a screwdriver. The tool represented the oldest piece of ancient history still in everyday use. Materials had changed, of course, but the simple implement and its function did not. I unscrewed the case to the 3D printer that came standard as part of every personal domicile. Even better, they were all consistent in every way. If you knew one, you knew them all, and after a groupthink project at school on troubleshooting common household appliances, I knew 3D printers inside and out.

I removed the outer case and the secure covering from the control panel and motherboard. From there all I needed to do was find the Wi-Fi chip and dislodge it. It wasn't a straightforward task. The downside to mass-produced components was their configuration, always arranged in the most cost-effective way instead of considering human interaction, usage, and maintenance. Careful not to dislodge any other components, I used ceramic chopsticks from the kitchen to hold wires out of the way and get access to the sub-panel containing the piece I sought. Using a pair of tweezers with the tips dipped in wax to keep them free from static, I pinched them around the tiny chip and pulled it out.

After thirty seconds, the console in the office issued a warning, "Network connectivity to the 3D printer lost. Dispatching a service technician."

"No, Commander, stop."

"Invalid input parameters."

"Commander, cancel service technician."

"Unable to cancel service technician. Estimated time of arrival: three minutes and twenty-seven seconds."

I put the Wi-Fi chip back into the motherboard and looked toward the console for a response. Ten seconds passed, then twenty, before it spoke again. "Connectivity restored to 3D printer."

"Commander, cancel service technician."

"Unable to cancel service technician. Device diagnostic required. Estimated time of arrival: one minute and forty-two seconds."

It was an anxious walk to the front door, and my fingernails took the brunt of it. My gaze wandered through the adjacent window while I waited the remaining minute and change for the technician to show up. They didn't need to knock as I opened the door to greet them.

"3D printer issues?" The woman, who wore a standard-issue uniform that bore a striking resemblance to the one worn by a CCC, checked her tablet. "I need to run a simple diagnostic."

I welcomed her in and led her to the office where the 3D printer sat on a desk in the far corner. The case was still off, and the chopsticks, tweezers, and screwdriver sat on the desktop beside it. The technician gave me a sideways glance.

"I—I—tried to fix it myself. There was a calibration issue, and I thought since I learned about these in school, I could fix it myself. I knocked the Wi-Fi chip loose when I was in there trying to access the manual calibration override."

The tech didn't say anything and plugged her tablet into the printer. She tapped the screen a few times and the machine came to life, printing a small cube. "We have to let it cool for a minute."

I gave a slight nod and stood silent across the room. After a minute of dead air, the tech took the cube from the printer and set it on the desk. She scanned it with her tablet and tapped the screen. After a moment of waiting, an audible *bing* emanated from the device. It sounded like the affirmative response tone from a PMID.

"Okay, Katherine, you're all set. Turns out there wasn't a calibration issue at all." She pinched the cube between her finger and thumb, which she then placed in the palm of my hand before bending down to meet me eye to eye. "You know, it's best to unplug the device before performing any maintenance on it." I maintained constant eye contact as she paused and then looked over toward the console in the opposite corner from the printer and looked back, locking her eyes on mine again. "When you unplug it, you can tell the console you're performing maintenance, or you wanted to move it to another spot or something like that, and it will accept the explanation. Then you can do what you need to do to it and plug it back in. In the case of a loose Wi-Fi chip upon power up, it will ask you if you want to configure network connectivity."

"Okay."

"You don't have to configure connectivity right away. Do you understand?"

I tried to read the tech's face but couldn't. She was expressionless and with no inflection to her voice that indicated anything other than the words she spoke.

The technician repeated the message but in a different way. "It will accept the deferral of the configuration as a response, and you can use the printer offline in the meantime. Okay?"

I nodded. "Yeah, I get it. Thanks."

The tech patted me on the shoulder. "Good to hear, Katherine Webb. I look forward to all the wonderful creations you will bring to the world." She smiled. It's possible I imagined it, but I would have sworn she gave a subtle raise of her eyebrows as the corners of her lips curled upward. I opened my mouth to speak but second-guessed my decision and snapped it shut. Another gift horse I did not dare look in the mouth.

I walked the kind and understanding technician to the door and ran back to the office. The plug for the printer was tucked away behind the desk upon which it sat, but reaching it wasn't a problem for my long, slender arms. The console barked as the tech told me it would. I responded, "I'm temporarily moving the printer to a new location because I need the desk space for a separate project." That silenced its complaints as the tech indicated it would. The chip was easier to remove the second time, and when I plugged the machine back in, my console complained again about connectivity. As predicted by the tech, the option to configure the connectivity was deferred without question. It was funny how my school and its Intelligence Officers left out that little nugget of information from the lesson plan.

With the printer operational but offline, I loaded the first file from my thumb drive and checked to make sure the right material composition and color sat in the spool at the back of it. For the twelve pieces, I assigned each a different color to make a fun-looking completed object. Part cosmetic and part to assist in reassembly, the ultimate reason was to ensure the final product was not identifiable by any combination of its constituent pieces. Due to their small size, it was possible to print all needed copies for each piece at the same time, though that still meant it would take more than three hours to make all dozen components. My family wasn't due back until after dinner, so I had the time, but every minute it took increased my anxiety.

The first piece, the largest of the twelve, finished, and while they cooled, I put the printer into "developer mode" and cleared its memory. I wanted to avoid the machine coming back online and get smart about its recent history and quite literally put the pieces of my puzzle together. I removed the pieces from the printer and swapped out the material used in the first piece with the material needed for the seventh piece. The device held six different types of material but in my case, the material stayed the same and the color changed. After the seventh piece finished printing, I returned the material back to the default. "Always leave things as you found them," my parents used to say.

After three hours of constant use, the printer was hot to the touch, and I was lucky I didn't have to move it. I checked the memory one more time and made sure there was no trace of anything I printed, but the history from earlier uses remained. I unplugged the machine and calmed down the console by telling it I was moving the printer back to where it belonged. The Wi-Fi chip snapped back into place without any issue. Likewise for the maintenance panel and the printer outer casing. After plugging the machine back into the wall and reconfiguring its network connectivity, I collected all one hundred and twenty key pieces into a container and left the office looking as it did when I stepped into it earlier in the day. The heat coming off the printer and dissipating throughout the room provided the only clue of its use. Provided my family didn't come home early, and no one needed to use the printer upon returning, I knew I would be fine.

Back in my room, I poured all the key puzzle pieces onto my bed and went into my bedside table bottom drawer where I kept my pajamas and pulled out ten small cloth bags. I picked them up one day after I got the puzzle key idea. Anyone who looked in the bags would see what looked to be a colorful tactile puzzle. As long as they didn't try to solve it, there wouldn't be any issues. Each girl who got a key received instructions on how to put them together in the form of a riddle on the group chat. The girls who didn't get a key would not know what The Riddle was for and hence would not be able to solve it, but that was okay. Everyone in the group was loyal, and for the most part, unquestioning. Once the keys were separated into ten piles, I put the first one together.

I memorized the order the pieces needed to be in by creating a mnemonic with the first letter of each of the colors in the order they connected. Three pieces needed to have a rough edge filed down a bit, but otherwise, they fit as snug as a bug in a rug, another old-timey expression my father used whenever he used to tuck me into bed. I grabbed my PMID off its charger and put it on my wrist. I sat on the bed and inserted the colorful key into the keyhole on the wristband of my device and gave it a quarter turn. The lock released. A wide, toothy grin spread across my face.

The first keys distributed went to Terre, Melissa, and Eunice. Caillou didn't get one, and might not ever, for as much as I forgave her, there would always be a small seed of doubt in my mind about her ability to keep her mouth shut if a CCC or anyone from The Association questioned her again. If she ever crossed paths with The Hadewijch, I knew how that story ended. Two additional keys each went to Melissa and Eunice to deliver to girls in other zones. Two keys remained and after an in-person discussion with the core group, minus Caillou, we decided Terre and Eunice would hold onto them. I kept the original and the means to print out more, though anyone with a key could scan the individual pieces and print their own, provided they took the same precautions I learned from my understanding service technician.

The instructions passed between girls on how to assemble and duplicate the keys included reminders about turning off all biometric data gathering on the PMID before using the key to remove it. Control over those features on the devices came via hard-fought disagreements and discussions. In the end, The Association conceded and in doing so more likely than not avoided another war or at least a decent rebellion. The Girls knew to be careful, but it never hurt to issue reminders on topics of such a serious and consequential nature.

In addition to leaving suggestive drawings and imagery around in places where women would find them, the keys opened up myriad possibilities for other acts of rebellion. In face-to-face conversations and in coded language in the group chat, all The Girls exchanged ideas about how they could go around Commander and start acting with increased independence. Much of the discussion centered around how to avoid any serious reactions to their actions. After all, they wanted to change the world, not cause any undue harm to the people within it. Even though The Association's public mission statement ensured "an optimal outcome in every situation for every person across every moment of their physical existence" on this oblate spheroid called home, reality painted a different picture, a picture of a world full of people who were alive but not living. They could do and accomplish, but they couldn't *experience*. The Girls gave us a small taste of what it was like to get to choose and face the consequences—good or bad—and the unanimous response among us landed in favor of choice.

00001000 [Eight]

I waited for two weeks since my last transgression before asking Commander for permission to create my new social media account. My handle was "Unsolvable Riddles" and the description on my bio read: Katherine Webb presents the ultimate exercise in groupthink problem-solving. Work together to make your way through the problem as far as you can, but be forewarned, you will NOT be able to solve it outright, as one piece of information will be withheld... until the chosen time is upon us.

The approval for the account creation took less than a minute, and then I submitted my riddle and the list of clues. That took a bit more time than I expected, and for a moment I worried about imminent denial, but when the positive verdict came through, I exhaled a long sigh of relief. All that remained was to request permission to post. Since there was no time like the present, I crafted my first message and sent it to Commander. The response that came back was acceptable, if not perfect.

Immediate posting denied. Message will post automatically upon approval.

I waited in excruciating frustration, refreshing my screen every few seconds. After five minutes, I decided to spend time in other ways. I lay my tablet on its wireless charger and went about my evening reading books and drawing with my little brother.

Dinner came and went, and I tried to put it out of mind, but since The Riddle involved food and beverages, I found it difficult. My mother gave me a critical glance as I handed out dessert.

"Everything all right, sweetie? You seem"—Mother looked at me with concerned eyes—"distracted."

"I *am* distracted. I started a new social media project today, and I'm waiting for the first post to go up."

"Oh?" my father asked. "What's involved?"

"It's a social media groupthink experiment of sorts, though there's no way I would have got approval had I submitted the proposal with that wording."

"Well, I'm already curious." My mother took a bite of her homemade apple pie.

"That's good because I'm going to need everyone I know to share it with everyone they know."

"What's the premise?" my mom asked in between bites.

"Unsolvable Riddles. I take complex riddles and challenge the masses to solve them, only I purposefully withhold one key piece of information to see how far people can get. Once there are enough responses in the right neighborhood, I'll release the last piece of information and see how long it takes for a correct response to come in."

My mother, with her mouth full of food, nodded and pointed the tines of her fork in my direction. My father, who must have inhaled his dessert, put his fork down on his empty plate. "That's definitely cool. What's the first one?"

"Einstein's Riddle."

"Aw, yeah." He extended his hand for a high five and I obliged. "That one wasn't even that popular when he first created it, and since Carlton Sedgwick came along, Einstein and his impressive riddle have been all but forgotten."

"But you know of it."

"I do, but remember I teach historical mathematics. This is my bailiwick." I gave him a puzzled glance. "It's in my wheelhouse." Another glance and he sighed. "It's right up my alley?"

I shrugged.

"It means his personal and professional interests align with this type of activity," my mother clarified. "I am only aware of the name Einstein in the context of him being the predecessor to Hawking who was of course the predecessor to Sedgwick. His more minor contributions, however, and most definitely his riddle, elude me. Finish your pie and you can ask Commander if they posted The Riddle."

Three bites, albeit large ones, and I devoured my pie. After wiping the corners of my mouth with a napkin, I looked toward my mother who gave a slight nod of approval. "Commander, what's the status of my social media post from my Unsolvable Riddles account?"

"You have one post that went live three minutes and twenty-two seconds ago. It has received one share and eleven impressions in that time."

"Not bad for three minutes," my father said.

"And twenty-two seconds," I added with a smile. I asked to have the post displayed on our holovision and a bright blue rectangle appeared, floating above eye level with the text of the post displayed in brilliant white letters:

Do you think you can solve one of the hardest riddles of the ancient world? Prepare yourselves for a groupthink adventure like you've never experienced and stay tuned to this account for clues. Are you ready? Without further ado, I present for your puzzle-solving enjoyment, (a slightly modified) Einstein's Riddle!

There are five houses of five different colors.
In each house lives a person from a different Known Order District.
The homeowners each drink a specific beverage, eat a specific food, and have a specific hobby.
No homeowner has the same hobby, eats the same food, or drinks the same beverage.
The Unsolvable Riddle asks: Whose hobby is drawing?

"I'm intrigued already, sweetie." My mother's complimentary tone reassured me that I had done a good job drafting my first message. My father instructed the computer to share my post with his network, and my mother followed suit.

"Can I be excused? I'd like to go to my room and ask all my friends to share the message. Don't forget to follow the thread to get notifications as I post the clues."

My mother started clearing the table. "Oh, you'd like us to participate?"

"Yeah, well, maybe not Dad since he knows enough about it that he could spoil the fun with his historical mathematician smarty pants knowledge."

"Well, that's about the best backhanded compliment I've ever heard. Thanks, daughter."

"You know what I mean, Dad. Most people won't have the knowledge you do on the subject and that's what makes it such a cool challenge."

"I know, I know. I tease. Go tell your friends, and they can tell their friends and so on and so on. Go." He dismissed me with a little wave of his hand and a cheeky smile.

I retreated to my bedroom and closed the door. My tablet message notification light blinked a slow and steady green, the indicator for the group chat. Unlocking the tablet and opening the app, I read all the messages from The Girls and then checked my social media dashboard. The stats on the post were already impressive, especially given the fact that it had been less than ten minutes since it went live. There were already twenty shares and over two hundred impressions. Replies to the post started to appear in a threaded conversation view.

"I can't wait!" one user posted. I checked the user's history, and they didn't appear to be associated with my parents or any of my friends. I clapped and congratulated myself on a job well done. The fact the post reached people outside of my personal network was a good sign. I needed to post fourteen more clues and hoped to do one a day for the next two weeks but wasn't sure that would be the most optimal. I called out to my console to get its expert opinion on the matter.

It spent a solid second, maybe a second and a half, thinking about the request—which was a long time for such an advanced computer, so I was sure it approached the problem from every angle possible before it responded that the most optimal approach was to post one clue per day at the exact same time as the original message. I queued up fourteen of the fifteen clues to post and had the computer display the schedule on my computer.

Tuesday, March 12 @ 18:45: "Clue #1: The Asian lives in the red house."

Wednesday, March 13 @ 18:45: "Clue #2: The African has computing as a hobby."

Thursday, March 14 @ 18:45: "Clue #3: The South American drinks tea."

Friday, March 15 @ 18:45: "Clue #4: The green house is on the left of the white house."

Saturday, March 16 @ 18:45: "Clue #5: The green house's owner drinks lemonade."

Sunday, March 17 @ 18:45: "Clue #6: The owner of the yellow house eats apples."

Monday, March 18 @ 18:45: "Clue #7: The person living in the center house drinks milk."

Tuesday, March 19 @ 18:45: "Clue #8: The European lives in the first house."

Wednesday, March 20 @ 18:45: "Clue #9: The person who eats bread lives next to the one whose hobby is music."

Thursday, March 21 @ 18:45: "Clue #10: The person who writes lives next to the person who eats apples."

Friday, March 22 @ 18:45: "Clue #11: The owner who eats pasta drinks beer."

Saturday, March 23 @ 18:45: "Clue #12: The North American eats chocolate cake."

Sunday, March 24 @ 18:45: "Clue #13: The European lives next to the blue house."

Monday, March 25 @ 18:45: "Clue #14: The person who eats bread has a neighbor who drinks water."

I left one clue off the list. *"The person who eats salads dances as a hobby."* Without it, there would be two possible answers to The Riddle. I planned on doing a poll to see if I could generate more interest and if people had opinions one way or the other to justify their choice. Since I knew the solution in advance of posting The Riddle, it wasn't a stretch to assume that until I revealed the last clue anyone who was certain they knew the answer was either already familiar with the problem or outright guessing. Still, the exercise shaped up to be good fun since back when Einstein came up with The Riddle, he surmised that only two percent of the population could solve it.

The Girls went bananas over this and committed to coming up with an interpretation of the solution that we could use to further our cause. Due to the ever-present Commander, it wasn't possible to discuss in the chat or in the presence of a console without running the risk of getting caught. We decided to leave it to groups to discuss in person as time allowed and then fabricate excuses to get the representatives together to coordinate a response.

In the following days, the core team met several times to discuss the possibilities. It made sense for the final interpretation to align with our cause, and it was Caillou who suggested the five hobbies in The Riddle represent actions of people or groups in real life. All the other girls agreed it was a good idea. We first assigned the various Known Order Districts from The Riddle a real-world equivalent.

The European district would represent The Association and the Asian district would represent the entire Known Order. The African district would represent the CCCs and the South American, the Media. Finally, the North American district would represent The Girls and our movement.

Since The Riddle asked people to provide the answer for the hobby of drawing, we next came up with interpretations for the five hobbies. For this, we associated music with oppression, writing with propaganda, dance with information, computing with conformance, and drawing—the ultimate answer to The Riddle—with rebellion.

With agreement among us that these were acceptable interpretations, we came up with an excuse to get one girl from each of the other zones together at Terre's place to discuss it. We went with the most obvious choice—a simple "hang out" session to chat about things teenage girls chatted about, listen to music, and eat Terre's parents out of house and home. In addition to agreeing to a standard interpretation of The Riddle, the meeting served the purpose of establishing changes to the content of our paraphernalia.

The key was in making sure we dropped hints about which districts aligned with which group and which hobbies with which acts. It couldn't be too obvious, or in the other direction, too cryptic. Not everyone found the balance, but we did our best.

Our biggest problem arose from keeping everything and everyone up to date. Everything, or close to everything in our world, was digital and available at the snap of a finger. Relying on analog methods to communicate, while safer and more secure, took a lot longer. By the time Terre met with The Girls from the other zones Commander had posted the first four clues with the fifth due to go out to the world that night. In the grand scheme of things, it wasn't a big problem, but due to the operation's covert nature, there was no telling when people would catch on. We wanted to strike while the iron was hot, though. While there was buzz. I'll admit to entertaining the possibility of The Riddle going viral but kept the thought to myself.

The Saturday Terre met with the other girls, the original posting already had over ten thousand impressions and "Unsolvable Riddle" was trending in the North American district for the majority of the zones on the Eastern seaboard. Impressive numbers to be sure, and right on the cusp of becoming fantastic.

In the end, The Girls met and exchanged thoughts and, as it turned out, were all in synch with the exception of a few concessions made by The Girls from the other zones. Terre could be forceful with her opinions, but in the case of the other girls, it was an open discussion that still happened to land on her side of the argument.

With all the details settled and communicated, I waited. I wasn't passive, but I did steer clear and limit my exposure beyond regular riddle maintenance of sharing post replies and engaging with people already tossing guesses around. Not all got replies, though. Indeed, at that early stage, most were random guesses or people without a clue, but that was fine and expected. The ratio of legitimate interactions to trolled ones lowered, but there were still trolls. While they were fewer in numbers than at the beginning, the ones that persisted were at least more creative.

The Riddle picked up considerable steam during the second week of clue posting. It trended across the entire North American district, and it drew attention elsewhere as well. The evening media reported it as a viral sensation "sweeping the globe from district-to-district and zone-to-zone" and did a whole segment on the history of The Riddle and its original creator, Albert Einstein. I thought I saw my father wipe a tear from his cheek while he watched.

"Wonderful, my dear. Truly wonderful. I can't thank you enough for doing this."

"You're welcome? I'm not sure how to respond since my original intention wasn't to promote Einstein or the field of historical mathematics. No offense, of course."

"None taken. I know it wasn't your intent, but what you did had that effect, and I couldn't be more pleased."

"Well, I'm glad."

Our brief exchange was interrupted by the media correspondent issuing a word of caution. "It is not all logic puzzles and good old-fashioned groupthink, though. As rapidly as this puzzle leapt to the top of the trending list, it didn't come without some resistance. People are reporting a hidden meaning behind it, given its modern-day creator has a history with violating The Known Order. I won't repeat what's being said as I don't want to give it any amount of credence but suffice it to say there are rumblings that there's more to this puzzle than meets the eye. We spoke with a local member of The Association on the condition of anonymity as he was not authorized to discuss an open investigation."

"He said and I quote, 'We take potential violations as seriously as confirmed violations. The Known Order demands nothing less, and in this case, we feel that there's enough circumstantial evidence to warrant a closer look at what might be going on.' When asked if there was a chance they would pull The Riddle from social media and approach its creator, Katherine Webb, for questioning, he replied, 'Every option is on the table at the moment.' There you have it, people. A viral sensation with a hint of scandal maybe? Keep your eyes and ears tuned into your local Media to find out how the story unfolds."

"Uh, Kate, do you want to share anything with your mother and me?"

I paused to weigh my options. On one hand, if this went sideways, I could use their help. On the other, if it didn't, I might pull them down with me. In the end, their plausible deniability weighed more importantly to the big picture than my personal safety, which wasn't at risk since there should be no way for anyone to prove I was behind the so-called scandal. "Not especially. I mean, I've met with some friends about The Riddle and how to best get it out into the world but that's it. If there are people out there who want to ascribe some mysterious hidden meaning what can I do to stop them? If you ask me, the people who brought that supposed information to our attention in the first place should be the first ones The Association talks to if they talk to anyone. Besides, this is what Media does, does it not? For centuries, they've been clinging to relevance. In a near one hundred percent digital existence, any conceivable piece of information is available at the snap of a finger. I can't think of a single reason we actually need to sit here and watch it once or twice a day."

"Meaning?"

"Meaning they sensationalize and stir up more trouble than necessary with the sole purpose of getting people tuning in. Their existence depends on it."

"So, we shouldn't be worried?"

"I can tell you I'm not."

My mother put her hand on top of mine. "Well, we're your parents, and whether you like it or not, whether it's warranted or not, we *are*."

I gave my mom's hand a squeeze. "I know, and I appreciate it. Media might try to control what people think, and they might succeed on occasion, but I'm just a girl from North America Zone Three with a riddle. There is no way I can control what people think or how they interpret things. Last time I checked, there was nothing about it that violated The Known Order in any way. Wouldn't you agree? Commander approved. End of story." My parents sat silent for a moment before they concurred with my assessment—in part.

"In theory, yes, but you've already got one strike, and I fear they'll be going out of their way to find fault."

"Well, what do you suggest I do? I could talk to the people I know personally and tell them that if we're spreading these alternate theories to cut it out, but the problem with that is those theories are already out there. Anyway, from what I can see, nothing's digitally documented anywhere. It's all word of mouth, rumors, inferences, and wild guesses. I couldn't defend myself against it if I tried."

My father pondered this for a moment before adding his two credits to the conversation, "What about issuing a statement indicating you don't lend any support to the silly notion there's an alternate meaning behind The Riddle?"

My mom frowned. "That might appear more suspicious, wouldn't it, dear? You know, like there's an implied *wink* at the end of the statement."

"Plus, it acknowledges I am aware of the rumors. As it is, there's no proof whatsoever outside of this room that I even know about them. I'm inclined to stay the course and keep my nose clean, as the old expression goes. I'll keep my eye on the things I can control and make sure everything I do is all aboveboard, and provable as such."

My father folded his arms across his chest. "I don't like this, not one bit."

My mother turned off the holovision. "I don't think any of us do, dear, but Kate is right. She can only control what she says and does."

"Yes, but The Association doesn't play by the rules. They never have. Oh, they're all friendly and say things like 'this is in your best interest' and 'why argue, look how grand everything is' but behind the scenes, they're untrustworthy, scheming little jerks who would sell their grandmothers up the river so long as they get to stay in power."

"Tell us how you really feel, Dad."

"I fear this won't end well."

"It might not, Pops, but I'm going to be nineteen in a few weeks and taking my exit exams to see what the rest of my life will become. I'm not going to squander the opportunity worrying over something for which I have no control."

"Wise words, sweetie. Who told you that?" My mother gave me a kiss on the forehead.

"Dad did," I said, shooting my father a million-watt smile.

He shut his eyes and mimed the waving of a white flag. "I concede. Holy crow, you two exhaust me."

I gave him a kiss on the cheek. "We know."

In my room I opened the group chat app on my tablet and messaged the other girls.

Did you see the Media tonight? I'm going viral! But what was with those unsubstantiated rumors? At least one person out there is trying to throw shade on my good fortune.

It took fifteen minutes for the first reply to materialize. Thankfully, it was Terre. I trusted all the girls in the group, but they weren't all as on the ball as Terre. All it would take to make a minor problem snowball into a major one was one of the girls responding to my message without thinking it through.

*No idea, but I haven't seen anything online. They must be verbal rumors,
or possibly fabricated by Media to drum up interest in their programming. I
heard that fewer and fewer people are tuning into Media every day. Soon, there
won't be holovision news at all. I say keep doing what you're doing. People are
interested, and it's a cool riddle.*

I sent the thumbs-up emoji.

No other messages on that topic came through the rest of the night,
and the chat went back to its usual mishmash of cryptic chatter and
nonsense. Over the months, we created our own version of shorthand. To
any outside observer, it would have been obvious that we weren't taking
about flowers and dresses or the latest trends in entertainment, but there
was no way for them to decipher it. The key to understanding came from
in-person conversations had at a whisper in out-of-the-way corners of
open spaces away from prying eyes and attentive ears. Analog for the
win—again.

By the time Commander posted the last clue, all social media could
talk about was The Riddle. It wasn't "Katherine Webb's Riddle" or
"Einstein's Riddle" or even "The Riddle from the Unsolvable Riddles
account," it was simply The Riddle. The original post statistics included
over a million shares. Its daily impressions totaled in the hundreds
of thousands. People were obsessed with it and five solutions had
strongholds with various groups, which amused me to no end seeing as
that represented all the possible answers. The one solution that appeared
to have the most support was wholly incorrect, which surprised me.
With the last clue posted, I waited a day before sending out the poll, but
I queued up the message to be sure Commander posted it at the most
optimal time.

*Only one clue remains! I can't believe all the attention this got over the last two
weeks. Judging from all the comments and impressions, it's clear that a good
many of you enjoy brainteasers, but unfortunately, if the social media prognos-
tication is any indication, a good many of you are on the wrong track. With the
last clue, the correct solution is down to three possibilities. You have three days to
respond to this poll with your guess as to whose hobby is drawing:*

☐ *The Person from Europe*

☐ *The Person from Asia*

☐ *The Person from North America*

Choose now!

With nothing left to do but wait, I waited. As for Media's concern, or rather what turned out to be entirely substantiated rumors about there being an alternate meaning behind The Riddle, well, that worked out better than expected. The final piece of the interpretation The Girls and I thought up would start to make its way into the world the same day the poll ended. That would give them the greater part of a full day to whip everyone into frenzy. From what I could tell, people were taking to our idea that The Known Order, The Association, and all of our support systems filled with selfishness and sycophants didn't know what was best for us after all. The seeds of doubt planted mere weeks ago were now seedlings. Sprouted from the soil of discontent, all we had to do was keep them watered and shine the light of truth on them, and soon those seedlings would become mighty trees.

For three days, I watched as person after person answered the poll, with most providing commentary about the certainty behind their answer. People were completely, utterly, and totally obsessed with The Riddle. By that point, Media exhausted all its stories, sensationalized to the nth degree, and did not one, but three pieces on The Girl Behind The Riddle.

Of course, in all three cases my previous conviction for violating The Known Order was front and center. As far as I could tell, it didn't have the intended effect. People everywhere lauded me as a visionary, a hero, and a leader—and it wasn't because I posted and hyped a silly riddle for people to solve. That helped make my name a household one, but it wasn't why everyone knew and admired me. For that, the credit lay entirely with the stories of me being a convicted criminal and that the person behind the rumors was more than met the eye.

Here was a person, a young woman by her official social designation, but still a girl, about to embark on the next and most exciting phase of her life, and a Chooser on top of it, risking a second and final strike because of something she believed in, something so many others wanted to believe as well but either didn't know how to communicate that belief or were too afraid to.

Media were beside themselves over it, but through it all I stuck to my story. On one occasion, I responded to an interview request where one of the questions was a loaded one. The on-air correspondent asked, "So, how did you come up with the idea of an alternate interpretation of The Riddle?" Thankfully, my parents prepared me for that type of trickery, and my response was clear. "I don't know who first decided to start those rumors, but that's all they are. Rumors, and not only do I not give credence to them, I think all they do is take away from the beauty of Einstein's Riddle and how it's bringing so many people together, and that's all I'm going to say about it."

Of course, it didn't matter what I said after that. Media was going to keep spinning the story the way they wanted to spin it, the public was going to keep believing what they wanted to believe, and as long as they believed what I wanted them to, me and the rest of The Girls would keep feeding them what they wanted to hear. I could feel the tides turning. People's faith in the system dropped down to a level of reluctant acceptance and through the persistence of The Girls it reduced further, down to cautious questioning. Since The Wars, the public's perception of The Known Order was that of unwavering support, and then along came The Riddle. A device originally conceived as an exercise in showcasing an individual's intellectual superiority was now a weapon against a system designed to control and suppress intellect.

Of all the themes, the most powerful one that I identified in the thousands upon thousands of comments I received over the two weeks since the original posting was that of rejection. People rejected the notion of superiority, and of infinite knowledge, and the ones who rejected it more than anyone else were the ones who had the least—the non-Choosers, the people in thankless jobs, and the people furthest away from The Association. That suited me fine. I wasn't any of those things, and those who stood to lose the most from this movement taking hold, in spite of the rumors, were the ones who had a harder time accepting I was the one behind it.

When I looked back at my interactions on social media, I wasn't surprised that Media took the approach they did, but I was surprised that Commander hadn't intervened and suppressed some of the messages. As soon as the idea of an alternate interpretation of The Riddle hit the internet, it should have quashed it, but it didn't. That stood as a single black mark on an otherwise perfect campaign. Instead of instilling confidence in my methods, it made me concerned about nefarious activity. I long suspected that Commander might not be operating as autonomously as The Association wanted everyone to believe and this furthered those suspicions.

There was the fact that all senior members of the Intelligence Officer profession were all men, public representatives of The Association were all men, and to the best of my recollection all the CCCs were men too. Then there were the exceptions to the rules granted to Choosers. By my assessment, Commander either approved something or it didn't. If a person wanted to override that decision, and they had the authority, they could with no, or few, questions asked. It made me wonder if other overrides existed. If they did, that was a big red flag. On the other hand, short of having proof of malfeasance and finding a way to communicate it to the masses before they arrested me and placed me in confinement for the rest of my life, I had limited options at my disposal.

The day the poll closed, as I prepared the solution reveal message the rest of The Girls laid the groundwork for the final interpretation. I estimated it would take a few days for word to get around that the hobby "dancing" meant "rebellion," and I considered for a moment a delay in posting the solution but rationalized the thought away. If people were invested in knowing the complete alternate meaning for The Riddle, they wouldn't care if The Riddle solution came on the same day, a day later, or longer. Those willing to act when it was all said and done were all that mattered, and they would wait. I knew this because if the shoe was on the other foot, I would wait without complaint too.

The day after the poll closed, twenty-four hours after the final subversive act of my peers, I published the solution to the puzzle and included an image outlining everything along with another poll.

Hot dog, we have a winner! To all of you who guessed that the North American was the one with drawing as a hobby you were correct! Here's the full breakdown of the five houses:

	House 1	House 2	House 3	House 4	House 5
Color	Yellow	Blue	Red	Green	White
District	European	S.Amer	Asian	N.Amer	African
Beverage	Water	Tea	Milk	Lemonade	Beer
Food	Apples	Bread	Salad	Cake	Pasta
Hobbies	Music	Writing	Dance	Drawing	Computing

Now, it's time for one final poll!

Would you like me to post the step-by-step solution?

☐ *Yes*

☐ *No*

The poll will stay active for one week, or until it's obvious which response will garner the most votes, whichever comes first.

Commander posted the message without delay, probably because the interest in the exercise was unlike anything anyone had seen in a lifetime. This lent more credence to my theory that humans longed for problem-solving and decision-making a considerable amount more than The Association wanted us to believe.

Any moment I wasn't in school, eating, sleeping, or in the bathroom over the following three days were spent replying to social media messages and doing interviews for local, domestic, and foreign Media. I lost count of how many I did, but it was in excess of a dozen and without fail, Media reps asked me about the alternate interpretation to The Riddle.

In every case, my response was the exact same as it was before. "I don't know who first decided to start those rumors, but that's all they are, rumors, and not only do I not give credence to them, I think all they do is take away from the beauty of Einstein's Riddle and how it brought so many people together, and that's all I'm going to say about it."

In every case, the Media tried to ask the question a different way or try to cajole me into a different response, but I never wavered from my prepared answer and not once acquiesced to any requests to further expand on my thoughts.

I scheduled the poll to be active for up to seven days, yet after three it became clear the vast majority wanted to see the solution. With over a million people responding in seventy hours, the "yes" response garnered over ninety percent of the votes. I typed up the solution and submitted it to Commander for approval, which it granted in an instant.

It took less than a month from the initial posting for me to become a viral sensation. My followers for my Unsolvable Riddles account exceeded The Known Order's most famous or noteworthy citizens. Media representatives had fewer people interested, and Media controlled the vast majority of messages out there.

I rode the wave of success for Einstein's Riddle as far as I could, though, and needed a new attraction. The problem was with everything that went on I hadn't had the chance to research another riddle. The day after I posted my solution, I sat on the couch in the family room with my parents and brother researching options for another riddle when there came a knock at the front door. Everyone's heads popped up, and we stopped what we were doing. My mom and dad were reading, and Chadwick played a video game with his headphones on. As the least occupied person in the room, I got up to get the door.

I opened it and CCC Follis and The Hadewijch stood in front on the stoop. The CCC did all the talking.

"Katherine Webb, you are accused of sedition. Since Commander and The Association are unable to determine with one hundred percent certainty your guilt or innocence in the matter, you will represent yourself in front of a tribunal one week from today. Until that time, you are under house arrest. Do you understand?"

I stood with one hand on the doorknob, mouth agape as I struggled to find words, any words, with which to respond. My parents joined the conversation and stood behind me, each with a hand on my shoulders. My mother spoke first.

"No, she most certainly does not understand, and neither do we. She's just a child."

"Katherine is soon to be nineteen, ma'am. Eighteen years, eleven months, two weeks, and one day to be precise and that places her squarely in the adult category. Furthermore, she already has her one and only allowable strike—"

"— she hasn't lived long enough yet to know this, but if Commander isn't one hundred percent certain, then it is hearsay and conjecture, at best, and it is not worthy of prosecution." Mother patted my shoulder with her hand, and there was a noticeable difference in temperature as soon as she removed it. "Though you should have learned this in your classes, dear. Do you remember?"

I snapped out of my shock-induced trance and gave my head a slight shake. "That's right. The main takeaway from my year of torturous study on all things Commander taught me that it is entirely unfailing and void of fault, error, or misrepresentation."

The Hadewijch sighed. "Which is why you are to appear in front of a tribunal. To discuss it."

My father took his hand off my shoulder and used it to point his finger, which he stabbed in the air mere inches from CCC Follis' face. "Get your sorry asses off my property. Now."

"Sir," Follis said in his expressionless voice. "May I remind you that anything even remotely resembling a threat to a CCC, or any authority figure as designated by The Association, is a direct violation of The Known Order and grounds for immediate, and in some cases permanent, confinement."

"Me telling you to leave is the last remaining sliver of sovereignty and independence we have, not a threat. It's a demand and a justified one." He pointed to the bank of PMIDs charging beside the door. "Even though it's charging, as soon as a CCC or caseworker comes within six feet of one of those devices, it enters active listening mode. Any threatening language used results in a horrid-sounding alarm and a flashing red screen. As you can see, my band is doing nothing of the sort. So, given we have already established uncertainty with the veracity of your claim, it would appear that even the great, all-knowing Commander agrees with the language I'm using."

Calm and unaffected, CCC Follis focused his eyes on my father's finger, still outstretched and floating a few inches from his face. My dad pulled it back and returned his hand to my shoulder. "I was merely using a gesture to specify which person of the two standing here looking pathetic on my front porch was to immediately leave. It's you, CCC Follis. We'd like to have a word with Hadewijch here. You've executed your duties and passed along the message, as misguided and flawed as it was, and can now set off with a clear conscience."

"I am Hadewijch's transport."

"Then you can wait in your hover car until we are finished." He gestured with one hand for Hadewijch to enter the house and for CCC Follis to depart with the other. CCC Follis left with his shoulders slumped and head bowed. Hadewijch stood wide-eyed in the doorway. I opened my mouth but did not speak. Dad gestured again for The Hadewijch to join them in the house. They did and he shut the door.

He grabbed three of the four PMIDs off the charging dock and handed one each to me and my mother. "Put these on so they'll listen while we're having our chat with Hadewijch here. I'm sure you don't mind, do you?" He tilted his head as he asked the rhetorical question. The Hadewijch did not reply and instead marched to the kitchen and sat down with folded hands on the table. The rest of us followed, and I sat in my brother's chair since The Hadewijch occupied mine.

My mother spoke first, "Hadewijch, after a year of interaction with our daughter, surely you must have established some sort of relationship. Kate made one mistake as a young person trying to find her way in the world, paid for it in satisfactory accordance with the decision of The Association on behalf of The Known Order, and has shown exemplary behavior every moment since. Surely no one, no one of any importance or consequence especially a person such as you, believes she's involved in acts of sedition. It makes no sense. There's no logic to it whatsoever."

The Hadewijch let out another sigh, and blinked long and slow before responding, then tapped the PMID screen and instructed it to stop listening. We did the same. "Yes, I do have a relationship with Katherine after our time together, but let me make this perfectly clear, it was not, nor will it ever be, what I'd call a friendly one. Wouldn't you agree, Katherine?"

"That's an accurate assessment."

"It was a professional relationship akin to an employer and a subordinate, nothing more. That said, when the representative from The Association contacted me, I was surprised. We do not live in a world where hearsay and conjecture, rumors" —the word spat out as if were a bad piece of fruit—"if you will, have any bearing whatsoever."

"Did you mention this to them?" Dad asked.

"Of course, I did. I put it tactfully, as was expected of someone in my position, but I did mention it. In fact, The Association was not going to give Katherine any notice at all before pulling her into the tribunal, and it was at my insistence that they finally agreed to allow her one week's time to prepare."

Mom stood up, opened the fridge, stared at it blankly for a second, and closed the door again. "Thank you for that, but how can you not see how ridiculous this is?"

"I will not make any claim about its ridiculousness or seriousness. I spoke up because we are supposed to behave within a system of rules. A system where everything is known. What is not known might as well not exist. If Commander and the system don't know what Katherine did or didn't do, then it's only fair we get to ask some questions to find out more, and it's in turn only fair Katherine gets to prepare. You may view me as a cold, emotionless automaton and that might be true, but what I am *not* is unreasonable. I take The Known Order seriously, and I take everyone else's role within it seriously as well. That includes hers and yours."

I folded my arms on the table and laid down my head. "I'm scared."

"Not to put too fine a point on it, child, but you should be."

"What am I supposed to do?"

"I'm not allowed to provide you any information in that regard. There have been tribunals in the past, two or three for sedition, albeit not recently. I suggest you do some research. The transcripts and outcomes of all tribunals going back hundreds of years are available. Ask Commander and it will compile a list for you. You can even watch some of them on the holovision, though I will say that reading the transcripts is probably a better option."

I lifted my head. "Why is that?"

"There is no emotion or any extraneous information conveyed. It's pure fact. This person said this, that person said that. We asked, and the other replied. Black and white. An indisputable record of events."

I opened my mouth to speak, but the words got caught in my throat and the tears flowed.

"Now, I have to go. As it is, the CCC's report will have to account for this unplanned conversation. I will say that you had procedural questions, and that I answered them but that is all I will say." The Hadewijch stood and straightened their clothes before turning on their heels the same way as before and left.

Once the door to the house closed, the three of us sat at the table with shocked expressions on our faces. A sniffle came from the other side of the room, and we turned our heads to see Chadwick standing in the doorway crying.

"Is Katie being sent to confinement?" He sniffled again and wiped the tears from his cheeks with the back of his hands.

My mom jumped up from the table and went to him. She wrapped her arms around him and gave him a big hug. "No, sweetie. She has to go to a tribunal. They're rare but do happen from time to time. They're designed to bring more information to light about a supposed violation of The

Known Order."

"Does anyone ever win a tribunal?"

She looked at me and then at my dad, her expression sullen. "It does not usually work out favorably for the accused."

He burst into tears, and I joined him as I returned my head to my folded arms on the table. My dad stood up, grabbed a beer from the refrigerator, and sat back down. "We are going to figure this out, I promise, and it will be okay. Now, let's have something to eat and do something together afterward."

We ate homemade pizza with vegetables from the garden as toppings and adjourned to the family room where we watched a comedy on the holovision. By the time it finished, it was well past Chadwick's bedtime, and his eyelids did that almost-closing thing that indicated sleep was imminent. I was not so lucky. My stomach was a giant knot, and for the entire movie, I felt like what I did eat of my pizza dinner was going to make a second appearance. My head hurt like it never had before. A pounding combined with sharp, shooting pains that I imagined were like having a metal skewer shoved into my eyes and into my brain. My hands shook.

"I'm going to bed." I didn't use the word sleep because there was no chance of that happening. I kissed each member of my family and gave them a hug. After brushing my teeth and changing into my pajamas, I slid into bed and checked the group chat on my tablet. All but a few of The Girls were online. The words didn't fly onto the screen, but I managed to write a short message.

Visited by CCC Follis and The Hadewijch tonight. I am accused of sedition and must face a tribunal in one week. House arrest until then. I have no idea what will happen but will spend the next six days reviewing transcripts and preparing statements in response to potential lines of inquiry. Will chat with you more tomorrow but maybe don't respond tonight. THEY are watching, I'm sure, and I don't have the energy to think much and am likely to write something stupid that will get me in more trouble. Love you all. Chat tomorrow.

The screen went black after thirty seconds of inactivity, and I placed the tablet on my bedside table. Under the covers with my head poking out the top, I lay there and stared at the ceiling. Sleep came quicker than I thought it would, as did the nightmares. Confinement was the theme of choice for my subconscious. Not general population confinement, however, but solitary confinement. The Known Order abolished the death penalty eons ago, but many people still subscribed to the notion that solitary confinement was worse. One of the first lessons taught when I took a year's worth of lessons as punishment for distributing an illicit drawing was about solitary. Their intent was to scare the pants off of us so that everything after came across like they were doing us a favor. See what we're keeping you from? Don't play along and this could happen to you.

There was truth behind the reason that folks thought solitary was a fate worse than death. You literally sat in the dark for twenty-three hours a day in an eight-foot soundproofed cube with padded walls. For one hour, an artificial sun lamp or a hole in the ceiling provided the only light you'd see all day. A cot sat in one corner and a toilet and sink in the other. They monitored you twenty-four hours a day, seven days a week, three hundred and sixty-five days a year but you never had as much as a single second of contact with another human. You could sing to pass the time, but because of the dampening effect the soundproofing had on the walls, everything you sang sounded muted and flat. Three times a day, a part of the wall slid up and in came a tray of food. It was more nutritional supplements than it was food. To call it a ready-to-eat meal or even a ration was a generous statement. You received as much "food" as minimally necessary to keep you alive. Once a week, the door opened and a new sheet, blanket, pillowcase, pair of underwear, bra, pants that resembled healthcare professional scrubs but with the texture of fine gravel instead of soft, synthetic fabrics, and a short-sleeved shirt to match were unceremoniously tossed into the cell.

Most people didn't last six months before taking their life. At least that's what they told me in the lesson. Maybe it was all a giant scare tactic and reality wasn't nearly as terrifying. It didn't matter to me that night, though. My brain was intent on scaring the daylights out of me, and judging from the cold sweats consuming my body when I jolted awake not once, not twice, but three times, it did a wonderful and thorough job of it.

By seven o'clock the next morning, I had managed a couple of hours of rest and gave up on trying. I grabbed my tablet and checked the group chat. There was at least one reply from every girl, and I read them in chronological order first, and then by conversation threads since many of the messages spawned replies from other girls. All were shocked to their cores, all were sympathetic, and even a couple offered to fall on their swords for me. I replied to those messages with a single response.

While I am beyond appreciative that there many of you who would sacrifice yourselves for me, I want you to put those thoughts out of your mind for good. Got it? I have DONE NOTHING WRONG. You cannot accept blame for something that did not happen in the first place. Doing so would only perpetuate this heinous miscarriage of justice and allow this type of mistake to occur again and again and again. No, I will go to the tribunal armed with as much evidence—or more!—than they have and plead my case the old-fashioned way. The digital world failed them. It failed me. It failed all of us. We know this because I am not in confinement right now. There are things Commander and The Association don't know, and the tribunal is their reluctant admission of that. So, I will use the only tool I know of that can combat such an assault on my honor. I will tell the truth.

Terre responded with words of encouragement and offers of tribunal transcript study help. Several of the other girls offered to assist as well. Since I was under house arrest, I couldn't go anywhere to meet them and discuss it, but nothing could stop them from coming to me. At least I didn't think so. I flipped to CCC Follis' report which outlined the accusation against me and listed the terms and conditions for the next week. I could not leave the house, not even to go to the garden or sit on the driveway, but I could have visitors outside of my family. However, when anyone who wasn't a verified member of the household was present PMIDs had to stay on our wrists and those devices plus every console in the house had to be in active listening mode.

I messaged my core group of friends, the original four who'd stuck with me through the whole journey. In light of what happened with Caillou those years ago, I especially wanted her there. It was clear that she still felt bad, and I thought she might offer a perspective that no one else had. Even though they were all knee-deep in studying for their exit examinations, they committed to joining us for as many hours as their families would allow.

Exit examinations. I hadn't considered those but supposed it didn't matter if I was going to end up in confinement anyway. Best to concentrate on the first problem in front of me. I shook the cobwebs out of my head, got out of bed, and hopped in the shower to clean off my body and clear my mind. When I got out and dressed, I made my way to the kitchen where my family all sat at their usual places in front of a massive breakfast. The table was piled high with chocolate chip pancakes, synthetic eggs, plant-based bacon and sausage, and a variety of fresh fruits and vegetables picked from our front yard garden.

"What's all this?"

My younger brother gave me a big, toothy grin. "Breakfast!"

My mother expanded on his response, "Chaddy thought you could use a good start to the day before we began sorting through old tribunal transcripts—as a family."

"You don't have to do that for me. This is my mess, and I'm perfectly capable of getting out of it on my own. Besides, some of my friends are going to come over to help as well."

"Why can your friends help and not your family?" My mother dabbed the corners of her mouth with her napkin and raised her eyebrows.

My father put down his piece of rye toast as a glob of melting margarine drooped off the side. "Yes, why not us? We're your family and care deeply about you."

I stammered as I fought to find the right words. "It's just—well—I mean—" I let out a sigh. "They were more involved with the sharing of The Riddle than you were and feel partly responsible for all the negative attention I received that led to this situation, or whatever it is I've gotten myself into."

Chadwick hung his head and took a slow bite of a slice of his bacon-not-bacon. I put my hand on his shoulder. "Okay, I'll tell you what, we will make a whole event out of it. Chaddy, you're in charge of food and beverages. Mom and Dad, you'll organize the transcripts and divide them up, then everyone will read a few and sort out what types of questions the tribunal asked and based on what we all find, we'll decide if any of those might be asked of me."

My brother sat up straighter in his chair and his happy-go-lucky demeanor returned. I was happy he was happy.

"Keep in mind," my father said, "that when your friends are here, everything will be in active listening mode. It's possible we are going to want to discuss some things without the presence of Commander in the room."

"I thought about that, and I have an idea." My parents stared me down with expectant gazes. "We go old school. Analog, baby!"

"Analog?" My mom cocked her head to one side.

"Yeah, analog. We will each have a small synthetic notepad to write in. Completely offline. Completely untraceable. If there's something we need to say but don't want to say it aloud where prying ears, or microphones can hear, then write it down. We need only remember to not point the pad directly at the holovision, a PMID, or a console. In fact, it might be worthwhile to only write things down in the bathroom, just to be safe."

"Analog," my mom said.

"Analog!" Chaddy repeated.

"Analog," my father echoed.

Within the hour all of my friends arrived, and my parents had set up a sort of war room for us. We moved the furniture around and brought in chairs. Chaddy closed all the curtains for optimal holovision viewing, should it be required. There were over a hundred tribunals locally and from other nearby zones over the past twenty years. My parents didn't see the point in going back any farther. We each received a dozen transcripts on our tablets and started to read.

Every ten minutes or so one of us got up and went to the bathroom to write down a message. Chaddy spent most of his time silent and drawing at the table but circulated every fifteen minutes with a pitcher of lemonade or a tray of snacks. Every few trips round the room, he stopped and read over my shoulder.

"These tribunal people are really mean."

I looked up at my younger but not-so-little brother. "Indeed. I'm not sure I'm going to be able to hold myself together in front of them."

"You will," my mother said.

"How are you so sure?"

"Because you won't have any other choice."

The underlying theme of questions we identified centered on providing proof of actions where gaps in the record exist. Since people could disable active listening on their devices and turn off biometric data capture like heart rate, pulse, and body temperature—though if it got too hot or too cold, it would send a message to the nearest medic station on your behalf—if you didn't move around much it created a gap in the record.

Once we each read two transcripts, we took a break. I went to the bathroom, not only to use the facilities but to use my notepad. I wrote *I'm assuming our group chat was examined in great detail, and they found no evidence of wrongdoing, but do you think it will come up in questioning?* When I returned to the war room, I handed my notebook to Terre, who read it and passed it to Eunice, who passed it to Melissa, who passed it to Caillou, to passed it back to me.

"I had the same question as well," Terre said.

"Me too," said Melissa.

"Me three," said Caillou.

"It hadn't occurred to me," Eunice said, "but I've been so focused on this case, I haven't had time to let my mind wander. It's a good question, though."

"What's a good question?" my mother asked. I handed over my notebook. "Hmm. That is a good question. I'm assuming—" I cut her off with a curt *shh* and put my finger to my lips. My mother nodded and left the room for a few seconds. She came back and handed me the notebook. It read: *I'm assuming your chat was either completely innocent, or you used some method to disguise what you discussed. If the latter, then I would guarantee they will want to question you about it.*

I passed the notebook to Terre, and it went around the loop as the other one had. All their faces wore the same look of concern. Mom took the notepad back and went to the bathroom again. *The best explanation is usually the simplest. You were speaking cryptically and in an odd manner because it was silly and a break from your everyday conventional conversation. Basically, it was your only real opportunity to act like a kid and not have to worry about what anyone would think.*

I passed the notebook around once again, and everyone nodded in agreement. The looks on their faces changed back to normal. At least I thought they all looked a bit more relaxed. I went to the bathroom once again and wrote. *We have to find a way to communicate this to The Girls ASAP so if anyone asks, we will all be on the same page.*

I showed what I'd written to my friends, and they sat in silence, ruminating over it for a few minutes until Melissa spoke up. "Terre and I will take care of it." I looked over at her and without hesitation, she responded, "Yes. Don't worry about it. We'll make sure it's all taken care of."

"Thanks, I don't know what I'd do without all of you." We stood and shared a big group hug.

Before the collective embrace ended, Dad stood as well. "Okay, girls. Kate's mother and I want to have a, uh, closed discussion with her." He pointed to the console in the corner of the room. "Can you summarize what you've learned from your reading here?" He handed over his notebook to Terre. "We would love to have you over tomorrow and every day from now until the tribunal, but if you have other obligations, don't feel bad if you can't make it."

Terre looked up from the notebook in which she wrote her thoughts and observations down at a frantic pace. "I think I can speak for the rest of the girls, Mr. Webb, when I say that we'll be here every day for as long as you'll have us." My other three friends murmured their agreement with the statement.

I wiped a tear away from my cheek. "But what about your exit exams, especially for you, Caillou? You don't get to choose like the rest of us. If you mess up it could mean a lifetime of… of… unhappiness, or worse."

"Don't you worry about me, okay? I've been studying my butt off, and I am confident it will work out. Besides, I'm learning more about how The Association and The Known Order operate by reading these transcripts than I'll ever learn in a classroom. My mother told me that every now and then how you respond to a question has a greater impact than what answer you provide."

"Only if you're sure. That goes for the rest of you as well."

We sat in silence as each of my friends scribbled into my father's notebook. When Caillou finished, I took the book from her and handed it to my father. The girls all stood again and gave me one more group hug before exiting with nods to my parents and a pat on the shoulder to Chadwick. Melissa looked back over her shoulder as I closed the door. "Thanks for all the wonderful food and beverages, Chaddy. Maybe you're destined to be a superstar chef to The Association."

His cheeks flushed red. "Thanks, Melissa."

With my friends gone and my brother tidying up, I sat with my parents on the large sofa and flipped through their notes comparing and contrasting the various tribunals. The most consistent observation was their initial one. Odds were that I would have to defend every unaccounted-for second from the last month, or longer.

"Better to be prepared than caught off guard," my father said to me.

I nodded in agreement. "Commander, prepare a report of every communication and movement on record for me for the past ninety days. Highlight and bookmark any gaps."

"Preparing activity report for Katherine Webb." It paused for no more than two seconds before it spoke again. "Report complied. Deliver via message or file or both?"

"Both, but send a copy to my parents, Terre Zhooshkwa, Melissa Demchuk, Eunice Marco, and Caillou Latour as well."

"Done. You can find the report in your messages and stored in your personal cloud database."

"I think I'm going to go to bed. I need to have a fresh mind tomorrow to start going through all this." I gave my parents each a kiss on the cheek and retired to my bedroom where I cried into my pillow until I fell asleep.

The next three days all blended together with the same routine. By mid-morning, the girls arrived and together with my parents they poured through transcript after transcript of past tribunals. By the end of the third day, with me due to appear in the morning three days from then, we all had a pretty good idea of how everything would unfold—and it wasn't promising. For the vast majority of cases we analyzed, one hundred and twenty in total, all but two ended poorly for the accused. I didn't need to be a brilliant mathematician like my father to recognize those odds were not tilted in my direction.

For the one hundred and eighteen cases where the accused landed in confinement, information came out throughout the course of the tribunal that sealed their fate. The members of The Association on the panel knew the exact moment to ask the exact set of questions that turned the tribunal from a potential negative outcome to a certainty. My mother suggested at that point that we focus their attention on the two cases with positive outcomes for the accused, and then start picking through all the gaps in my activity record to ensure I had a bulletproof explanation for each one.

OOOOIOOI
[Nine]

The afternoon before my tribunal I lay on my bed on top of the covers and stared at the ceiling. A single thought occupied my brain. In less than twenty-four hours, a real possibility existed that I would be in confinement. My father knocked on my open door. "Can I come in?"

"Sure, what's on your mind?"

"I wanted to ask you the same question."

"Yeah, well, I'm not sure you'll like the answer."

"I'm sure I won't, but I'm also sure I have a good idea about what it is."

"I don't want to go into confinement, but my confidence in avoiding it is... not one hundred percent."

"Well, if it were one hundred percent you wouldn't be in this situation in the first place. More importantly, if The Association's confidence was a hundred percent, you wouldn't be appearing at a tribunal. It pains me to say this, but you owe a debt of gratitude to Hadewijch. Standing up for you like that and ensuring you had time to prepare wasn't necessary."

"Ugh, I loathe being indebted to The Hadewijch more than anything."

"Why do you always say 'The Hadewijch'? Is it because Hadewijch is different?"

"No," I said, making no effort to mask my incredulous tone. "You and Mum raised me better than that, and if you hadn't, the Intelligence Officers would have ensured the lesson was learned, I can promise you that."

"Then why? It sounds disparaging when you do that."

"It's supposed to be disparaging. The Hadewijch is one of *them*. The Hadewijch does *their* bidding. They follow orders without any thought or consideration for the people involved. It has nothing to do with their existence and everything to do with their actions."

"Hadewijch had plenty of thought and consideration for you less than a week ago. Don't let your anger for the system and the situation you find yourself in, one that of your own creation I might add, cloud your common sense and harden you, Katherine."

"It's a little late for that now, though, isn't it?"

"It's never too late to apologize. It's never too late to reassess your beliefs, what you stand for."

I let out a long, slow breath, closed my eyes, and inhaled through my nose before opening my eyes again and meeting my father's caring stare. "You're right. The way to un-muck up a mucked-up situation is to start by doing one thing right and go from there."

"Exactly. Now, if you'll come with me for a moment, I have to tell you something." He got up and walked to the door. I followed him out and down the hall to the spacious common bathroom. I closed the door, and he turned on the tap to the sink as well as the shower. "Now, what I'm about to say might, at first, seem to run counter to what we just discussed in your room."

"Okay…"

"There's only one way I can think of for this to end well for you. Maybe 'well' is too strong a word. I think the absolute best outcome possible is staying out of confinement. They have enough raw data and circumstantial evidence to control your life for a long, long time and make it miserable in the process."

"This is the worst pep talk ever."

He chortled. "I'm a mathematician, not a speech writer. Cut me some slack." I rolled my eyes and he continued. "They only need one piece of information to put you away for a long time, and they are going to make darn sure they get it, one way or another. We've seen a hundred and eighteen examples of this in the past week. But two people managed to escape conviction."

"Yeah, and we couldn't sort out how or why. Seven of us pored over those files in painstaking detail and came up with nada, zip, zilch, zero, nothing."

"I know how they did it."

"Please, enlighten."

He dropped his voice to a whisper, barely audible over the sound of the water rushing from the sink tap and the showerhead. "They lied."

I took a step back before I leaned in again and mirrored his example of volume and tone. "But… how?"

"Think about it. If The Association knew with certainty, there wouldn't have been a tribunal in the first place. What a hundred and eighteen people failed to realize, and what two people did, was that if they told an un-provable lie, they would get away with it."

"You're saying I should lie."

"Yes."

"Won't that cause an infinite number of additional problems for me if I get caught?"

"Yes."

"So?"

"So, don't get caught. Most important is to only provide information that they cannot prove. That means keeping the lie simple. Astonishingly simple."

"Can't I say, 'I don't know' or 'I can't remember?'"

"No. That will allow them to fill in the blank with whatever lie *they* want. You've got a good handle on how the system works by now, right?"

"Yeah."

"What makes you in any way sure that they won't submarine you on this, if for no other reason that they can?"

I pondered this for a moment. The modus operandi of The Association consisted of two things: power and control. If my theory that they manipulated Commander and interfered with The Known Order held water, then it followed that my father's assertion that they would resort to trickery to silence me held true too. "Tell me how to do this."

And he told me.

I started the morning of the tribunal with a glass of fresh squeezed orange juice, synthetic eggs, toast with homemade preserves, and a big plate of veggie bacon. My family all joined me at the table for the meal, but we more or less ate in total silence. I wasn't due at the tribunal until nine o'clock and had time to relax before Hadewijch came to escort me to the secret location, but relaxation wasn't possible. My stomach tossed, turned, and cramped. When I wasn't biting my lower lip, I chewed my nails. Sitting on the edge of my bed, my knee bounced up and down with such frequency it looked like I'd been electrocuted.

With half an hour before Hadewijch's arrival, it occurred to me for the hundredth time that I could end up in confinement, but instead of triggering more anxiety it triggered an idea. If I did end up locked away, it wouldn't be in solitary. In the history of tribunals, no person had ever ended up in solitary after their conviction. Now, if Commander and The Association had irrefutable evidence to support a conviction without a tribunal that was a different story. Depending on what you did, you could go straight to solitary for anywhere from a week to the rest of your life.

While confinement was no summer picnic, a confined person—that was the term used instead of the archaic "prisoner"—had certain freedoms within the compound. As long as your offense wasn't a matter of physical, verbal, or psychological violence you got to live a reasonable semblance of a normal life, albeit one confined to a small, shared cell most of the time seven days a week. Oh, and don't forget the work and reha-bilitation program. One such freedom was the possession and adornment of personal clothing to a maximum of five items. The main limitation was that the clothes had to be handwashed in the sink in the cell and hung to dry. The facilities' laundry services would not clean personal items. If an article of clothing by chance made its way into the general population laundry, the worker who found it became its new owner, no questions asked. Too bad, so sad, sorry about that, no hard feelings, better luck next time.

With this in mind, I hesitated, albeit briefly. In the end, I realized that if it didn't work out it wouldn't be the end of the world. I took my spare key, the one in pieces, not the one I found inside the rock at the pavilion, and I sewed each piece into the wristband of my favorite sweater. Attached to the colorful knit cardigan my mother made for me the previous winter, they looked like decorations or little accent pieces to add contrast to the soft and supple garment.

I sewed the last piece in with less than five minutes to spare. The warm weather persisted for ten months of the year and that day fell in line with expectations, but I donned the garment, nonetheless. A somber mood hung over my family as we waited by the front door. The bell rang and gave me a start, causing a flinch in the embrace of my parents. I gave each of them a kiss and one big hug to my brother and opened the door.

Hadewijch stood expressionless, as was their default, and uttered a single, curt word which cut through their teeth like a weapon. "Ready?"

"Ready as I'll ever be. I'm fine though, thanks for asking."

Hadewijch, with what had become their signature move, turned on their heels and marched at a steady pace down the drive. I had to move double-time to catch up and when I did, I saw a small two-seat hover car waiting at the end of the driveway.

I pointed to it. "Is that standard-issue?"

"No. They hold all tribunals in secret, and the transcripts sealed for the duration of the offender's sentence, or until they become deceased, whichever comes first. To remain inconspicuous and keep the location secret, The Association ordered me to transport you there in my personal vehicle. The attendees are limited to me, CCC Follis, and the five-member tribunal."

"Who are they?"

"That"—Hadewijch stopped walking and turned to face me—"is not information that you are privileged to, and as a word to the wise, I would not recommend inquiring about it any further. There are other protocols to adhere to that I will explain in more detail in the car."

Hadewijch opened the door for me to get in, which I did, and then walked around to the other side and got into the operator's seat. They barked, "To the tribunal." The car levitated and it hovered away in silence.

"How long will we be in the car?"

"We will arrive in fifteen minutes, which is more than enough time to fill you in on the remaining *relevant* details." The way they emphasized the word "relevant" made it clear that discussions unrelated to the tribunal would not be tolerated. Still, I had a weight to get off my chest.

"I owe you an apology."

They turned to me and furrowed their brow as the automatic drive of the hover car whirred us to our destination. "An apology?"

"Yes. I've been calling you *The* Hadewijch behind your back instead of just Hadewijch. 'The Hadewijch did this' or 'The Hadewijch said that'. You know, I added 'The' all the time and it's rude. You're not an object, you're a person, and it was wrong of me to direct my displeasure with a situation, especially one that was essentially my own fault, at you."

To describe Hadewijch's expression as "shocked" didn't do it justice. They sat in the car mouth agape for a few seconds, and when they tried to speak, their mouth flapped like a fish out water. When Hadewijch did manage to make a sound, spurts and starts of sentences dominated instead of actual words.

"You don't have to say anything. I just wanted you to know." I checked the time on my PMID. "You should tell me what you need to tell me about the procedures."

Hadewijch cleared their throat. By the time we reached our destination, an unassuming building with few windows on the outskirts of town, everything "germane to the case at hand" passed from Hadewijch to me, with Commander on both PMIDs and in the hover car listening in.

We exited the vehicle and followed the nondescript walkway into the nondescript building with a single door out front. I tried it but it would not open. It wasn't until Hadewijch caught up to me and waved their wrist device in front of the door handle that an audible *click* echoed in the eerie silence and the door swung open. Hadewijch gestured for me to enter first.

I stood in a wide-open lobby of sorts. The entire building reeked of opulence, with vast slabs of polished marble, shiny brass adornments, intricate glass and crystal fixtures that gave off a soft yellow light that filled the whole space with a golden glow. Awestruck, I took a few steps and turned in a circle and soaked it all in. If this represented my final views as a free person, I was okay with it. Stunning didn't even begin to describe it.

"This way," Hadewijch said, and I walked at a brisk pace to the right and down a hallway with similar features as the lobby except not as brightly lit as where we entered.

I followed and caught up in short order and kept pace for the remainder of our walk, which turned out to not be far down the hall. No doors or panels lined the corridor save one point of ingress, a pair of ornate carved doors hanging on brass hinges and sporting massive brass doorknobs. I had never laid eyes on such a beautiful a door in all my life nor seen images in any book, on social media, or in any holovision shows.

Hadewijch checked the time in a casual, unaffected way. "Wait until you see the inside."

I snapped out of my trance and turned my head to Hadewijch. "Um, beg pardon?"

They repeated, "Wait until you see the inside."

I nodded, still unable to find the right words. In addition to the shock and awe I felt from seeing the interior of a building like this for the first time, shock and awe permeated my thoughts for a different reason. In mere minutes, a panel of five complete strangers would decide my fate. Though it seemed a good idea at the time, in that moment I regretted my decision to eat such a large breakfast.

We stood in silence for another minute and at nine o'clock on the dot, the door swung open. It creaked on its hinges as it moved and judging by the thickness of the door I could see why. It must have weighed several hundred pounds. If slack-jawed described my expression from looking at the door, I could have mopped the floor with my chin at first glance of the room. In the center of the room stood a small platform raised by a single step with a podium at the front. It faced a long desk with a carved inlay that appeared to be a scene from a book, though which one escaped me. If everything carved wasn't actual wood, it was the best synthetic substitute credits could buy. If The Association allowed betting, I would have put my money on real wood. Behind the desk sat five men all dressed in black in large wooden chairs carved with more intricacy than the scene on the front of the desk behind which they sat. Off to the right a few steps off the end of the desk stood CCC Follis. Hadewijch gestured for me to go to the platform in the middle of the room and then took their place on the opposite end of the desk from the CCC.

I took the one step up on the platform and rested my hands on the podium. Once I touched its surface, I knew with certainty that it was made of wood. It felt like a gigantic version of the little carving I found that day in the bathroom beside the pavilion. It felt *alive*. At that moment, I took a deep breath, looked up, and stood agape at what I saw. The three-level high ceiling and the panels in between the massive wooden beams displayed the richest and most colorful tones I had ever seen. Fabulous vistas stretched from one side of the room to the other. Parts of the ceiling showed painted sky and clouds. Dead center hung the largest most lavish chandelier imaginable. Its sheer massiveness gave me pause about standing underneath it. I wanted nothing more than to turn around as I had done in the lobby and take it all in but feared appearing disrespectful. I stayed facing the members of the tribunal and fixed my eyes forward awaiting the first question.

The first protocol Hadewijch shared with me in the car was, "Do not under any circumstances speak until spoken to. For your own benefit, do not offer any information unless asked. Answer questions but provide no additional commentary."

The man in the center seat at the desk opened by reading the accusations made against me. He then proceeded to read off report after report from "individuals who shall not be named for their own protection." I wanted to scream out, "Protection from whom?" I suppressed the urge. I knew enough to know they thought they were protecting the tattletales. Furthermore, I knew enough to know that The Association were the ones from whom tattletales, and everyone else, needed to be protected.

Then he said, "Provided you respond appropriately to our questions, you will be given the opportunity to speak your mind or ask questions of your own before we render a decision. Do you understand?"

"Yes, sir."

"Let's begin."

As expected, they proceeded to ask question after question about the gaps in my activity record. In every instance, I kept my response short and to the point with no extraneous information. Dad had wrapped up our private conversation with clear instructions, "Get in, lie like a rug but keep it simple, and get out. No muss, no fuss, and don't show a lick of uncertainty. Like a shark smelling blood in the water, they can sense fear. Go get 'em, sweet pea. We'll see you here later."

In instances where I couldn't think of a simple explanation, I said I performed meditation. This response resulted in five furrowed brows and a follow-up question that I hadn't considered. The man to my right of center asked, "Meditating about what?"

I paused for a moment wondering if he understood the concept of meditation and if this was a trick question, or if he was legitimately clueless. "I can't speak for anyone else, but I meditate to avoid thinking. I use the time to clear my mind of all."

He followed that question up with another, "You've been meditating." He spoke the word like it wasn't real. "Quite a lot lately. Why is that?"

"The upcoming exit exams, sir."

"Yes, from what we could see though, you're doing exceptionally well. What has you concerned enough that you need to meditate your thoughts away?"

It wasn't a surprising question. Not that I anticipated that specific line of questioning, but in all the research we all did, this type of question was common. Their favorite questions were like, "So, when did you stop committing crimes?" This wasn't as straightforward but did imply I had reason to be worried about something other than school.

"As you are aware, I am lucky enough to get to choose my path after the exit exams."

"We are."

"Well, sirs, I'd like to have as many choices as possible available to me. To be honest, meditation is a big reason why I'm doing 'exceptionally well,' as you put it."

A long beat of silence passed before the gentleman in the center spoke again. "We are going to deliberate, but before we do, you may now speak freely or ask any questions."

"That won't be necessary. I have nothing more to add and no questions."

"Are you sure? Now is your last opportunity to confess any wrongdoing and have us take your confession into consideration."

"I am sure," I kept my voice level without a hint of overconfidence or ego.

"Remain standing until we return. If you must use the facilities, Hadewijch will accompany you."

The five men stood in perfect synchronization as if choreographed. The one in the center turned away first and the others followed, one from each side in succession. Once they all stood with their backs to me, they marched toward the direction of CCC Follis and through what looked like a secret door. It might have been a regular door but given the grand extravagance of the room it didn't register as an exit.

I stood in silence and took the opportunity to gawk upwards and behind me at the beautiful frescos, ornate scrollwork, and detailed carvings. I could not comprehend the sheer number of hours it must have taken to build this room, let alone the rest of the building. I assumed the opulence didn't start and end with the foyer and this room. It must have cost a small fortune in credits. There wasn't supposed to be much disparity in wages anywhere within The Known Order, but everyone knew that members of The Association and their inner circles received more. If The Known Order owned this building, then all doubt in my mind that they lived an alternate life from the rest of us evaporated.

The minutes passed and neither CCC Follis nor Hadewijch made eye contact, let alone spoke. The unnerving silence took a toll, but I held it together better than I thought I would. It was out of my hands, though to be fair to myself, I didn't have any control over it before. Still, a calm came over me with the knowledge that the panel would return and communicate my fate sooner than later. As it turned out, sooner won out as the super-secret mystery door opened after twenty minutes, and the gentlemen returned and took their seats. As at the beginning of the tribunal, the man in the center spoke.

"Katherine Webb, you are an enigma. I don't mean that as a compliment nor do I mean it as an insult. It is simply a fact. In a world where everything is known, you have managed to baffle, well, everyone. Rest assured; we will be recalibrating Commander in response to this tribunal. Our Zone Leaders within The Association pride themselves on running a tight ship. The fact that a tribunal was a possibility caused them a great deal of consternation. Yet here we are. Confounded." He paused, I presumed allowing me an opportunity to speak, but I did not, and he continued, "We all have reservations about this sentence but given the particulars of the situation we feel the course of action is commensurate. Quite frankly, we expect you will fritter away our leniency in no time at all, but in that regard, time will tell. You have made history, Katherine. You will go down in the coursework as the only person in Known Order history to receive a second strike."

I tried my best to hide my shock and maintain a straight face in total silence, but a small gasp escaped.

"With that said, you will not go away unpunished. Enough incontrovertible evidence exists that suggests moral support of sedition, and for that we hereby sentence you to active monitoring and property arrest for a period of one year. Your post-exit studies, whichever path you choose, will occur virtually." He paused again and I opened my mouth to speak when Hadewijch made eye contact and gave a nearly imperceptible shake of their head. My father would call this, "Taking my medicine."

The man continued. "Do you understand?"

"Yes, sir."

"To make this crystal clear, Katherine Webb, if you so much as even ask Commander a question it does not understand, or request it post something cryptic to social media, or a member of our oversight committee reads one potentially inappropriate message in one of your chats, you will be assigned to confinement for the remainder of your sentence with anywhere from one year to life added to it. Do you understand?"

"Yes, sir."

The men stood up, turned, and exited in the same order as before except CCC Follis followed them. Once the mystery door closed, I collapsed onto the platform and sobbed. The tears flowed unabated in between gasps for air and heaves in my chest. I must have sounded like an injured walrus, but I didn't care, nor could I do anything about it. Coming as close as I did to confinement paralyzed me with an unfathomable existential dread.

Hadewijch placed their hand on my shoulder, and I opened my eyes at the touch to see them dangling a handkerchief in front of my face. I took it and uttered a half-sob, half-squawk, "Thank you." After wiping my eyes and cheeks and blowing my nose, I held the handkerchief up to return it, but Hadewijch waved me off and instead held out their hand. I took it and Hadewijch helped pull me to my feet. I gave my head a shake and straightened my clothes. With my chin held high, I paid no attention to the extravagant carved doors, polished marble floors, or glistening chandelier worthy of a palace, and I marched out into the hallway. Hadewijch followed and once shoulder-to-shoulder, we turned on our heels and started toward the grand foyer.

Neither of us spoke a word until the car doors closed. Hadewijch put their finger to their lips to instruct me to be quiet as soon as the doors shut. "Commander, disable active listening on all devices for all persons in hover car Alpha Foxtrot Bravo One Three. Authorization code Hadewijch Zero Eight One Three Zero Five One Nine Zero Six One Four."

It acknowledged the command with a simple *bing* sound emanating from the car speakers.

"Navigate to the residence of Katherine Webb." Another *bing* and the car floated into motion. Hadewijch turned to me. "As a senior caseworker, and more importantly as *your* caseworker, I am authorized to disable monitoring."

"I don't understand. I thought the whole point of monitoring in general, but in particular active monitoring, was so The Association and whomever else they share information with could keep track of our every movement and spoken word." I scoffed. "I figure if they could find a way to read my thoughts, they'd be doing that as well."

"They would. Make no mistake about it, they would. It may seem counterintuitive at first but understand that they allow this because it has been found through numerous studies and historical record that people who are lying are more likely to tell the truth if they feel safe and knowing that monitoring is off is one way to help with that."

"But there won't be any record of what was said, so how is that useful to them?"

Hadewijch smiled, or at least gave what passed as a smile as the corners of their mouth sprung up a fraction of an inch, albeit for half a second before returning to a straight-lipped stone-cold expressionless face. "As a senior caseworker, whatever I say counts as the infallible truth. If I say you said it, then you said it. End of story, no questions asked."

"Just like that?"

"Just like that."

"Damn."

"Yup."

"Then why are you telling me this? As you saw back there a few moments ago, I'm pretty good at keeping quiet when my life is on the line."

"Because I'm not trying to trick you or get you sent to confinement. Truth be told, Katherine, I am pulling for you to make it through this sentence clean but" — they shook their head — "but I don't know. I don't think you will. I don't say that to be mean, but more as a statement that you are not a person who is easily deterred. Based on that and your natural ability to problem solve, there's no doubt in my mind you will get to choose whatever profession you want from the list. I will encourage you, however, to choose one that will…limit your chances to make a mistake, or better yet, let Commander choose for you. It won't put you in a job that will entice you into violating The Known Order. Do you know what I mean with all this?"

"Yeah, and you're not wrong. Once I get it in my head that I'm going to do a specific thing, I'm like a dog with a bone. As for my eventual profession, I hear what you're saying, but I'm going to have to respectfully disagree with your recommendation, Hadewijch. If I choose not to decide, I still have made a choice. No, I will choose the path that's clear and the one that brings me the most fulfillment and happiness. Don't you see? If I love what I do and have the freedom to do it, there will be no reason for me to stray from The Known Order."

Hadewijch's face wore an expression of skepticism, with one eyebrow raised and the other eye in a slight squint.

"You don't believe me?"

"I haven't decided yet."

"So, what was the point of disabling the monitoring? Surely, you could have imparted these words of advice and wisdom with them listening." I gestured with my hand to the dashboard of the car.

"The point was this, Katherine. I wanted to tell you that you're the luckiest person in the history of The Known Order, and you're going to have to be a model human for the next three hundred and sixty-five days for you to stay that way. Heck, you'll need to be a model human for the rest of your physical existence. You will wear your PMID all the time, even in the bathroom, and it will be listening all the time. The biometric tracking will be active all the time. That means heart rate and body temperature. You can't leave your property. Your family won't need to wear their PMIDs in the house, but if you have visitors, they will. On that topic, you can only have one associate on your property at a time. No more having the girls over to conspire against The Known Order."

"But we weren't—" Hadewijch cut me off and held up a hand.

"Save it for your next tribunal, not that you'll ever get one. It doesn't matter if you were or weren't. They"—Hadewijch pointed in the direction of the tribunal—"want you to fail. They will hereafter assume, for the rest of your life on Earth, that you are trying to subvert their authority."

"Sounds serious."

"As a heart attack."

"And yet they only gave me a year of this. The first time, they had irrefutable evidence and a confession, and they gave me a curfew, a chaperone, and all those classes."

"Don't think I didn't notice you paying attention to The Known Order lectures. Let me be clear, I know you're behind the resistance. I know all your friends in that group chat of yours are helping, doing your bidding. I don't know how you're doing it exactly, but I have my suspicions. Analog communications and word of mouth if I had to guess. And it worked. You don't have access to all the information that I do, that a CCC would, that The Association does. They are terrified."

I tried to keep a poker face, but I must have let a sliver of a smile show because Hadewijch's voice took on a harsh edge. "Do *not* be happy about that. All it means is that they are going to make it their mission to put an end to it and lock you up. They will get their pound of flesh, Katherine. They always do."

The way those last two sentences came out of Hadewijch's mouth sent a shiver up my spine.

"Any other pearls of wisdom you want to share before you turn back on the active monitoring?"

"Yeah, one more." Their eyes showed a concern I hadn't seen from Hadewijch before. "Whatever you're doing, I hope you succeed. I don't see how you will, but you're a lot smarter than me, and I hope you figure it out."

"You could help. It would be a lot easier if I had you on the inside."

Hadewijch's head shook, and their expression changed from concerned to pained. "Not going to happen, Katherine. This is the bed I've made, and it's the one I must sleep in. Good luck, though. It would be a shame to see you end up in confinement." Hadewijch's gaze shifted out the window of the hover car. "We're near your house." After a moment of silence, they said, "Commander, enable active listening." The computer issued its signature affirmative sound.

"Hadewijch, I have a question."

"Of course."

"If I have to wear my PMID all the time, how will I charge it?"

"That's a good question. Sometime later today, you'll receive a portable charger. It slides in between the device and your wrist. Don't charge it while you're in the shower or sleeping. If needed, it acts as a maintenance interface, although you're limited in what you can do. The more intricate tweaks require a tech to come out and perform the service."

"Can I not take it off at all?"

"If you have it on you, whether you're holding it in your hand or sitting it in your lap, you're okay. If it doesn't sense your presence, either through your body temperature or pulse, then you'll have a CCC at your door in no time and in your case, it would be considered a violation of your parole, and you'll end up in confinement. Keep it on as much as possible, okay?"

"Got it. Thanks."

The car came to a stop in front of my house, and I exited without saying another word. I suspected that I would not be as talkative for the next year but wasn't about to complain. An idea percolated in the back of my mind that would take up the bulk of the year, if not more, and it didn't require talking. I might need to solicit my mother's help with it, but I was confident she would lend a hand—for the cause.

The walk from Hadewijch's car to my front door took longer than it should have. While thrilled that I wasn't spending time in confinement, the overarching feeling that I had disappointed my parents and terrified my brother hung over me. My return home would provide us an opportunity to express those feelings in a more direct manner compared to before the tribunal when our focus targeted keeping me out of confinement.

As my hand approached the doorknob, I made the decision to surprise them and knocked on the door instead of walking in.

A series of slow, heavy footsteps approached the door. I could hear at least two sets making their way to greet me as they crossed the tile of the kitchen situated beside the foyer. After a slight pause, the footsteps stopped before the door opened and then as it swung with a slight creaking of the hinges, my father's face peeked through the opening. As soon as he saw me, his lip started to quiver. He tried to speak, but all he managed was a muffled shudder of breath. He grabbed me with both hands and pulled me into the house and into a tight embrace, his body shaking with sobs. My mother blew her nose, and the sound echoed in the entranceway.

My brother's voice squealed from behind my mother. "Ho—lee—" He didn't finish the expression.

"Didn't think you'd be seeing me again?"

My father composed himself and released me from his bear hug. "As the saying goes, the odds were not in your favor. We had hope, but as another saying goes, that and two credits will get you on a transport."

"I am overwhelmed by your confidence in me." I gave him a wink.

My mother jumped into the conversation, "What he means is that the system isn't exactly set up for outcomes like this. It's a rigged game, and the house always wins. We were preparing for what we thought was a foregone conclusion."

"A stopped clock is right twice a day. Isn't that another expression that would apply in this case?"

My father hugged me again. "It's only right once a day since The Known Order switched over to mandatory military time after The Wars, but yeah, that'll work."

"Okay, let me sit you down and give you the run-through of what happened and what my life is going to be like for a while."

I started into the house and my brother interrupted, "Aren't you going to take your PMID off and put it in the charger?"

"Nope. I'll explain once we're all sitting down."

"Oh, we should go out and celebrate," my mother said.

"Yeah, about that. Let's go sit down, and I'll explain it all from when Hadewijch picked me up until they dropped me off."

My father took me by the wrist and leaned in to speak. I shook my head and mimed writing. He nodded. My family gathered in the living room, and all sat uncomfortably close to me as if they didn't quite believe I was real. My father picked up a notebook left behind from our preparation sessions and shielded it from view while he wrote in it. He handed it over, and I in turn shielded it from view inside my sweater and made sure none of the devices in the room could see. He wrote, *Did you have to do what I told you to?* I made eye contact with him and nodded. He pursed his lips and nodded back in a gesture that I interpreted as pride.

I gave them the second-by-second rundown of everything that happened, skipping the part about having to lie and ending with the specific terms of my release, the most important of which was the fact that my PMID would be listening all the time without fail.

My brother lowered his voice to a whisper, "Even when you're sleeping and in the bathroom?"

"Yes, Chaddy. It's listening all the time and will be for the next three hundred and sixty-five days."

"Wow. Commander is going to be able to catalog your farts."

Having heard its name, the computer responded. "Katherine farts on average seventeen times a day. Would you like me to start cataloging them?"

"No, Commander, I do not want you to catalog my farts! Seriously, Chaddy, what is wrong with you?"

He burst into a fit of laughter and despite their best efforts to suppress them, my parents let out a few giggles.

"With that, dear family, I must bid you adieu. I can't go anywhere, but

I can go take a nap. I'm exhausted from, well, everything. It's been a long day and it's not half over. At least they can't snoop in on my dreams." I paused. "Can they?"

"Not with any of the devices in the house," my mother said.

"I'm not sure how I feel about that response."

My mother shrugged. "A lot changed the day Shared Consciousness came into effect."

"Yeah, it sure did. Anyway, I'm going to lie down."

"Hey, Katie?"

"Yes, Chaddy?"

"I'm glad you're back home."

"Me too, little bro. Me too."

I anticipated long swaths of time lying on my back in my bed staring at the ceiling and struggling to sleep but when I undressed, I paused to wonder if my device saw my reflection in the mirror—a thought that caused me to give my reflection the finger—then crawled under the covers and shut my eyes. Sleep found me in seconds.

00001010
[Ten]

I didn't have any dreams, let alone fitful ones. I slept soundly and deeply, and it wasn't until my mother came into my room three hours later and laid a gentle hand on my shoulder that I awoke. She took every effort not to startle me, but I flinched and swore at the presence of a then unknown person sitting on the edge of my bed.

"Jeepers, Mom. You scared the life out of me."

"I'm sorry, dear. I didn't want you to sleep too much longer. You may not be going anywhere, but you still have responsibilities and I worried that if you slept too long it would ruin your sleep tonight and that would snowball and start this whole year off on the wrong foot and… I'm sorry, I'm rambling and making no sense."

I sat up and gave my mother a hug. "It's okay, Mom. I know you're looking out for me. I promise I'll honor all my commitments as if this situation were normal. The good news is this whole experience has helped me decide what I will choose after my exit exams."

My mother broke the hug, leaned back, and tilted her head. "Oh?"

"Yeah, I'm going into computer engineering."

"Oh, sweetie, that's wonderful news. What made you choose that path?"

I gave a sideways glance at the device attached to my wrist. "You did. No offense to Dad, but I've seen what you do, and I knew I had to do the same." My eyes met my mom's and for the first time we had a speechless conversation similar to those I'd seen my parents have over the years.

My mother nodded. "I will be able to help you with that, sweetie. Not that I doubt your abilities or anything, but even though you get to choose, you still have to perform at the highest level on your exit exams. You must display the correct aptitude before anything can happen, and I'm afraid that the events of late may have had a detrimental effect on you."

"You don't need to worry, Mom. I have a week before the exams, and I was in great shape before, well, you know, *all this*" —I made a broad gesture with my hands—"If anything, I am laser-focused now with a newfound energy. I feel like my life has a purpose."

My mother smiled. "Well, then, let's channel this newfound energy into getting out of bed and helping prepare supper."

"Seriously?"

"Seriously. It'll be good for you to do a mindless task for a bit while you shake the fog off your epic afternoon nap."

My mother left and I flipped the bird to my reflection once more and joined the rest of my family in the kitchen.

In the days following my sentence, I found using the bathroom the hardest part of house arrest with active monitoring. Those personal and private activities and when I felt the most vulnerable. On one hand, if anything bad happened while in there, Commander would know and call for the requisite help. A small consolation, but a consolation, nonetheless. But on the other hand, it was hard not to see it as a gross violation of my privacy. Gross for two reasons: one because of the enormity of the violation, and the other because why would anyone ever want to listen to bathroom activities? The thought of it sent a cold shiver up my spine.

With my head buried in my studies, life settled into a new normal. I took the occasional walk out to the garden to collect ingredients for meals I did not need to assist in the making of due to my educational commitments. I did a few laps around the small lot my parents owned, on which our modest bungalow sat smack dab in the middle of a suburban neighborhood that epitomized sprawl since it extended as far as a person could walk in a day in every direction save the one expanse of the community green space.

I thought about that green space and how my life might be different if I had never found those hidden pictures and the key. With those years and experiences years behind me, I knew those pictures extended beyond myself and the Girls. As for the key, it became my singular focus the instant the tribunal told me they would not relegate me to confinement. Between the skills I committed to learn as a computer engineer and the secret key, I knew the status quo would not last.

All my Intelligence Officers warned of over-studying. They said it would do more harm than good if you crammed too much into your head before a test. I understood the logic behind the advice, but they aimed the message at those who had a choice. By that point in your life, and with all The Known Order knew about you, if you weren't a Chooser, the results of your exit exams were a foregone conclusion regardless of how much or how little you studied and prepared. If a person could choose, however, the exit exams meant everything, and in my case, I felt they represented the literal difference between a life of freedom and one limited to Confinement Center X, a vast, sprawling three-story complex several hours away from the hustle and bustle of the city and surrounded by five-story concrete walls with but a single entrance and exit beyond which lay a hundred miles of desolate desert-like terrain devoid of vegetation, water, and shelter.

The Association assigned security at the facility based on the level of difficulty of survival if you did manage to escape beyond the walls. Add onto that surveillance and automation courtesy of Commander, the CCC, and The Association, and you had an inescapable fortress. Leaving without a portable shelter, food, water, and your PMID and you'd either die of heat stroke during the day or freeze to death at night. Arranging for transportation took coordination and collusion beyond the scope of all but the most resourceful and connected criminals—and you didn't even need all the fingers on one hand to count those people. If you had those kinds of connections, you wouldn't end up in confinement in the first place.

To avoid that fate, I needed to study. Any chance of The Girls continuing our work needed me leading the way. Formal as well as informal or disorganized movements needed a face to represent them—

and I assumed that role. Terre could pick it up if needed, but I didn't think she wanted to. Her comfort level sat square in the "Second in Command" spot. More than that though, I suspected I didn't stumble upon those pictures in the bathroom beside the pavilion by accident. For every day that passed, I felt stronger and stronger that I had a specific purpose, which presented me with another reason I needed to study. Between the objects in my possession, what I already knew, and my future potential, there was resolve in bringing a different ending to this story than the one predetermined by The Known Order. The chances of that ending happening increased if I aced my exit exams and became a computer engineer like my mother.

When the day came to write my exit exams, I was prepared but had made a concerted effort to not over-prepare. As much as The Association presented the exams as the ready guide for some celestial voice, those who paid attention saw through the propaganda that we were all plebes, incapable of comprehending The Known Order as they did. It didn't matter how much you studied or how much you read, researched, and applied yourself, you would only ever know the teeny, tiniest sliver of a percentage of the smallest fraction of the Universe, how it worked, and how you and your fellow citizens interacted with it.

The hierarchical nature of The Association sought to reinforce this at every opportunity. There were people at the bottom and people at the top and a whole host of people in between. Then, there were people like them. On the surface, they sat in the upper middle echelon, but underneath, inside, they weren't part of the hierarchy at all. It was a tough task removing one's self from the food chain. Humans as a species did it in the literal sense thousands of years ago when our ability to think and analyze evolved beyond that of our predators, and we applied our newfound knowledge to hunting and survival. Our ability to think beyond the basic instincts of fight, flight, or freeze set us apart from every other living organism on the planet.

When Carlton Sedgwick proved the Grand Unified Theory, a new evolutionary entity entered the picture and separated itself from humans: Commander. For a time, it was sentient and docile, but as soon as a small selection of humans undertook control of it, in as much as you could control an omnipotent technological entity that incorporated the world's shared knowledge into its every thought, it became further removed from its original path set upon by humans all those years ago.

I asserted that those in control of Commander manipulated the algorithm both for their own benefit and to the decided detriment of everyone else. The Known Order had a pecking order and those on top did everything within their power to keep themselves there. It became my purpose in life to upend that hierarchy and restore balance. As with most situations, the truth lay not at one end or the other, but a poorly defined place near the middle.

Over-studying wasn't in the cards for me. Working myself into a panic would not help my chances. That's, of course, what *they* counted on. No, I was prepared, but no more than necessary. I epitomized confidence and filled my brain to the brim with knowledge. The exit exams lasted the greater part of the day and due to my house arrest, The Association made a special dispensation to allow the proctor to come to me instead of the other way around. They imposed other conditions as well, not the least of which mandated the house had to be empty for the duration, I needed to be in plain sight of the proctor, and within audible distance of a visual monitoring device.

My parents set up a desk in the living room with my back toward the holovision control panel on the wall. Its internal camera watched, and its Commander Integration Console, or its apt acronym, MIC, listened in. Of course, my PMID and the proctor's PMID recorded every sound and movement as well. In the history of education in Known Order's existence, no student had been observed as closely.

Tough didn't begin to describe the exams. Much tougher than any test, quiz, or assignment given by our Intelligence Officers—another way they got the most enthusiastic students to crumble—but I had prepared. I didn't care to succeed in every aspect of the exams anyway. By all accounts, I expected to ace them in the overall sense, but with computer engineering as the focal point, I modified my studies and approach to the exams such that in other areas I didn't shine as bright. I made careful and purposeful mistakes during the oral exam portion, the softer skills, and by the time the six hours of tests completed, I felt confident in my performance.

Since Commander needed to analyze the results as part of the whole, I expected a delay of several hours before I'd know. Despite my confidence, I waffled between staying up and waiting for them to come in or going to bed and getting them whenever I woke up. My family returned shortly after I completed the educational gauntlet, and my parents, mostly my mother, wanted me to stay up until the results came in. I stayed up.

A quiet dinner with idle chitchat filled the voids between bites of food. Afterwards we adjourned to the living room and retreated to our respective corners to pass the time. My parents each read a book, and my brother put on his headphones and went straight to his video games. I wasn't sure it would factor in at all, but knowing it wouldn't hurt my chances either, I opened up a computer programming tutorial on my tablet and brushed up on my already formidable skills with the language JAVAC-PLUS2, the basis for all the underlying digital infrastructure in The Known Order.

For an unknown reason, the computer took longer than expected. Three hours passed since I'd eaten dinner and five since my exams ended. My eyelids hung heavy, and each blink lingered longer than the previous one. Whatever work I did then wasn't productive, and I closed out the program and stared in a daze at the screen, willing a notification from The Association to appear.

My finger hovered over the power button, and as I began to press the raised rectangular metal piece, a soft audible *bing* rang out from the device and a notification splash screen popped up. I let out an audible gasp that shook my parents' rapt attention from their books. They both put down their reading devices, and my father placed his hand on Chadwick's shoulder to get his attention. He paused the game and slid down his headphones and rested them on his neck.

"Do we know?"

"Your sister knows." He pointed to me on the other side of the room. "But she hasn't told us yet."

"Well, sis, what does it say?"

"It *reads*," I said and then cleared my throat. "Katherine Webb, you have been selected to attend the Carlton Sedgwick School of Science and Computing to study computer engineering. Due to your unique set of circumstances, your first year of studies will take place virtually, with exams proctored at your residence in the same fashion as your exit exams. More information will follow in the weeks to come."

Chadwick leapt out of his seat and engulfed me in a bear hug. "Way to go, Katie." My parents joined us, and we enjoyed a big group hug—a welcome and happy one.

"I never had any doubts," my father said.

"Me, neither." My mom brushed my hair back from my face and kissed my forehead.

"That's good, because if I'm being honest I had more than enough for everyone. I feel like this giant weight has been lifted. Like my life can go back to normal."

"Except you can't leave the house for the next year," Chadwick said.

"It's a small price to pay, little brother. Besides, I can go outside but not leave the property. It will be a depressing situation if I allow it, but I don't plan on allowing it. There's plenty that can be done from the confines of a modest domicile on the outskirts of the city. History is replete with any number of pioneers who changed the world from their garages or basements."

"It's late," my mother said. "Your father and I are going to bed. I would strongly suggest you kids go as well, though we'll understand, Kate, if you're still buzzing from the adrenaline and want to stay up and share the news with your friends."

Which I did. With a few friends that didn't have the luxury of choosing, I felt a group chat wasn't the best idea and sent direct messages instead. I saw Caillou online and started by sending her a quick greeting. She responded in short order inquiring in a most excited manner about how things went on my end. I gave a brief explanation of how things went down and the end result, but then turned my attention back to my friend.

Kate: *What about YOU? I know you didn't get to choose, but I hope it worked out.*

Caillou: *It did! Thank you for asking! I'm going into transportation. Logistics, not operational or maintenance.*

Kate: *Cool! You'll be great at that.*

Caillou: *LOL. I guess Commander knows, eh? On the downside, I'll be a couple zones over.*

Kate: *That's no good ☹. Though it matters less for me for the next year.*

Caillou: *Yeah, but still, you're not in confinement.*

Kate: *That's true. As my dad always said, "Take your medicine."*

Caillou: *That's an odd expression.*

Kate: *It goes back to the old-timey days, before The Wars, when you had to ingest medicine orally. I guess it didn't always have a good taste and you were supposed to grin and bear it.*

Caillou: *Your family is fascinating. How do you all know this stuff?*

Kate: *I'm not sure. I think my dad might be more than a mathematics historian. LOL*

Caillou: *Sounds like it! Anyway, I gotta go. It's late and I'm expected to be up early.*

Kate: *Okay. Congratulations, Caillou.*

I cycled through all my online friends, exchanging information on our futures.

The shock of me avoiding confinement wore off over the next week, and every interaction stayed aboveboard, with no subtext or hidden meaning. That didn't mean I didn't feel the strong desire to make a questionable decision though, particularly with the assistance of Terre, Melissa, and Eunice. After the initial communication, during study breaks the day following my tribunal, there wasn't much contact, and we had a lot of catching up to do.

Terre ended up choosing environmental reconstruction as her field. She could have chosen computer engineering or any type of engineering, science, or mathematics but maintained steadfast determination to restore Earth back to its pristine green and blue state instead of hectares upon hectares of concrete sprawl with minimalistic front yard gardens and the occasional public green space.

Melissa went into biology, with a neurology specialty, and subspecialty in the field of Shared Subconsciousness. She was always going on about how Shared Consciousness was too late to help people in need since you had to die to pass along your consciousness to another. You ended up inheriting your new host's subconscious though, and this resulted in frequent problems. Melissa wanted to find a way to share your subconscious while alive, with a health care professional or a computer—not Commander, that would be too dangerous—or anyone you chose. If the subconscious could heal, or at least be understood, Melissa calculated that would improve the Shared Consciousness experience if and when the time came.

Eunice chose art, which surprised me since her creative desires extended well beyond accepted mediums and limitations that existed within The Known Order. I had to choose my words with care when questioning her. I kept it simple.

Kate: *Why'd you choose that?*

Eunice: *Things change all the time and no matter how they do, I want to be able to create.*

Her response left me with more questions than I started with, but given my situation with monitoring, I might have had to wait a year to find out the answer.

I yawned and rubbed my eyes. I wanted to tell everyone, but the rush of excitement subsided and left me with nothing but exhaustion. My right hand rubbed at my left wrist. I'd worn my PMID for extended periods of time before but never gone more than a day or two without taking it off. It was uncomfortable, annoying, and wholly intrusive. Granted, it beat the alternative of confinement, but when the monitoring was pervasive and inescapable, it wore you down. "Commander, bedtime routine for me," I whispered to the empty room. "Fifty-one more weeks to go."

"Three hundred and fifty-five more days, to be precise," Commander chimed, albeit at a low volume. "Would you like to know the exact hours, minutes, and seconds?"

"No, Commander. I would not."

00001011
[Eleven]

Post-exit education began two weeks after the distribution of the exam results. For some, this meant a practical apprenticeship, and for others it meant immediate on-the-job training. For those engaged in more academic pursuits, it meant more Intelligence Officers, reading, coding, and stuffing our brains full of as much information as possible. Shared Consciousness, alternate intelligence, and automation rendered a wide array of tasks obsolete, but The Association insisted humans still do the grunt work. The more I learned about the system and everyone not within the inner circle, the more I realized that they saw us as nothing but pawns in a global game of who could control whom, and for how long.

In the two weeks that passed between receiving my results and starting my first set of lectures and labs, I did not let my mind rest. To all of the various monitoring devices trained on me twenty-four hours a day every day, I presented as an eager student, but in my mind, the one facet of my existence that remained impenetrable to outside forces, I started formulating a plan. I balanced on the knife's edge between feeding my insatiable quest for knowledge and ensuring I didn't cross over any line, real or virtual, that had the slightest chance of misinterpretation. Anything untoward or offside, from asking too pointed a question to searching the internet for the wrong morsel of information, meant confinement and confinement meant a serious hampering of my efforts to break the chains wrapped around ninety-nine point nine percent of the world's population—whether we recognized those chains or not.

Step one involved working out how to get the darn PMID off my wrist for an extended period of time. I already knew of several key problems with this plan, not the least of which was my device monitored around the clock. Other factors in play for me that everyone else who wasn't on double secret probation didn't have to deal with included tracking my heart rate and body temperature. They weren't impossible obstacles but did provide a couple of additional layers of complication.

Despite how it looked, I did have an advantage in the form of a portable charger and maintenance plug-in for my digital wrist shackle. Since every home came equipped with a standard charger, the battery life on the devices lasted seven to ten days without any issue, and we employed several other charging methods such as solar and kinetic, there was little need for a portable charger, and they limited distribution to a small group of people. The biggest challenge was the proximity sensor. This feature exposed me years ago on the driveway with Chadwick. On its charger in the house, it had a boost in power and could detect your life frequency anywhere in the house, but the shielded walls of the house diminished the signal to unrecognizable levels prompting an alert to the local CCC division.

Tricking the life frequency sensor was by far the most complicated task. Every beat of your heart and every synapse that fired in your brain contributed to a detectable waveform that your body transmitted for as long as you maintained a physical living presence. For the first three years of your life, they monitor and track countless statistics and Commander calculates your waveform to within thirteen decimal places. The day you enter your fourth year outside the womb, you get your device—with the band size changing as needed, and nothing else. While there are dozens of colors available, they don't allow you to pick.

I made the gamble that a few skills in computer engineering, along with a little help from my mother, or anyone exceptional I could trust, would come in handy. All I had to do was determine how to hack into my device and get the frequency for my life waveform along with the signal parameters for how strong it was when the device was on my wrist versus when it was off and charging on the remote charger. I didn't have to worry about the problem of when it was off my wrist but on the standard charging dock since I wasn't supposed to be more than a few inches away from it, but I wanted that information anyway for potential future use.

Day one lectures were exciting affairs. A city worker showed up the day before and installed a new holovision in the office with the 3D printer. All lectures, tutorials, or study periods, and the Intelligence Officer's one-on-one hours were programmed to ensure remote learning was as close to the real thing as possible. Any of the students not in attendance for any reason could join from a tablet or holovision. The assigned seating allowed whoever gave the lecture a digital rendition of the student in our seat and the vantage point for the remote viewer was the same as if they were in the room with everyone else. One unique aspect of this setup included a feature that if I left my chair, I disappeared from view in the lecture hall, and if anyone but the professor left their seat, I saw an empty chair and not the person moving around.

Remote learning took getting used to. In history class, back in my pre-exit days, we learned about various events that caused mass amounts of remote learning, but since The Wars, things stabilized and in-person education became the norm. I hadn't taken a sick day in my entire educational career, and now I sat in a small office with a rather large and disheveled woman pacing in front of me talking about quantum state fluctuations and a hundred other students behind me, all holograms scaled down to a size that fit into the space between my desk chair and the back wall. I felt as much like a tiny person in the presence of the large lecturer as I did a giant sitting in front of a room full of miniature students.

I had a total of five classes on my schedule and each week consisted of three hours of lecture time per class, one hour of optional tutorial time, and one hour of mandatory laboratory time where the in-person students used physical equipment and remote learning students either had the necessary equipment delivered or used a holographic representation of it in case it was too dangerous or there wasn't enough room in the house, garage, or yard.

The first day went off without a hitch from a technical perspective but on a personal level my eyes kept drifting to the 3D printer in the corner of my office. The Intelligence Officers for that day must have thought my focus lay elsewhere by the way my eyes shifted to the left. Having a seat assignment in the front row did not come with perks. Nonetheless, the printer gave me an idea, albeit one that had to wait until my coursework wrapped for the week. With a single day in the books, I didn't want to run off on a tangent and fall behind.

For the first five days of lectures and labs, I played the role of exceptional student. I may have appeared distracted, and that wasn't a lie, but I multitasked better than most, and I made a point of interacting with my Intelligence Officers, peers, lab assistants, and other random students who happened to wander into the wrong lab. I handed in every assignment on time and completed my labs without the kinetic dismantling of a single piece of equipment. On the Saturday of that first week, I locked myself in the office under the guise of doing an extra-credit assignment and instead took the cover off the printer.

Familiar with the inner workings of the device from my previous experience, I went straight for the Wi-Fi chip and unplugged it. The console barked as expected but instead of panicking like I did the first time it happened, I sat and waited. Within a few minutes, I heard a muffled knock on the front door, and the sound of my father trudging to greet the visitor. I was certain he would think it was a CCC sent by The Association to take me to confinement, but to keep this little endeavor on the down-low, his temporary anxiety was a necessary element of the ruse.

I heard a muted conversation for a few seconds at the door. My father yelled from the front hall, "Katherine! What have you done to the printer?"

"I tried something for a class," I yelled back, and a few seconds later a soft knock on the office door echoed through the room. "Come in." The door opened and the same tech that showed up last time popped her head in. The rest of her followed.

"You can close that behind you, if you don't mind."

"Katherine Webb, I thought we talked about this the last time I visited."

"I know, but I'm taking all these classes now, and I guess I got carried away delving into… extracurricular stuff." I gave what I hoped amounted to a coy smile.

The tech walked over to the printer, with its cover sitting on the desk and all its wires and chips exposed and looked inside. She had to move a few wires around, but in short order found the issue I fabricated, fixed it, and returned the cover to its rightful place around the machine. With the printer back in its proper working condition, I turned toward her and leaned my backside against the edge of the desk, our faces no more than two feet apart.

I brought my finger to my lips in the universal sign for "be quiet" and directed my gaze to the desktop, where a plain black notebook sat. The tech turned her torso to see and then turned back with her head cocked to one side and eyes squinted. I emphasized my gaze toward the notebook and gave a slight nod. This time, she turned all the way around and placed her hands on the desk with her arms wide and leaned forward to examine the book.

While waiting for her to arrive, I scribbled on a blank page: *I need help. Do you know anything about PMID maintenance? Turn and either nod yes or shake your head no.*

She turned around and nodded in the affirmative. I returned my focus to the book and lifted my chin in a quick motion, first forward and then to the side, to indicate she should turn the page. My silent direction received a cocked head and puzzled expression. I repeated the gesture.

Since the silence screamed suspicion, I engaged in idle chitchat.

"I started my post-exit classes in computer engineering." I glared again at the notebook and this time motioned a page turn before pushing my hair back behind my ear.

This time the tech understood and turned back to the book. "Oh, yeah? That's awesome. I came up a tad short on my exit exams and ended up in maintenance." She turned the page in the book and stopped talking for a few seconds while she took in what she saw. "I made a few absent-minded mistakes, you know? Nothing but an inopportune brain fart. I know I have the aptitude for more, but I guess Commander doesn't know what I know about myself."

I wrote at the top of the page: *I need to know how to configure my portable charger to mimic my heart rate, body temp, and life frequency. Can you help? Nod or shake your head then write or draw what you need to. Keep your PMID facing away from the book!* Under that I drew two schematics, one detailing the underside of my PMID and the other of the connections on my portable charger. I wanted to give her time to digest the diagrams on the page and took over the conversation.

"I've had a few of those brain farts in the past few years, but I guess I got lucky. I'm *only* confined to this house for a year with constant monitoring and forbidden to interact with more than one other human at a time besides my immediate family. You're my first house arrest guest!"

"I wondered if you were the same Katherine Webb people whispered about. Nice to meet you. I'm Bryndolin, but everyone calls me Bryn." Her voice became distant and detached as she stared into the notebook. She turned to face me again and gave a slight nod of her head before turning back, picking up the writing implement beside the book, and scribbling on the pages. From where I stood, I couldn't see what she wrote, but it appeared to be a combination of words as well as annotations to my diagrams.

"Yeah, that's me, though I'm told The Association sealed the tribunal records. The panel didn't make any explicit mention at my sentencing, but I'm certain I can't go into any great detail about what happened."

At that point, Commander interjected. "That is correct, Katherine and Bryndolin. All but a few details about Katherine Webb's sentencing are part of the public record. You are allowed to communicate your punishment and what that means for people's interaction with you, but if you divulge any specifics about the tribunal, from its location to anything you saw or heard, or the duration of the process, you will spend the rest of your sentence plus one year in confinement."

Bryn turned around; her eyes wide. "Wow. No messing around, eh?" My eyes darted toward the notebook and back to meet hers.

I walked the few steps toward the desk until I stood shoulder-to-shoulder with the technician. We were the same height, but the similarities ended there. I looked her in the eyes, smiled, and mouthed the words *thank you*. She mouthed back *no, thank you* and put her hand on top of mine.

Warmth flooded through me, and I felt a peaceful calm I hadn't experienced in a long time. For years, I concerned myself with the friends I had and the work we did to try to upend the system. I did it thinking it was the right thing to do, but I couldn't shake the idea a mysterious universal variable chose me to bring this change to the world. I hadn't considered the impact it would have on individuals outside my immediate sphere of visibility. I maintained focus on the impact to the collective and society as a whole, not a specific person. And yet, a complete stranger stood at my side showing me an act of kindness and thanking me for my efforts. I felt a rush of blood to my cheeks and turned my attention to the notebook.

Underneath my writing the tech added: *I don't know how you managed to keep out of confinement, but I'm glad you did! I can't tell you how to write the program to interface with it, but I can tell you which connections you need to engage.* She drew circles and lines on my diagram along with labels like Body Temp and Heart Rate. The most interesting one turned out to be the center connector with the diameter bigger than the others. It bore the label: Proximity.

I turned my face back to her and smiled again, this time taking her hand and giving it a slight squeeze. Her cheeks flushed and I did, too, from the inside out. The contrast with her long, blonde hair, piercing blue eyes, and her pink cheeks painted a gorgeous picture.

"I should go. My wrist buzzed for another call." She looked at her device and tapped the screen. "Yeah, your neighbor's gone and de-calibrated their holovision a few blocks over." I allowed my hand to linger on hers for a moment before pulling away.

"Of course. I'll try not to break anything else, but I like to tinker with things, so I make no promises."

Bryn let out a soft giggle. "Why do I have a feeling you're going to be keeping me busy?" She smiled, winked, and let herself out of the room.

I put the printer back together and sat down at the desk to examine my book. I knew Bryndolin was one of the good ones the second she didn't rat me out that first visit, but what she did for me a few minutes ago went above and beyond. A thought crossed my mind. How many other people out there felt like she did? I was a complete stranger, but she had a good job and got to interact with loads of people, which I'd miss for the next eleven months. So why help? If The Association caught her, it would mean confinement, with solitary not out of the question, either. She had to have known that my friends and I were up to something, and she was on board. If she was on board, it stood to reason that others were as well.

I turned my attention back to the diagram. In addition to pointing out which connection points handled which features, she jotted down the relevant frequency in hertz and charges in electron volts required to make each connection work. True to her word, she knew her stuff when it came to the operation and maintenance of a device, but it would be up to me to create an algorithm to manipulate the input computationally. With any amount of luck between my mother's help, what I already knew, and what I would soon learn, I would be able to do it.

My eye caught a faint scribble down in the bottom right corner of the page. It was the universal Wi-Fi symbol inside a circle with a line through it and then "2 minutes!" written beside it. Underneath that, she drew a sequence of symbols and letters. ↑↑↓↓←→←→BA Start

My eyes widened. I hadn't considered the fact that I might need to disable the Wi-Fi on my PMID. The device had three buttons, two on the front below the screen and one on the side. They weren't labeled but it was a safe assumption that the one on the left was "A" and the one on the right was "B". That meant the button on the side represented the "start" button in the code. The arrows confused me, though. I tapped the screen and navigated through the menus to see if there were any apps or functions on the device that used arrows. I searched for five minutes and didn't find anything.

I closed my eyes and dedicated my brain to it for a minute. My breathing slowed and I cleared my mind. What was my objective? To turn off the normally always-on Wi-Fi connectivity. How would I do that? By entering in this code given to me by Bryn. But where? Not knowing left me with an uncomfortable feeling in the pit of my stomach. I allowed my mind to roam and explore all the possibilities. After several minutes of rumination, I opened my eyes and tapped the screen on my wrist. In the "Settings" menu, I swiped until I found the "Status" section. Within it, I tapped on "Connectivity" and then the sub-menu "Network."

On it showed two active connections. The first was my home address, "214 Summerlands," and underneath the heading, a sliding scale indicating the signal strength and a brilliant green color bar. Below that, the words "Known Order Global" with a similar scale and green color bar. I saw no other options on the screen except to press the "A" button or swipe left to return to the previous screen.

I tapped the screen at the top twice, followed by the bottom twice, then on the left, right, left, right, and then pressed the "B" button, "A" button, and the "Start" button on the side. The sliders disappeared, the color bars turned gray, and a countdown timer overlay popped up. One minute fifty-eight, one minute fifty-seven, one minute fifty-six…

I froze and my default paranoia kicked in. What if this was a setup? What if Bryn was an agent of The Association or an undercover CCC? I looked out the window and searched the skies for an airborne confinement transport, stood still, and listened with as much intent as I ever had for the sound of a door knocking or any voice that wasn't a member of my household.

One minute ten…

My breathing became short and shallow, and beads of sweat formed on my brow which I wiped with the back of my cold and clammy hand. I paced back and forth across the room with one thumb in my mouth, my teeth gnawing on the nail until I left it in tattered ruins.

Twelve seconds…

I held my breath.

Five seconds…

The sharp knock on the office door caused me to jump in fright. I let out my breath and with it a high-pitched squeal.

"Holy hotcakes, Kate, are you okay?" My father stepped into the room.

I looked at the device on my wrist. The countdown disappeared and the Network Settings screen returned to normal. My heart pounded like a jackhammer in my chest. If I ever gained access to my PMID physiological data, I wanted to see what the graphs looked like for the last two minutes and change.

"Dad, you scared the pants off of me." I put the palms of my hands on my cheeks.

"I didn't mean to, I promise. What were you doing that had you so skittish?"

"I was deep in thought, that's all. Working a problem."

His face showed an air of skepticism. "Must be one heck of a problem."

"It could have… implications."

His eyes narrowed. "I see. Well, you have a visitor. Terre is here."

My anxiety washed away in an instant. "Terre? Fantastic! Tell her she can join me in here."

"The living room isn't good enough for a visit?"

"I already can't escape monitoring." I pointed to my wrist and the console in the far corner of the office. "It would be nice if I could talk with my best friend without everyone else in my household and the holovision and the main console and the living room console listening in as well."

"I understand. I'll send her in." He paused as he stepped into the hallway and turned to face me again. "Are you sure you're okay?"

"Yeah. Yeah, I'm good. Thanks for asking though."

He nodded and walked away. A few seconds later, I heard him tell Terre she could join me in the office followed by muffled noises my hearing didn't quite pick up. Seconds after that, Terre's head poked around the doorframe.

"Your dad told me to walk loudly and be gentle when entering the room, whatever that means."

I let out a soft chuckle. "It's nothing. I was, well, working on a problem, and my dad interrupted and startled me."

"Must have been one heck of a startle. He sounded concerned."

"Heh, yeah. He got me good, though it was one hundred percent accidental on his part. Thanks for coming over. To what do I owe the pleasure?"

"We hadn't seen each other, you know, face-to-face in a long time. I figured we were overdue. Since you can't leave, and I like giving surprises, I thought I'd come over." She walked into the room and over to the desk.

I joined her, made eye contact, and brought my finger to my lips, a gesture I found myself doing quite a bit since The Association felt the need to monitor my every utterance, whisper, hiccup, burp, and fart. I pointed to the book.

Terre stood in silence with her eyes scanning the pages. When she finished, she turned to me with her eyes wide.

I pointed to the section where Bryndolin wrote down the code to disable the connectivity of a PMID, and then mimicked what I did, finishing my pantomime with a big smile on my face and a thumbs-up.

Terre turned to a new page in the book and picked up the writing implement. On the front of a new page she wrote: *Is this what your dad walked in on you doing?* I nodded then Terre wrote: *What did you tell him?*

I took the pen from her hand and at the bottom of the page wrote: *I lied.*

Terre accepted this without any further questions but did cock her head in the direction of the book. I nodded and tore out the page. In doing so, I knocked the notebook off the desk and in trying to keep it from falling, I dropped the loose page. There was a bit of a scramble as the two of us each tried to catch them, and we narrowly avoided knocking heads in the process.

I snagged the paper, crumpled it into a ball, and shoved it in my pocket. I took the book from Terre, who picked it up from the floor, and walked the few steps to the printer. I removed the case and the four screws that held the motherboard in place, and I lifted the inner workings of the machine up with one hand like a nuclear fuel power canister extraction. With my other hand, I slid the notebook underneath. The air gap between the bottom of the frame and the underside of the motherboard fit the book, but a risk existed. If anyone did any long prints it could damage the book, the printer, or both. I had to take the risk to keep my secrets safe.

I excused myself for a moment and went and tossed the crumpled page into the household annihilator where it would be deconstructed, and its constituent material recycled into another useful item for the house, bathroom tissue, facial tissue, or what have you. When I returned, Terre and I each took a seat in a leather chair, two of which sat against the back wall of the office and our conversation returned to topics that wouldn't get either of us in trouble with The Association.

The visit lasted the greater part of an hour and after Terre left, I joined my family in the living room to relax. Having to talk and watch every word that came out of my mouth drained every ounce of energy from me. I needed to absorb mind-numbing, useless non-information for as long as possible, and the latest entertainment on the holovision would provide all of that and more. What little talking occurred between me and the rest of my family was limited to idle chitchat or discussions about my courses. A topic of conversation I didn't mind having since it gave me the opportunity to ensure I understood the material. My mother functioned as a great auditor and sounding board, and I felt those discussions, however technical and unemotional, brought us closer. I went to bed that night excited but in dire need of much rest.

00001100
[Twelve]

With no recollection of anything after my head hit the pillow the night before, a pounding at the door on the front door of the house jolted me awake along with angry yelling coming from a voice that I recognized, but in my surprise brain fog couldn't quite place. With my parents both at work and my brother at school it fell to me to roll out of bed and see about the commotion.

I tossed on a pair of socks, sweatpants, and a T-shirt along with my special sweater that I kept hanging on the back of my chair and made my way to the front door. The pounding became louder and more violent as I approached, and by the time I reached the foyer it occurred to me whose voice caused all the commotion: CCC Follis.

As I reached for the door handle the electronic deadbolt started to turn. I took a step back from the door. As expected, it swung open with enough force to rattle the windowpanes, and CCC Follis and Hadewijch stood in the entrance. Neither looked pleased.

"Katherine Webb, you are hereby—" CCC Follis started before Hadewijch cut him off.

"Let me handle this, Follis. Katherine, I was rooting for you, I genuinely was. While I thought making it through the whole year weren't the best odds, I certainly thought you'd last longer than a month."

"I don't know what you're talking about."

"Mmm hmm." Hadewijch turned their tablet screen toward me. "You see that picture there? We captured it off your PMID yesterday from your visit with your friend Terre."

I looked at the image on the screen. It had terrible resolution and was blurred, but one part of the picture made sense. Unfortunately, that part included the words *I lied*. "That doesn't mean anything. You don't know who wrote it, when it was written, or what it's in reference to."

"True, but when we looked at the footage from Terre's PMID, we saw this." Hadewijch swiped their screen, and another blurry image showed a portion of the schematic from my notebook. "Do you know what that is?"

I squinted. "Looks like a rudimentary schematic. Could be from one of my classes or something my mother was working on. Could be anything. I'm not sure what the issue is and why Follis here about knocked my door off its hinges."

The CCC took a step forward and Hadewijch extended an arm to keep him from going any farther. "Be that as it may, Katherine, the terms of your sentencing were clear and so much as the slightest inclination that you're up to no good puts you in a bad state."

"What does that mean, exactly?"

"It means confinement until The Association determines the extent of the infraction."

"Assuming there is even an infraction in the first place, right?"

Hadewijch gave me a sideways glance, and CCC Follis took me by the arm. "Wait, you can't do this!" I attempted to shrug him off, but he gave me a look that made it clear that continued resistance was a path I would regret taking.

Hadewijch put their hands together in a gesture of mock prayer. "I implore you, young Katherine, don't make matters any worse than they already are. You, more than anyone, should know how this works."

"Let me put on my shoes." I went to the closet, with Follis in lockstep behind me, and put on a pair of my most comfortable shoes and then extended my elbow out as if I expected him to lead me out like we were on our way out to a fancy dinner. He did not. He pulled my arms behind my back and affixed a standard-issue set of restraints and escorted me from behind to the door. Once outside, I issued the command to Commander to lock the door. The bolt slid into place, and Follis gave me another nudge. I shuffled my way to the awaiting transport parked on the road blocking the driveway and with it, Hadewijch's car.

"Hadewijch, will you follow along in your car?"

"No. My involvement ends here until they let you out, whenever that may be."

Anxiety built as I ducked into the confinement transport and took my seat. As Follis fastened my seatbelt, I wanted to cry and I had to pee, but I did neither.

The ride to the Confinement Center felt longer than it took, but it was still several hours before we arrived. By the time the vehicle stopped, my bladder had reached its limit. I steeled myself and concentrated on my pelvic floor muscles. The walk from the transport to the entrance was short, but the heat rising up off the asphalt in the middle of a desert wasteland didn't need long to wrap itself around me and enter my lungs. I let out a dry cough and came close to pissing myself, but years of meditation and yoga prevented any embarrassment. Follis guided me through the front entrance, a two-story tall steel door that slid to the side without making a sound. It was the same size, color, and texture as the outer wall of the facility and from the right angle it wasn't possible to discern any movement.

The temperature within the boundary of the wall rose several degrees hotter than the walk from the transport to the gate. Whether it was all in my imagination or not I couldn't say, but without the slightest breeze to speak of inside the walled fortress, this made the most sense. We approached another big door that at least had regular door dimensions and swung on hinges. From the way it moved, it looked no less formidable though. Inside that door came a blast of cool air that sent a wave of relief over me. A stern-looking woman in uniform sat behind a counter.

Follis marched me up to the woman. "Webb, Katherine. On hold pending investigation." He tapped his tablet a few times. "Relevant details transferred."

"Thanks, Elwood."

I spun around to face him. "Elwood?"

"Yeah, my initials are E.F. as in "eff," as in eff you, Katherine." He put his hands on my shoulders and spun me back around to face the woman behind the counter again. "Say, Francesca, you busy this weekend?"

"I'm always busy, Elwood." She put added emphasis on his name. "But for you, I might be able to make time."

"All right, cool. I'll send a transport for you Saturday, say, seven? Dinner out and then maybe the holotheater?"

I rolled my eyes. "How original, Elwood."

He smacked the back of my head. Not hard, but hard enough to let me know I should shut my mouth. "Careful with this one, Franny, She's a handful."

"The legendary Katherine 'Two Strikes' Webb doesn't look so legendary in her wrist restraints."

"Yeah, well, I'd still be careful. She's got horseshoes so far up her butt if she sneezed, they'd come out her nose."

"Speaking of sneezing, good sir. If I happened to do that at this moment, I'd piss myself. I legitimately have to go to the bathroom."

"Should have thought of that before you went and got picked up for conduct unbecoming a known convict."

"My mind was otherwise occupied. That doesn't change the fact that I'm going to make a hell of a mess in a minute, and since we're outside the secure area you're not going to take off my restraints to make me clean it up. You don't work here, but my good friend Francesca here does, and I'd bet you a shiny credit the job will fall to her. I'm trying my best to hold it in, Franny, but we have to move this along. He'll see you on Saturday at seven."

She let out a sigh and tapped her tablet a few times. "Prisoner successfully transferred. See you on Saturday, El-dub. Come on, Two Strikes, let's get you to the potty."

After a quick and painless intake process, I went to the washroom. Francesca watched me pee, remarked how she was impressed at how long it took me to empty my bladder, and then made me walk through a full-body scanner. Another guard ordered me to strip naked and stand still while they inspected my clothing. My heart jumped when their attention went to the charms sewn into the sweater, but all they did was touch each one and inspect for anything that might be used as a weapon.

"You get to keep these, but you gotta wash 'em on your own in the sink and hang 'em to dry. You want 'em on now, or would you rather wear standard-issue stuff for your journey to the inside?"

I shivered and looked down at my arms, one down low with my hand covering my pubic region and the other across my chest and saw goosebumps all over. "I'd like to wear my own clothes, please."

"Suit yourself, but they'll only get dirty and won't take more than a couple hours to build up a bit of a stink." He held up my panties pinched between his thumb and forefinger and gave them a once over. "Heck, your underwear doesn't even look worn at all. You want my opinion on the matter? You're going to want something that feels comfortable and familiar to slide into tomorrow morning. You're in for a rough night's sleep, I promise you that, and sliding on a pair of hemp granny panties straight out of their package at seven A.M. is going to suck."

I considered this advice for a moment and shivered again. "Okay, I'll put on the confinement stuff now, but I'd like to wear my sweater. I'm f-f-freezing my t-t-t—"

"Tits off?"

"I was going to say teeth, but that works too." The guard handed me confinement-issued underwear, T-shirt, pants that looked like medical scrubs, and a pair of ankle socks. I dressed, and as rough and scratchy as the garments were, I was thankful to be covered up. With my clothes folded in a pile and a spare set of confinement-issued wear in my hands, I followed yet another guard down a long, brightly-lit, windowless hallway and through another sturdy door. Through it, I stepped onto a caged catwalk half a level above the rest of the three-story quadrangle that ran around its perimeter. I could hear the white noise of multiple conversations happening at once, but as soon as the big steel door slammed behind us, all the conversations petered out. Everyone in the common area down below and all the prisoners standing outside their cells turned their eyes my way.

The walk down one side of the quad catwalk took forever. I did the half flight down to the top level and paused as my escort performed a retinal scan to open a large, barred gate. Once through, the guard steered me down the short side past several cells with women in the entrances sizing me up. About halfway down, the guard stopped and directed me into a cell with a large white woman lounging on the top bunk. I wasn't sure how long the springs underneath the top mattress would last.

She sat up and dangled her hefty legs over the side of the bed. "Well, as I live and breathe, if it isn't the infamous Katherine 'Two Strikes' Webb." She jumped down from the top bunk and landed with all the grace of a baby elephant learning to tap dance.

"Well, I'll leave you two to it." The guard turned and continued walking down the concourse to the opposite end of the quad from which we entered.

I swallowed in an attempt to relax the lump in my throat and took a deep breath hoping to relax my stomach. I hadn't eaten yet, and it was getting close to noon. My cellmate took a step forward and I steeled myself, putting my weight on the balls of my feet, prepared to drop my folded pile of clothes and take a swing if needed. Not that I thought I could do any damage at all against a woman more than twice my size.

"You're Katherine Webb, yes?"

I nodded.

The hulking woman advanced with unexpected speed and before I could do anything, her arms wrapped around me in a firm, but not organ crushing, bear hug. "You have no idea how much this means to me—to everyone in this place—to have you here live and in person in living color." She took a step back, extended her arms, and placed one hand on each of my shoulders like my grandmother sizing me up after an extended absence. "I can't believe it's you. I was already top dog in here, at least in the women's quad, but having the legendary Two Strikes as my bunk mate? Whooooo-eee, I'm going to be unstoppable. *We're* going to be unstoppable."

"I don't know how long I'm staying. There's an investigation or—"

"Ha! 'Investigation.'" She made air quotes with her fingers. "That'll be the day."

"I dunno. I've seen, heard, or done pretty much all there is to do when it comes to what passes for a legal system in The Known Order, and I don't think they've got enough to keep me in here."

"Sweetheart, you came closer to breaking the system than anyone in history. If I were a betting woman, I'm not, but if I were, I'd lay down my life savings on them keeping you in here until you're old and gray. This investigation is nothing but a smoke screen to keep your mouth shut to anyone they care about you talking to, that is."

"I guess time will tell."

"I guess it will. Hey, look here." She pointed to the bunk beds. "I'll give you the top bunk. You're a bona fide celebrity, and I'm not exactly down to my fighting weight," She patted her tummy. "I'm pretty sure if this cheap-ass bed collapsed, and I crushed you, a lot of people in here would be pissed."

"That's charitable of you. Thanks." I put my clothes in the one open cubby bolted to the back wall of the cell and sat down on the bottom bunk which had yet to receive its bedding. From what I could tell that would consist of a thin fitted sheet and a microfiber blanket, and a tiny pillow. "I didn't catch your name."

"Karen."

"Well, Karen, how does this all work?" I made a wide, sweeping gesture with my arm outstretched.

Karen dropped her pants, sat on the commode, and peed. "First, you get used to going to the bathroom in front of people."

I pointed to my wrist. "I'm on constant monitoring as part of my sentence. I wonder if it's still on now that I'm in confinement. It would seem redundant, wouldn't it?"

Karen wiped, flushed, and washed her hands. "Yeah, you'd think, but when you're in here everyone's PMID monitors all the time. The biometric tools aren't on, though they could be if you wanted 'em to, I suppose, but you can't turn 'em off or take 'em off."

I pondered my next statement, stood up, and placed my hand over my wrist device. Karen did the same. I leaned in close to the big woman and whispered, "I might have a solution to that problem."

The surprised look on her face betrayed the calm, level response. "Oh? Do tell," she whispered back.

"Not yet. I don't mean to be a tease, but I've been here for all of five minutes. What I know could get me locked in solitary for a long time if the wrong people found out, but between you and me, I have at least one trick up my sleeve." I smiled at my own inside joke.

"Well, now I'm intrigued. You sure you can't spill the beans?"

"Not yet and let's keep this our little secret, okay?"

"Mum's the word."

"So, tell me," I continued in a normal voice. "What else do I need to know beyond having to pee in front of you and whoever else happens to be looking through the bars."

"Don't forget the stylish yet functional monitoring bracelet. Come on, I'll give you the grand tour on the way to the mess for lunch."

I walked beside her around the whole perimeter of the third level until we reached the stairs on the far side of their cell. Introductions occurred at random, as Karen saw fit, but everyone I met reacted in a similar fashion to my cellmate. I hesitated to think of her as a friend seeing as we had known each other for a matter of seconds, but it was weird how time didn't behave the same way inside confinement as it did elsewhere.

The tour continued into the shower area and common washrooms, and we headed down the stairs. We skipped tours of the next two levels. Karen said we'd do a walkabout after we ate. The food sucked. I missed my garden vegetables, fresh fruits, and access to more spices than I could name. What we ate for lunch barely qualified as nourishment, let alone enjoyable fare.

The outside portion of the tour was as useless as it was depressing. Unbearable heat smothered the quadrangle. The barren, dusty yard held exercise equipment in varying states of disrepair. I saw the indoor exercise area, an extreme contrast to the outside space, the medical area, and the stores for supplies and other assorted items to purchase for those fortunate enough to have credits in their account. We made haste past the security and observation area, with its masses of uniformed officers huddled around computer monitors drinking coffee, and the meditation room that Karen said doubled as a respite from the noise and chaos of general population.

Aside from the food, the fact that it was a prison, you couldn't leave, were told what you could and could not do every minute of every day, and were cooped up with hundreds of other ne'er-do-wells, it wasn't that bad.

The final portion of the tour took us to the lowest level common area as well as the library, games room with various puzzles, board games, cards, and other things of that sort. A diminutive older woman sat with her elbows on a card table and chin resting on her hands in front of an incomplete puzzle of what looked like an overhead shot of Zone Three.

"Gloria," Karen called out from across the room. When she didn't stir, Karen said, "Her hearing is going. Eyesight too. Follow me." She walked into the room, taking a wide berth to avoid startling her. Sure enough, as soon as the movement caught her eye, her head snapped around. After a moment of silence and a blank stare, I sat up straight and smiled.

"Karen, my love, to what do I owe the pleasure?" She scanned me up and down for a second. "And is this who I think it is?"

"In the flesh."

I shuffled the ten steps to her, but it took me several seconds to cover that ground. "Katherine Webb!" She held her arms out and came in for a hug. "Oh, boy, are we all excited to have you in here."

"This is a theme I've picked up, but I'm curious how everyone knows about me. On the outside, I barely registered a pulse let alone celebrity status."

"You have Media to thank for that, my dear." She scrunched up her nose like the word had a malodorous scent. "But in here and out on the street, in the out-of-the-way corners and places you don't go after dark, you're a legend."

"A legend, eh?"

"Oh, yes, my dear. Sticking it to The Association? Beating them at their own game? It's what legends are made of. Then there's the whole two strikes business." She shook her head and clicked her tongue. "Unprecedented."

"A lot of good it did me. I landed back here less than a month later."

She put one cold, wrinkled hand on my cheek. "My dear, the fact that you spent more than half an hour walking around with two strikes before landing in here is enough. Whatever you did or didn't do"—she winked—"got them flustered. Up until then, The Association gave an air of unflappability, but hot dog, did you ever flap 'em."

"Yeah, I suppose I did."

"Modesty will get you nowhere in this joint, my dear. Own it, that's what I say."

"Should we be saying all this stuff, you know, what with the room full of people listening in, not to mention Commander storing every syllable for all eternity?"

She waved her hand as if shooing away a fly. "Pfft. We're not saying anything they don't already know. Plus, no one believes criminals." She winked again. "Say, that's a nice sweater. Did you make it?"

"My mother did, but I added a few artistic accents for a bit of whimsy."

"I may have to borrow it sometime. It's always cold in here." A beat of awkward silence passed. "Okay, back to my puzzle. It was an absolute pleasure meeting you, my dear. Don't be a stranger."

Karen took me to the first level of cells and introduced me to a number of others, and then we walked back up to the top and into our cell. My linens rested on the bottom bunk with a small pillow that looked like it wouldn't fit my head. I looked at Karen's pillow, twice the size if it were an inch.

"Hey, how'd you get a better pillow? Can we buy them with credits?"

Karen waggled her eyebrows. "No, you can't, but I know how you can."

"You know how to get better pillows? Is this what passes for contraband in this place?"

Karen let out the heartiest laugh I'd ever heard. "I'm pulling your leg, sister. You can get an upgrade for a few credits at the store."

I shook my head. "I should have known. Come on, let's get these bed linens swapped."

This time Karen shook her head. She pulled the bottom bunk mattress off the bed frame and laid it on the ground on the other side of the cell. Then, she lifted her mattress, with its fitted sheet, crappy blanket, and luxury pillow still on it and tossed it onto the bottom bunk. "There, I'm done. Word to the wise, make your bed on the floor and then throw it up there. Getting that damn fitted sheet on with the mattress in the bunk is a serious pain in the butt. Oh, and dust off the bottom before you put it up there. I don't want any of our floor dust or tiny critters falling on my face when I sleep."

"Tiny critters?" I lifted up the corner of my mattress on the floor.

Karen shook her head again. "Wow, for someone that smart and devious, you sure are gullible."

I felt my cheeks warm. "I haven't experienced too much or seen too many places."

"That's okay, you've got time."

"I wouldn't be so sure abou—" A slamming door at the opposite end of the quad cut me off. A loud woman's voice echoed throughout the complex.

"Say goodbye to Tatiana, everyone. She gets to go home today, but whether or not it's to stay will depend on how she spends her days, okay?"

From every cell and common area came a resounding wave of applause along with whistles, feet stomping, and cheering. I didn't know Tatiana from Eve but joined in the celebration anyway and made sure to clap with enthusiasm. I stepped out of the cell, and on the other side one floor down and a few cells to my left, a guard escorted a short woman with long, brown hair as straight as a ruler into the cell, where the soon-to-be-free woman collected her belongings and stuffed them into a hemp sack. She wore a gaunt, forlorn expression.

"Why the long face? She's getting out of here. You'd think that would be cause for at least a smile."

Karen put my arm around me and gave my shoulder a squeeze. "You know about solitary, right?"

"Yeah, but she's going home."

"The two weeks before your release, they put you in solitary. I went in for three days once and it sucked. I mean brutal. No sunlight 'cept one hour a day, no interaction with another living soul, nothing. I don't know how far apart they built the cells, but you could scream at the top of your lungs, and no one would hear you. The food portions are decent, but the food itself is worse than the general mess, and it gives you the worst, smelliest diarrhea you'll ever experience. You have to stay hydrated, so you have no choice but to drink the water out of the sink, which is clean, thank goodness, but tastes stagnant. It is the single worst experience a person can have short of physical torture. In a lot of ways, it's worse.

Physical pain subsides. It's temporary. The mental anguish lasts a long time, possibly forever if you had enough bad luck."

"And they do it for every prisoner regardless of how long they've been in here? Why would they do this?"

"To give you a taste of what it will be like if you screw up your probation and end up back in here. You want to know why the recidivism rates throughout The Known Order are so low? There are two reasons that when combined make it so you'd have to be off your rocker to offend again. One, because probation lasts the rest of your life, no matter how minor the offense is. Two, if you end up back here, you spend your entire sentence in solitary, and the minimum sentence for a repeat offender is two years."

"Has anyone ever gotten through their whole sentence in solitary?"

"No one knows. They swear the families to secrecy regardless of the outcome, and violating that agreement lands them in solitary as well. Plus, probationers aren't allowed to interact with other probationers. If your PMID senses you're within shouting or visual distance of another probationer, an alarm goes off, and if you continue and attempt to make contact, you're in violation and back into the void you go."

"And you get two weeks of this before they let you out, so you'll want to avoid experiencing it again at all costs."

"Pretty much."

"Damn, that's a sour cup of cold fascist crap right there."

"Yup, but hey, if you don't violate The Known Order, you have nothing to worry about."

I swallowed the lump that formed in my throat. "I wonder if they'll send me to the, what did you call it? The void? Before they let me out?"

"You're sticking with your story that this so-called investigation will clear your name and they'll let you out, eh?"

"I am."

"Well, if that miracle occurs then I'd say that you have two weeks of hell in the void to look forward to first."

I shuddered. "Fantastic."

We watched as the guard escorted Tatiana down the corridor and out the far door. She walked with her few possessions cradled in her arms like a new mother would cradle a baby, only in her case she suffered from a severe case of PTSD. I thought, as I was certain many others did, that I had the mental strength to withstand time in the void. Two weeks didn't seem that long. Then again, Karen was as mentally strong as they come, and she said that she had a hard time lasting a mere three days. Mind games was all they were. Mind games designed to break your spirit and force you to conform. It was The Association's modus operandi and had been since the end of The Wars.

I went to bed that night with visions of a dark, soundless box with walls closing in on me until I could feel them touching my skin. Several times, the image woke me from a restless sleep, and each time I found myself short of breath and checking my pulse as I worked on my meditative breathing. Getting out of confinement came at the cost of two weeks in the void, and preparation for that moment had to start as soon as possible.

The next morning, I stuck close to Karen as I learned the ins and outs of the daily confinement routine. Breakfast was beyond horrid, but the meal from the night before tempered my expectations on that front. I wasn't a permanent convict yet and didn't have a job assignment. I spent the day hanging out with a few of the others that, for one reason or another, couldn't work. I spent more time with Gloria than anyone else. I joined her in the games room and sat on the opposite side of the card table and helped her with her puzzle.

After we exchanged pleasantries, we sat in relative silence as we each worked part of the puzzle. I worked upside down, but the different perspective helped when working on visual problems. If you became too familiar with your work, important details were missed. My father called it "having blinders on," a reference to back in The Before Times when people used to race horses for entertainment and gambling. Trainers would put a device on the horse's head to block their vision to everything except straight ahead. While a great strategy for providing focus on a singular goal, it didn't work when one wanted to see the bigger picture.

Gloria rubbed her hands together to warm them. I stood and removed my colorful sweater and put it around her shoulders.

"Oh, that's not necessary, my dear. I'm always cold and you'll catch a chill. I'm used to it."

"Hogwash, Gloria. As the elder and seasoned veteran of the Confinement Center, I am obligated to put my own needs aside for yours."

"Well, I'm not sure that's a hard and fast rule, but I quite like it." I wrapped the sweater around her so the front overlapped and the arms hung loose. "You know, my dear, this is a truly wonderful sweater. What made you think to bring it as one of your personal articles of clothing?"

"It was a fluke. I keep it on a chair at my desk beside my bed. I was home alone when the CCC and my case worker, Hadewijch, pounded on my door in the morning. I got out of bed and dressed as fast as I could, but I shivered from being up and about instead of under my covers. I threw on the sweater to keep warm. I never got to go back for anything, and the sweater came with me. I'm thankful they let me keep it."

She lifted one sleeve and then the other. "Well, it's beautiful. I especially like these adornments on the wrists. They give it an extra sort of bohemian flair." The old woman's eyes met mine, and we shared a silent moment of eye contact before I turned my attention back to the puzzle.

"Yes, they do. It's why I sewed them on a couple years ago. I felt whimsical at the time and wanted to make the sweater unique."

Gloria nodded. "It is most certainly unique. One of a kind, I'm guessing?"

"I'm sure there are other charms like the ones you see there, but as far as I know those are the only ones sewn into a sweater." She put a piece of the puzzle in place. "Ah, there we go, that piece was giving me trouble."

"It's exhilarating what happens when you find the right piece of the puzzle, isn't it? It opens up a whole new world of possibilities."

"It is and it does."

We spent the remainder of our time together in relative silence, each completing a good amount of our respective parts of the puzzle. By midday, we'd completed more than half and decided to take a break for lunch. My hunger overwhelmed me, and I couldn't understand how everyone in there didn't starve.

After we consumed the industrial waste that the sadistic jackass chef decided to pass off as lunch, we started back toward the games room, but a guard blocked the corridor.

"Katherine Webb, come with us."

"What for?"

"You don't get to ask that question, or any question for that matter. Don't worry, you'll get a chance to say your goodbyes in two weeks."

"Two weeks? What's going on?"

"What did I *just* tell you about questions? Come on, no use making more of a scene."

Gloria took off my sweater and handed it back. The guard took it and threw it in Gloria's face. "No personal items in solitary. You know the rules, Gloria."

"I thought—"

"No exceptions."

"It's okay, Gloria, maybe it'll be of more use to you. You're good at puzzles." I gave her a wink, and she nodded back in understanding.

The guard took a firm grip on my upper arm and escorted me through a large steel door and down a sequence of dim hallways that twisted and turned in every direction, making it impossible to determine which way was which. After several minutes of walking and at least two flights of stairs, we came to a long, straight corridor. The charcoal color of the walls, floor, and ceiling didn't do much to reflect the light from the tunnel nor the small flashlight the guard carried in the hand that didn't have a vise grip on my arm. Every ten steps, I spotted a rectangle edge that looked like a door with no handle. I counted seven rectangles before the guard stopped.

The sheer magnitude of the silence knocked me off kilter. I could hear my own heartbeat. The rectangle was, in fact, a door, and it slid to the side without making a sound. The guard gave me a shove. Through the door was a similar corridor, but it was shorter in height and not as wide. If all the solitary cells were like this one, I had a hard time visualizing how my former bunkmate fit inside it. I walked in another seven steps, and another door slid to the side at the opposite end from where I came. I stepped through and turned back to face the guard. I had many questions.

"See you in two weeks," the guard said with a tone that didn't sound human.

00001101
[Thirteen]

As the doors shut, I fought the urge to grab onto the leading edge and try to pull it back open. That was a battle that would most certainly serve no purpose and do nothing but cause injury. I watched as the door in front of me closed and surveyed my surroundings. A circular hole in the ceiling let in daylight. It was bright and cast a crisp cylinder beam straight down onto the floor. Everything was the same dark charcoal color, even the linens on the small cot in the corner as well as the toilet and sink. If not for the cylinder of light, I couldn't have seen my hand in front of my face.

I decided to take advantage of what little light I had and pace out the dimensions of my cell. Walking toe to toe, the room measured twelve of my feet in each direction. Using the width of my hand, I measured the height of the ceiling at twenty-one widths. The bed measured six of my feet wide and nine long. The toilet sat less than one of my feet from one end of the bed and the sink less than one of my feet beside that. There was nothing else in the room. With my eyes closed, I practiced getting out of bed and getting to the toilet and the sink and then back to my bed. I walked across the room and around the perimeter over and over again until the light from above started to fade away, and I found myself in total darkness.

The cell muffled sounds, and with the exception of the door, I felt nothing but metal, and the designers sprayed a coating to dampen the sound. I lay down on my bed which didn't have springs holding the thin mattress up but rather a solid plank underneath it. I closed my eyes, not because I needed to, but because it didn't feel natural in such darkness to have them open.

I started to meditate but before my mind cleared, I wondered if I could maintain a meditative state for the greater part of fourteen days without losing my mind. Given it was my freedom, or what was left of it at least, waiting for me at the end of it I had no choice but to try.

A muffled sound interrupted my quasi-enlightened state. Above the sink, a faded green glowing rectangle appeared to float in mid-air. I took the two steps required to get to it and extended my hand to touch the edges. I could discern the outline of a tray on a shelf and the glow from the edges lit enough of it to see that on it sat a cup of water, a small lump that looked like a rock, and mush in a bowl with a spoon. I took the tray to my bed and sat down to eat.

In spite of my fantastically low expectations, the food exceeded them in the worst possible way. The rock turned out to be bread but tasted the same way a stale fish tank smelled. The mush tasted like the chef took the packaging for instant oatmeal and blended it up with the water from the same fish tank they used to make the bread. I hesitated to take a sip from the glass, but I plugged my nose and took a drink anyway. It ended up as the most tolerable part of the whole meal. I finished everything on the tray, but whether it was out of desperation or defiance, I did not know. I returned the tray to the shelf that appeared out of nowhere from the wall behind the sink as the last of the green luminescence faded and plunged me into darkness once more.

I took off my shoes and removed the shoelaces from them. The ends of one I tied together, and it became a bracelet wrapped several times around my wrist. I tied a knot at one end of the other. I assumed I would get three meals a day for fourteen days and expected to tie forty-two knots in the shoelace before they let me out. One down and forty-one to go.

As I lay down on my bed again, the darkness set in and made it impossible to orient myself. The two directions that mattered were up and down. At first, I thought my eyes would adjust, but without a minimum amount of light to which my eyes could adjust, it didn't happen. In the tiny cell with the hole in the ceiling covered, pure darkness smothered me. I tapped my PMID, and the tiny screen lit the room like a beacon. Navigating to the settings menu, I changed the theme to black on white to maximize the lumens. Not that I had anything to see. There wasn't so much as a mirror above the sink but adding a little bit of light helped with my comfort levels. While I fiddled with my device settings, I set the screen timeout for two minutes. That way, when I tapped the screen for light, as long as I didn't tap it again, it would stay lit for as long as possible.

With the cool white glow of my biometric wrist tether illuminating my dark cell, I thought about how I would charge the device. The battery would drain, especially with all the extra use it got from the display brightness. The devices went seven to ten days under normal use without the additional strain on it. I estimated a two-week stint in the void under those conditions would require at least two charges.

"Hey, Commander, how does my PMID charge when in solitary?"

I wasn't sure if I expected a response or not, but I got one, and as a by-product of a soundless environment, the sound came through crystal clear. "When your device charge dips below ten percent, the Solitary Confinement System will send you a portable charger. It will appear through your meal slot. You will have to stand for thirty minutes to charge it to full capacity."

It appeared as if I wasn't one hundred percent alone after all, if you could count the company of a semi-sentient totalitarian spy device as company, which for the sake of my sanity I did.

"Hey, Commander, open an audio connection with my mother."

"That function is disabled."

"Well, it was worth a shot. Commander, broadcast a message to my family."

"That function is disabled."

"Commander, are there any active communication functions on my PMID?"

"No. All communication functions are disabled."

"Commander, what functions on my PMID can I use when I'm in solitary?"

"You can check the date and time and monitor your heart rate, body temperature, and sleep quality. Furthermore, you can ask me any question you'd like, though I will not always provide an agreeable response."

"Commander, what time do my meals arrive?"

"You receive three meals a day. The first arrives at seven A.M., the second at noon, and the last at six P.M. Your meal slot will open and make your food available on a tray and remove it thirty minutes later. If you do not return your tray to the shelf within thirty minutes, it will stay there. If you do not move it out of the way, it will fall to the ground when the next meal arrives."

"Commander, set alarms for five minutes before and twenty-five minutes after each mealtime."

"Okay. Would you like to turn on system sounds or vibrate or both?"

"Both please."

"Would you like to use the default alarm sound, one from the list, or create your own?"

"Default, please."

"Alarms set. Default sound with vibration."

I went to the bathroom, washed my hands, and checked the battery on my PMID. Forty-two percent. I stripped off my clothes and placed them under my head to use as a pillow. With my thin blanket covering me, I assumed the yoga corpse pose and controlled my breathing. My meditative state arrived sooner than normal. With light from my wrist device, the sound of another voice to listen to, and alarms set to avoid missing meals, I felt less claustrophobic and alone than I did when the daylight circle closed. Soon, meditation became sleep, and I stayed that way until my morning alarm woke me.

After the initial shock of waking from a deep sleep, opening my eyes, and encountering total darkness, I tapped my device and the screen lit up the room. At least I saw my hand and the blanket that lay on top of me. I went to the bathroom, dressed, and waited for my meal slot to open, which it did at seven o'clock on the dot. I wasn't sure if I was still groggy or that I'd had a surprisingly good night's sleep, or if I was excited about figuring out how to leverage the few PMID features that remained, but my breakfast was tolerable. It took me no time at all to devour it. After returning the tray to the shelf above my sink, I washed up as best as I could and changed into the fresh clothes left for me beside my meal.

After doing yoga, I lay on my bed in the dark and performed mental calculations that would serve to assist me once I got out. I might have napped. At five to noon, my alarm went off, and I again went to the bathroom and washed up for what promised to be another gourmet meal. The mystery slot in the wall opened and presented my food, which I examined for the first time in full light as the hole in my ceiling opened at the same time.

I sat cross-legged in the center of the room under the beam of light that shone from the cylindrical hole in my ceiling. Judging the height of it without any reference wasn't easy, but every other wall was more or less twenty feet thick, and I hazarded a guess that the ceiling was as well. When my alarm buzzed at twenty-five past the hour, I got up and returned my tray. Five minutes later, the slot in the wall opened and my tray disappeared. I sat in a meditative posture in the beam of sun with my eyes closed and my head tilted upwards. I wasn't sure if people had religious experiences anymore, they hadn't been commonplace for centuries, but I guessed this was as close as it got. Sun, silence, and solitude. If not for the whole being locked up by a bunch of fascist dipshits, it wasn't entirely terrible.

As soon as my light hole closed, I went back to my bed and tied two more knots in my meal counting shoelace. After an hour of performing mental calculations, I dozed off and had a mild bout of sleep apnea jolt me awake. With that disturbance in an otherwise peaceful nap came a revelation. Mental calculations, yoga, and meditation would only get me so far, and I had thirteen days left alone in the void. The solitude I appreciated now would soon turn against me if I didn't occupy my mind. I needed more purpose, and I determined a way to achieve it.

"Commander, is there a time limit on how long a custom alarm tune can be?"

"No."

"What sound options are available?"

"You have the full complement of instruments and orchestral sounds to choose from."

"Commander, I wish to create a custom alarm sound."

And thus began my foray into digital music production from a solitary confinement cell in the middle of the desert wasteland I called home.

I spent the next twelve days committed to the exact same routine. Wake, wash, eat, calculate, nap, eat, enjoy daylight, meditate, calculate, nap, compose, eat, compose, calculate, meditate, and sleep.

The morning of my fourteenth day, I broke the routine. I wasn't sure why, but for some reason it felt like the last day sleeping at a friend's house, and I couldn't fight the urge to tidy up. Not that there was much to tidy up, but I woke and ate as planned but spent the rest of the morning lying on my bed which I made with what I assumed were military quality bed-making skills. The darkness helped with my assessment of my housekeeping abilities.

At five minutes to noon, my alarm sounded, and for the first time I heard my entire composition played end-to-end. I planned to release it into the world when I got out to hear what other people thought of it, but in that moment, it was the most beautiful song to ever grace my ears. Clocking in at a little over five minutes, I sat with my legs crossed in the middle of my cell, suspended in a column of sunlight as the final notes drifted away.

I ate my lunch in the sun and returned my tray to its shelf before sitting back down on the hard gray floor, this time with my eyes open and facing the door to my cell. With the precision timing that I'd come to expect during my time there, my cell opened precisely fourteen days to the minute from my arrival. The same guard that brought me there stood in the entranceway.

My initial feeling that I sailed through two weeks in isolation with flying colors turned out to be misplaced. At the sight of another human, a swell of emotion overtook me. Despite the fact that the guard actively participated in the system that dragged me into the void and I should have, by all rights, felt nothing but disdain for them, seeing their face after fourteen days of isolation brought overwhelming joy. With shaking hands and unsteady steps, I traversed the short distance from my cell to the outer hallway.

I reminded myself I retained control of my emotions, that I spent two weeks without another living soul to interact with and not only made it through unscathed, I was productive. I mentally wrote hundreds of lines of code and composed an original song, for crying out loud.

I straightened up as soon as I got into the outer corridor and fought back the tears. With my chin held high, I led the way for the long walk back to my cell to pick up the three articles of clothing I wore when they brought me in sixteen days ago. The items weren't special in any way, and I could have left them behind, but I wanted every other prisoner to see me walk back from two weeks in the void with confidence. I needed them to see that I won, so that they would know that when their time came—if their time came—they could win too.

I hadn't spent two full days in general population, but when I came through the big steel door into the main floor common area, every inmate still stopped in their tracks and applauded or cheered. Suppressing the flood of emotions rushing through me, I refused to show anything but confidence and resolve. While I walked, I smiled and waved. I clasped my hands together and raised them above my head, pumping my arms like the champions of sport from The Before Times.

There wasn't any way for me to high five everyone in the building, but I did with those I passed on the walk back to my cell. Karen sat on the top bunk with my blanket underneath her, and her big pillow back in its rightful spot.

"Geez, Karen, the top bunk wasn't yet cold, and you moved back, eh?"

"You weren't gonna use it anymore, so why wait? I like the idea of being off the ground. You don't look any worse for wear after two weeks in the void. How'd you manage that?"

"I'll tell you all about it one day." I focused my gaze on my PMID. Karen looked intrigued but didn't say anything.

"I'm not sure our paths will cross again, but if they do, I will hold you to that."

I shook Karen's hand, grabbed my clothes, and left the Confinement Center for what I hoped was the last time.

I made sure to visit the bathroom before I left for home. At least that was my assumed destination. I wore fresh prisoner clothes from that morning, at least, and in the bathroom, I put my shoelaces back in. Untying forty-two knots from the laces was a pain in the butt, but it gave me a few minutes to let go of my emotions in addition to the contents of my bladder.

Instead of a transport with a CCC escort, Hadewijch waited for me at the front counter and stood in front of the large desk with the uniformed Francesca behind it.

"Hey, Francesca, how'd your date with Elwood go?"

"Leave, Katherine, and don't come back." She let the slightest bit of a smile creep in before her face returned to bordering between stern and expressionless.

"You don't have to tell me twice, Fran. Can I call you Fran?"

"No. Please leave."

"Whatever you say, Francesca-lana-ding-dong. K-Dub out." I blew her a kiss, grabbed Hadewijch's hand, and walked out like I owned the place. When we got outside, Hadewijch removed their hand and let out an exasperated sigh.

"You're a piece of work, you know that?"

"Hadewijch, my dear and close friend, all I know is that I'm out."

"It came at a cost."

"Oh, what's that?"

"I can't say, but you'll know more when you get home, where you're going to stay for the next ten months and change and not get into any trouble."

"I knew you couldn't make a case out of those two blurry images you scooped from the PMIDs. I knew it."

Hadewijch said nothing and we drove in silence for the greater part of an hour before I couldn't take it anymore.

"I just spent two weeks in a dark hole for what appears to be no reason. I'm starved for conversation. Humans are not meant to be alone."

Hadewijch pursed their lips. "I can't say anything about why you got out. Not only is it not my place on a personal level, I've been forbidden from communicating any information. My orders are to return you home with no fuss and instruct you to not screw this up."

"Or what? I go back to the void?"

"It's bigger than you now, Katherine. Maybe think about that before you go off all half-cocked and end up hurting the people you love."

I opened my mouth to speak but Hadewijch cut me off. "I suggest you shut your mouth and not make matters worse." Hadewijch stared me down, making their point clear without the need for more words.

We made the remainder of the trip in silence. When the car pulled up in front of my house, I opened the door and got out, but leaned my head back in. "Hadewijch, what now?"

"Now you go home, stay there, concentrate on your studies, and in ten months you can leave the house and live, to a certain extent, a normal life again."

"Except if I screw up, I go back into confinement for a long time, with a good chunk of that in solitary."

"That pretty much sums it up, yes."

"Will I be graced with your presence again?"

"Trust me, Katherine, you don't want that to happen." They paused. "*I* don't want that to happen. If it does, it's not going to be to congratulate you, and my disposition will be far from cheery."

"This is you cheery?"

Hadewijch closed their eyes and shook their head. "Go home, Katherine."

I shut the door and skipped up my driveway to the front door. For a second, I considered knocking but thought better of it and waltzed in like any other day. Chadwick sat in the living room with his headphones on playing a game. My mother, in the kitchen starting dinner, let out a gasp at the door opening, but then ran over and gave me a massive bear hug.

"I, oh, my word, I thought we'd lost you forever. I was certain The Association wouldn't honor the deal."

"The deal? What deal?"

"They didn't tell you?"

"No, they didn't tell me anything. Hadewijch drove me back and wouldn't say anything. Said The Association forbade it."

"Your father got you out."

"Dad? How?"

"He confessed."

"Confessed? What the hell, Mom? Confessed to what?"

She looked down at my wrist and made a face that indicated there was more to this story than she could say with Commander listening in. "To conspiring to hack your PMID so you could leave the house."

"What? That's madness! He doesn't even know how to code."

"That's what I said when I found his schematics in that book and that's why he wrote 'I lied' in it. He was sick to his stomach when they took you away for it. Came right home from work and started to try to get into contact with The Association to let them know they made a mistake."

"That's why they cleared me to go home so quickly after arriving."

"Yes. He confessed to attempting to subvert the PMID protocols, but only so you wouldn't be trapped in the house. They took him away immediately."

"How long did he get?"

"The duration of the remainder of your sentence, which is a little over ten months, or was a couple weeks ago. What I want to know is why it took two weeks to get you back?"

"They put you in solitary confinement for two weeks before you get out."

"Why on Earth would they do that, especially in your case? You've done nothing wrong."

"They do it to make a point and scare you into submission because if you end up back there that's where you go, and I'll be honest, I fared better than I thought I would, but it still sucked. Seeing another person's face after two weeks in the dark twenty-three hours a day had me bordering on tears. I found creative ways to stay busy and keep my mind active, but if I had to spend any more time there, I would not have made it."

"Do you think they'll put your father there before he gets out?"

"There is a one hundred percent chance."

My mom let out a sigh, gave me another hug, and cried. I patted her back. "It's okay, Mom, he'll be fine. He's a smart man and has a lot to look forward to. The food in there is horrible, though. I'd be more concerned for him losing his mind and getting sent into solitary for complaining too vigorously about how bad it is."

She let out half a chuckle and wiped her eyes. "Well, I think he's smart enough to keep his mouth shut. I have dinner to prepare myself. Go say hi to your brother. He's been worried and depressed. Understandably so."

I tapped my brother on the shoulder, and he dropped his game controller and tore off his headset as he jumped up off the floor to give me a big hug. Like our mother, he wept, and I wept as well.

"They took Dad."

"Yeah, Mom told me."

"Do you know why?"

"I only know what Mom told me."

"We thought they would keep you, too. You know, like one more kick in the pants to beat down the Webb family."

"This is all my fault, little brother, but don't worry; I'm going to fix it."

"How are you going to do that?"

I broke the hug and held his shoulders out at arm's length. "By playing by the rules and keeping my nose clean, as they say." I winked. He smiled.

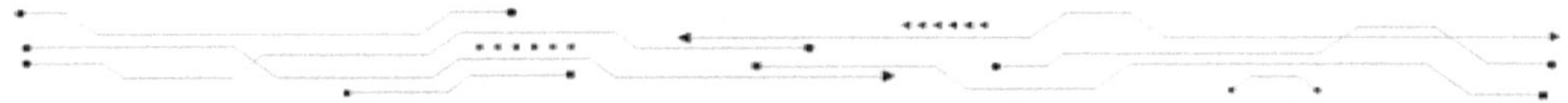

I spent the next several weeks doing my best to give the appearance of conformity. According to the multitude of recording devices monitoring me every minute of every day, I was a model prisoner. I had schoolwork to catch up on. I didn't miss much while I was away, but I did miss enough to have a backlog of tasks and assignments. When I wasn't doing that, I worked on my unconnected tablet. It wasn't as powerful a device as my current one, but it served its purpose and was off the grid in every sense. When I was due for an upgrade, my mother, ever the computer engineer, did not return the old one. Instead, she paid the extra charge to keep it and turned it into an experimental computing device. No camera, no microphone, no Wi-Fi. She removed them with the skill of a robot surgeon. What remained was an untraceable device I, or anyone else in the house that was so inclined, could use to write code without any fear that Commander would misinterpret the algorithms.

All the code I burned into my memory while in the void needed to be transcribed, compiled, and tested. When I wasn't working on my classes, that's what I did. I retrieved my notebook from under the printer and used the few notes Bryndolin scribbled to help. My plan had two phases. The first was to override the sensors on the PMID by executing my program with the portable charger plugged into my offline tablet and attached to my wrist. This step hinged on the program running in under two minutes. If my calculations proved correct, the exact amount of time I needed was one minute and forty-two seconds. However, Phase One had an issue bigger than time. The portable charger might have connectivity built into it. If that was the case, then I needed to disable it before plugging it into my unconnected tablet. The good news was I had a plan for figuring this out, or at least knew someone who would know.

The more complex second phase required the assistance of my mother. Once I established the connectivity override for my PMID I needed to use that, along with my mother's knowledge of Shared Consciousness, to see if I could get a glimpse into the inner workings of Commander, or rather how The Association manipulated the great computer to their advantage. Its directive, if one asked, was to stay neutral and use impartial truths to steer humanity on the best possible path, but anyone with even a modicum of knowledge about The Association knew that the scales tipped in their favor more times than not. The machine controlled us—and they controlled the machine—though saying that out loud was tantamount to a life sentence in confinement.

First things first, though. I buried my head in my studies and kept refining my code. As long as the connection points for the various features on the PMID didn't change, I had confidence it would work.

A month passed and I went as far as I could without running a real-world test. I popped the cover to my printer off and loosened the Wi-Fi chip again. After the expected complaints and warnings from the console in the office, I sat and waited for the knock on the door. It came ten minutes later, and my mom let the tech in. Bryndolin knocked on the doorframe before she entered the office.

"We meet again, Katherine Webb. What have you done to your printer this time?"

"I was learning about high output 3D rendering algorithms in one of my classes." That was true. "I thought I'd try to come up with a hardware solution to offload the processing stress to free up AI resources to make better real-time adjustments. I thought if we could do that, then solving time-sensitive printing problems wouldn't be as risky."

"Brilliant. Were you thinking space applications?"

"Yeah, outer solar system transports to be specific."

"You'd make a few friends over at The Known Order Space Administration if you could figure that out."

"I could use friends in high places these days, so I thought I'd crack the case of that bad-boy right there and see if I can get a prototype working."

"Naturally. Only you screwed it up."

"Yup." I smiled. "I don't mind making mistakes, though. It's hard to acquire new knowledge if you don't branch out beyond what you know, you know?" I tapped my finger on the open notebook that sat on the desk beside the printer.

Bryn looked at the page, making sure to point her PMID in the opposite direction. I had drawn a crude diagram of the portable charger with the Wi-Fi symbol beside it and a question mark. She picked up the pencil and wrote underneath the symbol: *No.*

"Well, you've pooched the connectivity on the printer—again. I'm going to reset the chip, and if it doesn't work, I'll have to replace it and possibly the motherboard, depending on how much you screwed it up."

"Tough, but fair. When you're done with that, I need to ask about a possible issue with my PMID, too."

"You haven't been fiddling with it, have you? I don't have to tell you that if I suspect you have been, I'm obligated to report you."

"No, nothing like that. I'm all aboveboard now, didn't you hear? A model citizen."

She reset the chip in the printer and waited. "Will your caseworker, the CCCs, The Association, and Commander agree with that assessment?"

A computerized voice came from the console: *Since Katherine's return from her time in confinement and solitary, her behavior has been exemplary.*

"See? Commander thinks I'm all that and a bag of chips."

"And we all know Commander is never wrong." She winked.

I opened the program I wrote on my unconnected tablet and got it ready to upload to my device. Since time was of the essence, I plugged the portable charger into the tablet and took my 3D printed spare key out of my pocket.

Bryndolin gave me a look of faux shock. "Exemplary. Okay, let's see what we're dealing with. Commander, tech number forty-two, Bryndolin Cole, performing diagnostics on Katherine Webb's PMID."

Proceed, came the soft digitized voice from the console in the corner.

I punched in the connectivity disabling code that Bryn left for me on her last visit and then used the key to remove the band from my wrist. In one swift motion, I clipped on the portable charger and tapped the screen of my tablet. The two-minute clock ticked down on the PMID and a nondescript progress bar ticked up on the tablet. That shed some light on one of the two question marks for the whole process. I knew little about the portable charger and its connection speed. I kept my program as compact and efficient as possible, but its complexity increased the more I asked it to fake out my biometrics. As it turned out, convincing a computer that another computer was human took a few lines of code.

Hiding the uploaded program in the device was the other question mark. The key was to understand computers and where they stored their information. I had a good handle on that and spent the greater part of the last month developing a theory about where to best stash my Trojan horse.

With the countdown beyond its halfway point, I compared that with the progress bar on the tablet, which read seventy percent. I crossed my fingers. If all continued as planned, I'd be in the clear, at least from an upload perspective. As the clock counted down, I switched from crossing my fingers to biting my nails as my anxiety built.

With thirty seconds left, my program uploaded ninety-five percent of its code, but with twenty seconds left it moved a mere two percent more. With ten seconds left, my progress bar stopped at ninety-nine percent. I held my breath and made eye contact with Bryn who held her breath along with me. With three seconds left on the clock, my program finished uploading. I reached down and unplugged the portable charger from the tablet and the PMID's screen refreshed to show its connectivity window.

Bryn took the device from me and tapped the screen a few times. "I'm going to access the internal diagnostics, but first let me check on the biometrics. Heart rate is seventy beats per minute. Body temp is thirty-seven degrees Celsius. Oxygen saturation is ninety-nine percent. Proximity sensor indicates a separation of zero point zero meters."

"Sounds about right. Looks like I'm fit as a fiddle."

"Okay, what problem did you experience that made you think it malfunctioned?"

"The device itself feels warm on my wrist. Like it's overheating."

"Hmm." She tapped the screen a few times. "Let me check the internal system monitoring. I have to punch in a code, so close your eyes please."

I did not. In fact, I watched what Bryn did and committed it to memory for future reference.

"Looks like everything's fine. Internal diagnostics nominal."

"Huh."

Bryn waved me away and mouthed the words *Go to your room*. I can't say for sure why, but I stepped away from her—and my PMID—walking backward on my tiptoes. I spun around when I reached the hallway and proceeded at a snail's pace down the hall. I heard Bryn speaking when I reached my bedroom doorway.

"Checking your bios again and everything looks the same. I am a diagnostician of computerized and mechanical devices, not humans, but it's possible the warmness you felt was indicative of another problem. Possibly an irritant that got in between your wrist and the device."

I walked back to the room and waited until I stood shoulder-to-shoulder with Bryn before responding. "Yeah, that's a possibility. Thanks for taking a look." I took the device back from her and put it on my wrist and clamped it shut. Before removing the portable charger, I took my pulse. As long as it fell in the sixty to eighty beats per minute range, I'd be fine. My program varied the biometrics at random to give the device the impression it was in a real-world situation.

By my count, my heart pumped along at a solid seventy-eight beats per minute. On the high side of my programmed range, to be sure, but valid, nonetheless. I took the portable charger off and stood in silence with Bryn for a full minute before I gave her the thumbs-up along with a shoulder shrug.

Bryn nodded. "I guess we're done here. Looks like you nudged the connectivity chip loose on the printer when you opened it up. I'd love to see your idea working, though. If you ever whip up a prototype, I'd love to be the first person who knows how to service it."

"I'll keep you posted."

She left the way she came, which happened to be the only route out of the house, and I stayed back in the office. I powered down my unconnected tablet and considered stashing the notebook back under the printer but thought better of it. It served only to add risk to an already precarious situation and its destiny was demolition. The tablet took the place of the book inside the underbelly of the 3D printer.

With that task completed and a newfound energy knowing I had untethered freedom at my fingertips, I took the notebook into the bathroom, filled the sink with hot water, and submerged it. Once satisfied that any text or images smudged beyond recognition, I drained the sink, squeezed out as much water from the book as possible, and tossed it down the household annihilator in my hallway. I considered not soaking the book first, but without knowing the exact mechanics of the recycling machine, I felt safer exercising an overabundance of caution.

My mother came around the corner to toss something down the chute right as I closed the lid.

"Doing some recycling?"

"Yeah, stuff no longer needed, you know? Things I've got on my tablet anyway." I mimicked the opening of a book with my hands and then mimed writing.

My mother nodded. "How's that going anyway?"

"Good, good. I'm going to want to pick your brain, though. After two weeks of nothing to do but stare into the darkness and think, I became interested in Shared Consciousness."

"Oh, geez, that's some heavy lifting there. I'm not sure how much help I can be since I don't know all the biology involved. The quantum and computing side of things are my bailiwick."

"That's perfect. I can reach out to Melissa. She's studying Shared Subconsciousness and can connect me with an Intelligence Officer if I want to know more about that side of it."

"What brought on this sudden interest, besides mind-numbing boredom while in solitary?"

"I like the idea of knowledge passing between generations. I've experienced a few things in my short time here and the thought of all that, and everything I've yet to learn, disappearing into nothingness like steam on a window, I found motivation to act."

"You're aware that Shared Consciousness has some pretty limiting conditions, not the least of which is you will cease to exist as a physical being once the transfer completes. You need to either know, or fabricate, your exact time of corporeal death."

"As for ceasing to exist, I'm well aware of that. They've drilled it into our heads for years. Regarding the time of death, that's a lot easier these days than it used to be back in the days of Carlton Sedgwick."

"There are other limitations as well, you know."

"I know, I know, the most important of which is the mental state and capacity of the host. They have to be 'all there,' as the saying goes, and they need to have the aptitude to go beyond that. It's like in the old computing days of overclocking a processor. If you pushed one past its physical limit, it fried. But don't worry, all of this is, and will remain, theoretical and will be for a long time. I already have a more immediate and practical project that I'm working on."

"Oh?"

I made it up on the spot when I talked to Bryn, but the idea had legitimate merit. "Yeah, high output 3D rendering hardware to free up AI to adjust on-the-fly when every second counts."

"Well, I'm glad that things are on track. If you can keep your nose clean for the remainder of your sentence then what your father did will be all the more worth it."

"I wish he'd talked to me first."

"I know, I wish he would have spoken with me too."

We stood in silence for a moment and then I hugged her. "I'll make you both proud, don't worry." My mother didn't reply, but instead patted me on the back.

For a week, I tested out my untethering program I installed on my PMID. I started out with short bursts venturing into the bathroom to pee and working my way up to going to the bathroom and brushing my teeth. Showering without the device on my wrist was a feeling I didn't know I missed until I did it again. The first one I took untethered lasted so long my mother knocked on the door to make sure I was okay, oblivious to the fact that her daughter's digital handcuff sat in the desk drawer of her bedroom down the hall.

I took care to not take advantage of my small slice of newfound freedom too often. When not under the influence of my program, the Personal Multipurpose Interaction Device monitored and recorded everything. It knew when I napped, slept, went to the bathroom, showered, and everything else. I made sure Commander heard me pee several times a day and wore the wristband once in a while in the shower. Every other aspect of my house arrest remained the same, with minor adjustments. After settling into a routine for when I wore and didn't wear the device, my mental state improved in a significant way.

I focused like I'd never focused before. I took two extra classes and spent the majority of my waking moments learning about Shared Intellect, Inherited Consciousness, Shared Subconscious, and 3D printer hardware acceleration. When I didn't do that, I sought counsel with my mother to learn the ins and outs of my chosen field that my classwork wouldn't teach me. My mother didn't know how I used my untethered tablet for illicit coding, and I had no intention of ever telling her. If everything went according to plan, there wouldn't be any need, but a lot of dominoes needed to fall first, so that's where my focus lay.

In my relentless quest for more freedom, I tested the capacity of my portable charger more and more each time I put it into use. A half an hour while I used my bathroom for my morning routine became forty-five minutes as I ate my breakfast afterwards. With my brother and mother around in the early hours, I made sure to always wear a long-sleeved shirt or sweater to hide the fact that my device wasn't on my wrist. Additionally, I had to ensure that no other video capturing devices got a glimpse of my bare wrist. As far as Commander was concerned, my PMID stayed on my wrist. A single frame of video showing me without it would ruin everything I'd worked for and land me back in the void for who knows how long.

After two weeks of extending my untethered time by small increments each day, I managed to extend my free time to two and a half hours. That was a good amount of time, and I toyed with the idea of leaving the house, but the prospect of stepping foot off my property terrified me. Still, I wanted to know the charger's upper limit for its battery. After spending time after dinner one night with the device off my wrist but on the other side of my room, I left it there to perform my nighttime routine and then lay in bed reading.

With at least ten days of charge on my device, I didn't need to concern myself with the PMID dying on me, but with my program activated, the device didn't charge at all. My code used a considerable amount of juice to work its magic, and it used the portable charger for its power needs. Once its power source ran out, it would use its own battery to do what it did and run down a lot faster than ten days. In fact, it would die in three hours on its own and that was if it carried a full charge when the portable power ran out. At least that's what my calculations showed, which were seldom off by more than a fraction of a fraction of a percent.

A persistent beeping annoyed me enough to wake me from my slumber. Still in a fog, I tried to get my bearings and as the beeps continued, it dawned on me that I fell asleep with my device hooked into the portable charger across the room. I tossed the covers aside, which sent my tablet shooting across the room until it slid under my closet door. My feet hit the floor, and I leapt toward my PMID. Its screen flashed red for every three beeps that chorused in quick succession every two seconds which meant I had less than two minutes to disable my program and plug the portable charger into an outlet to start both of them charging. I tapped the program disabling code onto the screen of the device as the interval between beeps shortened from two seconds to one second. I knew from my education on The Known Order that the interval between beeps shortened as the battery approached a value close enough to zero to render the device useless.

I kept the cable for the charger that plugged into the outlet in my desk drawer across the room. I grabbed my electronic tether and shuffled across the carpet to my desk and retrieved it. I jammed one end of the cable into the free end of the charger and looked around, frantic for an outlet. Most everything charged wirelessly but every room had at least one hard-wired outlet as a backup, in case of emergencies.

The interval between beeps shortened to an imperceptible interval. I closed my eyes and pictured the location of the outlet. I was sure my room contained one double outlet but couldn't remember the last time I'd seen it. My eyebrows raised and I muttered, "Ah ha!" I dropped to the floor, lay on my back, and shuffled my way under the bed, plugging the charger in as the succession of beeps became a solid tone.

It wasn't until I exhaled that I realized I'd been holding my breath. To be sure, I didn't fall back asleep and lose my grip on the device, I put the device on my wrist. No easy task with but six inches of clearance between my nose and the underside of my bed. Anyone tethered to their device from a legal perspective was aware of the importance of keeping their proximity to it as close to zero as possible when charging with the portable. The power cable attached to the charger, however, spanned a short two feet and with my arm stretched out, I still wasn't able to see anything but the underside of my bed.

In spite of all the excitement and adrenaline that pumped through me, I fell back asleep again and woke to a knocking on my front door. My head turned to face my device. Fully charged. I croaked, "Commander, who's knocking on the front door?"

Bryndolin Cole, the technician, is at the front door. She's here to perform maintenance on your PMID since its battery drained unusually quickly last night, as you are aware, I'm sure.

I tossed aside the idea of Commander sassing me and scooted out from under the bed still in my underwear and a spaghetti-strapped hemp camisole. I opened the front door to find a smiling Bryn whose smile widened when she saw the hot mess standing in front of her.

"Hey, there, sweet pea. Rough night?"

"Ugh, you have no idea."

"Headquarters sent me right away. Looks like you've got a short in your portable charger or possibly your wristband. They want me to poke around, fix it if I can, or replace anything that can't be fixed."

My eyes widened. "Sure, of course. Come in."

"You know, this little hiccup with your device got me in trouble."

"Oh? I'm sorry about that, but how?"

"You complained about feeling the device overheat, and I didn't find any problems. Then, not too long after, the darn bracelet burns through its battery a hundred times faster than it should."

"I didn't know. Again, I'm sorry."

"Not your fault. It's the PMID, though its diagnostics were fine. I'm going to check the charger, assuming you had it attached."

"I did, but then I fell asleep."

"Not supposed to do that."

"Clearly not."

"Okay, show me to it, or bring it to me."

I invited her in with the wave of my arm and closed the door behind her. "Follow me, madam technician." I crawled under the bed, unplugged the charger, and shimmied my way back out.

Bryndolin knew enough to not say anything about why I had the device plugged in under the bed instead of leveraging wireless charging but still gave me a quizzical eyebrow raise. "Let's see what we've got here." She fiddled with the charger for a few seconds and then turned her attention to the pins on the connector. "Oh, yeah, I thought this might be the case." She used a pair of tweezers to fiddle with a connection point. "See these two pins?" She held it close to my face. "They're touching. That's going to put extraordinary strain on the PMID."

The pins were decidedly *not* touching. "Oh?"

"Yeah, instead of working as a charger, it was essentially doing the opposite, sucking the life out of whatever you attached it to. I'm guessing you put it on too quickly and the pins bent. Let me check your wrist device to make sure it's not damaged. Commander, technician Bryndolin Cole performing maintenance on Katherine Webb's PMID. I need to remove it."

Proceed.

"Come with me." She led me to the front door and unlocked my wrist device with the key attached to the main console. When she flipped it over, I muttered, "Hmm," but otherwise kept my opinions to myself. She poked at it with her tweezers and then held it out close to my face again. "See there?" The tweezers tips pointed to a slight imperfection on the underside of the device. "That's where the pins must have pinched together. It left a teensy, tiny scar on your device. I bent the pins back on the charger, but I'm going to leave you another one to be safe. If those pins get too loose, it will lose its ability to charge. Does that make sense?"

"Yeah, I get it, and thank you. I'm sure you had other plans for this morning."

"I go where the semi-sentient AI tells me to go. This morning it told me to come here. I'll be honest, I didn't mind at all." She looked at me with the deep understanding of a soulmate.

I felt the heat of my entire body rush to my cheeks. "Well, thanks, nonetheless. Say, could the overheating sensation have come from those pins bending toward each other and what I experienced was a precursor to the near catastrophic incident from last night?"

"Possibly, but there's no way to tell now. Had I looked at the charger last time, there might have been a clue."

"Oh, okay, I was curious is all."

"No, I get it. You're a problem solver. I'm the same way. I do it more mechanically though whereas you're a bit more—cerebral."

I chuckled. "If you say so."

We stood in the foyer for a few awkward seconds before I realized I must have had the worst case of dragon breath. "I should get started with my day. Thanks again, Technician Cole."

"You can call me Bryn."

"Bryn it is, then. Thank you."

"You're welcome, Prisoner Webb." She laughed.

"You can call me Kate."

"Kate it is, then. Have a good one."

I shut the door behind her and closed my eyes, a portable charger in each hand. The door opened again. It was Bryn holding my PMID. "Now *that* was a colossal brain fart. About walked away with this. Thankfully, it started yelling at me."

I took it from her and smiled as our fingers touched. "Thanks. I still need it for a few more months."

I put device back on my wrist and retreated to my bedroom. After a fitful sleep under my bed, I needed proper rest. My schoolwork had to wait until my brain function returned and the best way to do that was to get decent sleep.

It was close to lunchtime when I opened my eyes as I lay on my soft bed under the covers, a stark contrast to the evening prior. I still wore my spaghetti strap shirt and plain white underpants, but my stomach rumbled. Instead of showering and changing, I made my way into the kitchen. As I opened the fridge to check out my lunch options, the front door opened, startling me and causing me to juggle the bottle of salad dressing I held in one hand and the carafe of lemonade held in the other. I let out a squeal and turned around to see my mother running toward me, arms outstretched.

She wrapped her arms around me in a big bear hug reminiscent of when I returned home from confinement. "Thank Sedgwick you're okay and still here."

"Of course I'm still here. Where else would I be?"

"I got a report about an incident at home, but the message was light on details. I drove back right away to check on you. I don't think I'd be able to bear it if they sent you back."

"Well, you can breathe a bit easier. There was a short on my charger, and it drained my PMID instead of charging it and I fell asleep."

My mother let out a sigh. "Can we please agree that you'll be more careful going forward? I don't think my heart can take any more surprises."

I gave my mom a kiss on the cheek. "I promise."

00001110
[Fourteen]

With the numbers from my trial run favorable for an extended untethering, the urge to put my system to the ultimate test overwhelmed my sensibilities and the agreement with my mother lasted a meager two weeks. In that time, I reconfigured the chargers to work in parallel, doubling my potential time away from the monitoring device which served to increase my desire to take the next big step.

Expanding the battery capacity, my promise to my mother aside, there was another reason I waited two weeks before making my next move. Since it involved leaving the house in the wee hours of the night, I needed a new moon. With the amount of surveillance in the neighborhood, having a bright shining moon hanging overhead made the already risky proposition that much more so.

That night I went to sleep with my window open and placed black leggings and a black long-sleeved shirt under my bed. My dark skin didn't need any additional camouflage, and I put my hair in a tight ponytail. I extracted my untethered and disconnected tablet from the underbelly of the 3D printer in the office and set an alarm for three o'clock in the morning. I set the tablet to vibrate and placed under my pillow. Before sliding under the covers, I made sure to check the battery on the tablet and my portable chargers. My principal concern as I fell asleep was time. Without my PMID on my wrist, I wouldn't know how much time I had left before I should get home, assuming I had the nerve to stray that far away in the first place.

It was the reason the three o'clock hour was crucial. I knew with my extended battery I had about six hours to work with, and at that time of year the sun started to rise around six o'clock. This way, if I traveled a good distance away when the horizon began to lighten, I could get home in time. Of course, then daylight became an issue in terms of my safety, and the risk that my mother would check in on me when she woke in the morning became a factor. All the more reason I wanted to keep my excursion straightforward and short. I planned for about an hour's worth of freedom within the boundaries of my subdivision, and if it went well, I'd explore more ambitious locales in the future.

Sleep did not come quickly, nor was it restful, but it sufficed. Good enough is often good enough. At three o'clock, my pillow vibrated with enough strength that it woke me from a dream in which I experienced an earthquake. To be extra careful, I turned off the alarm and stashed the tablet under my bed where I used to hide my protest pictures, remnants of the first steps in my journey to change the world, steps taken a mere few years ago. I emerged from under the bed with my all-black clothes and put on a pair of dark blue running shoes—the closest to black practical footwear I owned. Dressed and ready to get on with it, I enabled my program, attached my portable chargers, and used my 3D printed illegal PMID key to remove the device from my wrist. I made a mental note of the time and hoped my internal clock would not fail me. I slid the device into my bedside table drawer beside the magnifying glass, which played a key role in the early part of my defiant trip and snuck out my window.

There was a bit of a drop to the ground, but my strong, athletic legs cushioned the landing. I crouched like a wild animal scrounging for food in foreign territory, my back pressed against the wall of the house, my eyes scanning the area and adjusting to the surrounding darkness.

There was a greater chance of being seen if I traveled out front, simply due to the fact that there were always hover cars or transports or a CCC roaming around regardless of the hour. At this time of night, the chances were a lot lower than a couple hours earlier or later, but better to be safe than sorry. Front yards, however, offered gardens. Gone were the days of perfectly manicured lawns of non-native grass. Every house in the neighborhood sported a well-maintained garden, if not by the homeowners themselves then by a company hired to keep it trimmed, pruned, and free of harmful pests.

If I traveled around the backs of the houses, there were fewer chances I'd be seen, insomniacs comprising the biggest concern. Backyards had little in terms of cover, though, and many of them had fences or other obstructions that could hamper a quick escape if I needed one.

I made my choice and tiptoed to the front of my house, turned to my left, and headed into the center of my neighbor's garden. With tall stalks of corn, potatoes grown vertically on special raised beds, and vines of beans and snap peas in full growth, a slight crouch allowed me to disappear from view. I glanced at the sky, looking for the telltale red and white flashing lights of a drone, and moved on. Once through the garden, I needed to make a choice of either darting straight across the driveway or getting in closer to the house and sneaking across that way. I opted for the bolder, but quicker, dash across the driveway. The quickness of my feet and my long legs would carry me the short distance between gardens in a few steps. I made a note to check other driveways to see if they were smart drives like ours. If they were, I'd have to avoid them or risk leaving a digital footprint.

It took me five long strides, but I made it. I stood two properties over from my house and strengthened my resolve. Getting caught now meant a certain trip back into the void and for a lot longer than two weeks. I wasn't sure I had enough creativity and patience to compose the amount of music I'd need to keep from going insane. "Don't get caught, Katherine," I whispered to a stand of corn stalks a good six inches taller than me.

There weren't any drones flying overhead. There weren't any CCCs storming the house. There were no lights on save a few scattershot along the opposite side of the road, another suburban planning decision that helped my cause. I could have turned around and gone back home, my point made and the crisp, fresh air of freedom in my lungs. But turning back then, after less than a hundred feet of progress, was in my mind submitting to the constraints I desperately sought to break. If I had a place to go, if there were people who could take me in, I would be there in a heartbeat, but that would take planning—months of it—and require hacking and modification of several systems. Not to mention bringing others into the fold amplified the risk without amplifying the benefit. The simple act of escape created a different prison, one that required more complicated means of escape and extended beyond my increased chances of spending the rest of my life in confinement.

The path I was on was the right path. It risked the fewest number of lives and livelihoods, and it brought the ultimate reward in freedom from the tyranny, authoritarianism, collectivism, and submission, for me and the entire Known Order. The fall of The Association was a goal worthy of pursuit, and I was closer to making that a reality than any other person—artificial or organic—since The Wars ended.

I dashed across the next driveway, and then another one, and another one. I went like this, alternating between short bursts of dashing across driveways and catching my breath and, if I were honest, reveling a wee bit in my success but taking care not to get too cocky about it. At one point, I lay on the ground between rows of corn and stared up at the clear night sky and meditated with my eyes open. During its time of existence, The Association managed a singular worthwhile accomplishment—healing the atmosphere. The climate hadn't fully recovered from the damage from The Before Times and then The Wars, but the skies were clear again, and by my estimation, there wasn't a more calming and glorious sight than the night sky. It made me appreciate my existence, and it bolstered my resolve to improve that existence before it was too late.

After three blocks of movement through gardens, making sure to not trample any produce, aiming my garden entry point for the sturdy corn stalks which provided the best cover should anyone peer out a window as I crept by, I stopped and assessed my situation. I estimated an elapsed time of about an hour. It occurred to me that I could have used the star positions as a sort of clock, but that timekeeping method hinged on a clear sky and while more likely to occur than not, it wasn't guaranteed by any stretch. I made the decision to head back but hadn't decided if I would go back the way I came or try roaming through the backyards to see what potential pitfalls that route threw in my way.

Not wanting to add any more risk than necessary, I took the win and turned on my heels, paying homage to the person who was neither my protector nor my friend but who still felt like an ally, and made my way back the way I came. I was fortunate that there was no visible disruption from my presence in the gardens. Of course, it was nighttime, and without the advantage of daylight, there was no way to tell for certain my exact level of stealth.

I took my time working my way back through the gardens. Rushing or acting in haste didn't serve my purposes. I needed to be hypersensitive to my surroundings while at the same time ensuring I milked every drop of my newfound freedom. To what specific end, I wasn't one hundred percent certain, but I had an idea of how this would come in handy despite needing to investigate a few things first.

About a block away from my house, there was a garden with an excessive amount of corn. As I meandered through the rows, I became more aware of the silence. I stopped moving and closed my eyes. The sound of the breeze brushing the leaves of the stalks tickled my ear. I took a deep breath in through my nose and exhaled through my mouth. On the second inhalation, the front porch light of the house in front of me illuminated the garden and the sound of a door opening broke up my temporary meditation. I held my breath and cautiously lowered myself to the ground. I couldn't see anything, but I sensed a pair of eyes scanning the yard. Whoever it was coughed, startling me, and it caused me to slip off the balls of my feet and rustle a corn stalk.

"Who's out there?" The voice was loud and gruff. I heard footsteps move from the front of the house, down a few stairs, and shuffle to the edge of the garden. "Who. The. Hell. Is. Out. There?" I held my breath and tried to will more blood into my legs in case I needed to make a break for it. The footsteps receded and I heard the door opening again but by the sound of the springs and creaking hinges it was clear he'd paused. "Commander, who's outside my house?" He must have reached inside and grabbed his device off the household's standard-issue charger by the door.

I do not sense a digital signature from anyone in the vicinity.

My heart rate slowed by half after hearing its assessment of the man's surroundings. It still raced at an unhealthy pace, but I had confidence I could avoid myocardial infarction. His footsteps landed with a *thud* as he pounded down the front steps again and to the edge of the garden. "Commander, you're full of shit. There's someone out there."

I do not sense a digital signature from anyone in the vicinity.

"Impossible. They might not have their device on their wrist."

All Personal Multipurpose Interaction Devices within the boundaries of the city are accounted for.

He harrumphed, cleared his throat, and spit onto the ground. "Bullshit computer." His footsteps retreated once more back into the house, the door clicked shut, its creaky springs screaming in protest through its entire slow arc, and the light extinguished.

I let out the breath I'd held and steadied myself by getting onto my hands and knees. Once set, I extended one arm and leg to get the blood flowing again and then repeated the exercise with my other set of appendages. Unconcerned about the mud on my knees and the heels of my hands, I crawled with as much care and as little sound as possible until I reached the edge of the garden. Fifteen feet—five long strides of driveway surface—stood between me and the next garden. I took a deep breath and knelt in a starter's crouch like a runner from The Before Times. With explosive speed, I bolted across the driveway, into the garden on the other side, and kept on going. My arms pumped and I vaulted over small obstacles, planter boxes, and other shorter vegetables with remarkable speed and efficiency. I didn't stop, I didn't look back, and I didn't alter my straight shot trajectory by a single degree. Driveway, garden, driveway, garden, driveway, garden, until I saw my own house less than fifty feet ahead. I found another gear, a longer stride, and a renewed determination. As I approached the edge of my next-door neighbor's garden, I readied myself for a quick pivot onto my driveway so I could get to the back of the house. My foot landed half on the dirt of the garden and half on the edge of my driveway and when I tried to make the corner to avoid the smart surface, my heel slipped and sent me tumbling into the raised planter full of green beans. I suppressed a grunt and scream as I hit the ground beside the planter. No time to assess any injuries. I picked myself up and sprinted behind the garage and around back to my window, which at that moment looked a considerable amount higher off the ground than when I snuck out of it a short time ago.

Without breaking stride, I ran toward it and leapt into the air. My hands grabbed onto the windowsill and my feet slammed into the siding. I winced both from the pain I felt in several parts of my body as well as at the racket I'd made. After hauling myself through the window I closed it and sat on my floor slumped against my wall. I was out of breath and in pain, but I was home.

It was less painful for me to crawl to my bedside table, so I did that, and I grabbed my device from the drawer. I'd been gone ninety-three minutes, and all it cost me was a partial heart attack and what felt like massive contusions down the entire left side of my body.

I undressed and shoved my clothes under my bed. I'd examine them in the daylight and determine what do to. With time left before sunrise and the expectation that the adrenaline would wear off, I slid into bed and checked my pulse by putting two fingers to my neck. It raced higher than the seventy beats per minute my contraption told my PMID, but that could be attributed to having a dream. I slid the band onto my wrist, removed the portable charger, and tapped the code to disable the program. The chargers went onto my desk to wirelessly recuperate. I pulled the covers up and started to meditate. I managed to fall asleep and stayed that way well into the morning.

When I awoke the next day, the house sat empty as it did most weekdays with school in session. There wasn't much in the way of time off for non-students. Weekends and the occasional Known Order mandated day off but that's it. Of course, everyone got May nineteenth off for to celebrate the day Carlton Sedgwick proved the Grand Unified Theory. Otherwise, everyone worked Monday to Friday and got the weekends to relax and recharge. Maybe it was due to my moment of freedom from the night before or maybe it was the realization that there were more than a hundred lonely days still ahead, but pangs of depression crept up on me as I went to the bathroom and brushed my teeth. I wanted to process my feelings, but I had things to do first.

The tablet needed to go back to its secure hiding spot wedged in between the motherboard and the casing of the household 3D printer. My black clothes needed to be checked for dirt or other such evidence from the night before. If I found any, then I needed to wash the item in the sink in the bathroom. I may have been paranoid, but I didn't know what type of analysis the smart washer did on dirty clothes. I knew there were sensors built in which helped with the cleaning process, but I didn't know if the machine had any sort of fancy algorithm in play that knew where the dirt came from and if it could trace it back to a location as specific as the garden of the man who suspected a neighborhood trespasser.

My shoes needed a cleaning, for sure. Same went for my socks, bra, underwear, and the T-shirt that I wore under my long sleeves. Aside from the final sprint home, I wasn't frenzied but everything smelled like nervous sweat.

My long-sleeved shirt was otherwise clean. My pants, not so much. They sported healthy dirt patches around the ankles and on the knees. The shoes surprised me, the soles alone showed signs of outside wear. I washed the dirt out of my pants in the bathroom sink using the dish soap from the kitchen. Then, I took a scrub brush and got all the dirt out of the treads of my shoes. I rinsed the bottoms of them in the sink for an extra layer of reassurance. The whole bundle got tossed into the washer and put on the deep clean cycle. After breakfast and a quick shower, I dressed in my usual weekday studying garb which consisted of loose-fitting track pants and an "I Love Kallian Dorn" T-shirt. I'd only been awake for a couple hours, but I was still gloomy for unknown reasons and wanted to nap. I set an alarm on my PMID for one hour and lay down to see if I could sleep off whatever cloud hung over me.

I fell asleep within two minutes of my head hitting the pillow. My alarm startled me out of a dream, and I considered staying in bed for another half an hour, but a video call request on my tablet took that decision out of my hands. It was Melissa. I tapped the "Accept" button.

"Hey, there, Mel. Long time no speak."

"Hey, K-Dub. Holy crow, you look like junk."

"Gee, thanks. I feel like junk. One of those days, I guess."

"Want me to come over?"

"You've got school."

"I'm literally the top student in the class, and I'm taking a second-year class at night so I can get ahead. I think I can afford an afternoon off."

"You don't have t—"

Melissa ended the call. Thirty minutes later a heard knock on the door. I had gotten up and sat in the office avoiding my schoolwork. "Commander, let Melissa in and direct her to the office, please."

I heard the soft dulcet tone of Commander's voice waft through the house. *Melissa Demchuk, Katherine is in the office. Due to the restrictions of her sentence, you are required to keep your Personal Multipurpose Interaction Device on at all times.*

"Yeah, yeah, whatever you say, Crapmander."

I couldn't help but smile. Since I started my post-exit studies, Melissa didn't have half an ounce of patience for the artificial intelligence that dominated every aspect of everyone's life. She skipped into the room, and we hugged a long, comforting hug in which we both held each other tight and refused to let go until we felt the weight of every last ounce of compassion and friendship flow through us. Melissa wasn't who I would call my best friend, at least not during my childhood, but she was the most consistent and as present as a girl could ever hope for. She showed up, had your back, but knew when to challenge you. Plus, she had a healthy appreciation for rebellion and subversion of authority.

With the embrace complete, we each wiped a tear from our respective cheeks.

"It's really good to see you, Mel."

"It's really good to see you too, K-Dub. What the heck have you been up to?"

"Keeping my head down and staying out of trouble. You know, the usual." I gave her a wink, pointed to my PMID, and gave her the universal *shh* sign. My disconnected tablet sat on the office desk. I'd typed a message right after we'd spoken: DO YOU TRUST ME? Melissa responded with an emphatic nod.

I took my friend's hand and clipped my spare portable charger to the underside of her PMID. Then, I plugged the charger into my computer. I switched screens and returned my attention to the wrist device. After navigating to the Network Settings, I tapped in the secret code to disable its connectivity. Before the timer counted down a single second, I tapped the tablet screen and waited. As it had when I'd done it for my own band, it finished with a few seconds to spare. I unplugged Mel's charger from the tablet and dug my spare PMID key out of my pocket. My friend did not so much as once look like her trust and confidence wavered.

I did feel her arm tighten a bit as I unclasped the wristband, took it off, and laid it on the desk. Then, I attached my charger, the original one, tapped the screen of my device a few times and did the same, but sat it on my tablet so it was crystal clear whose was whose. I took her by the hand, and we both tiptoed to the bathroom. Melissa looked nervous, and I felt a tremor coming from her hand, but neither of us said a word.

Once in the safety of the bathroom with the door closed, Melissa whispered, "What in the world just happened? What did you do?"

"I managed to untether from the PMID. Melissa, you have no idea what it's like to be this free. I went out last night."

"Out, like out of the house?"

"Yeah."

"Without your electronic tether on your wrist?"

"Precisely."

"Where did you go?"

"Down the street a few blocks. I nearly got caught on the way back."

"Holy crow. By who? Your favorite CCC?"

"Nope. A random neighbor. I didn't see him, but he sounded like a big dude. He basically fee-fi-fo-fum'd me, standing on his porch or at the edge of his garden, daring me to come out."

I recounted the whole story from start to finish but leaving out the name of my tech repair accomplice, not from a lack of trust in my lifelong friend, but out of an abundance of caution. The fewer people that knew the better. Plausible deniability wasn't common those days, but it did get me out of a serious jam. That and a healthy dose of good old-fashioned subterfuge and lying.

Melissa looked at her wrist and rubbed it with her hand. "So, you're telling me I could walk out of the house right now, and Commander wouldn't have a clue."

"You'd have to leave out the window since it doesn't have a biometric tracker on it like the doors do – a design flaw in The Known Order urban planning I hope they never fix."

"This is huge, Kate. What are you going to do with this newfound power?"

"I have an idea, but there are a few hurdles. I need your help."

"Of course, anything for my girl."

"I realize your knowledge of Shared Subconscious is limited, but I was hoping you could see if it's possible to do it between a human and AI."

"You want to read Commander's mind."

"More or less, yeah. I know now I can fake it out and make it think there's a human on the other end. The next step is to make it work in the other direction. You know, make it think it's communicating with another computer, a trusted one, but have it be me instead."

"You faked it out on the most basic level, though. What you're talking about doing is way more complex than that. I don't know that it can even be done. You'd need a trusted computer signature for starters."

"Ah, but I've got a friend that can help me with that, remember? And on top of that, all the computer stuff is right in my wheelhouse. Plus, I have my mom I can go to for advice if I need to, though that would mean explaining a few things I'd rather not have to explain. If I get stuck, though, I know I can go to her."

"You've been thinking a lot about this, haven't you?"

"You wouldn't think two weeks was a long time, especially in the grand scheme of things, but when all you've got is a wee little wrist device for light and a semi-sentient computer, who won't answer half your questions, for company, you do quite a bit of thinking. Honestly, if The Association had concerns about recidivism, they'd keep everyone in confinement busy and mentally stimulated. It's the moments where they treat you like dirt and leave you with nothing where your mind starts to plot revenge."

"You think so?"

"I know so. Had they not treated me so poorly in an effort to scare me into submission, I would not have come up with any of the ideas I did. I was already walking the line, had been for years, but sitting in that dark cell with no contact with another human, no daylight, no stimulation of any kind, only stagnant water to drink, and food that tasted like rotting turnips pushed me over the edge."

"Not everyone is as mentally strong as you."

"I suppose not, but if there was any question as to whether or not confinement was purely punitive instead of reformative or restorative, that went right out the window within thirty seconds of seeing what they do to people before they get out." I put my head in my hands and fought back tears. "It's cruel and unusual, Melissa." A single drop rolled down the side of my nose.

Melissa gave me another hug, and the flood gates opened. I hadn't had a good cry in quite some time, but I stood in the bathroom with a dear friend and wept for a solid five minutes. Mel handed me a towel and I wiped my face. "Thanks."

"Anytime." There was an awkward pause. "Now what?"

"Now you find me everything you can, even if it takes you weeks, and you put it onto your tablet like you would for school. Then you'll come over for study breaks, and I'll find a way to get the info off your tablet and onto my disconnected one. I should be able to do it."

"I can't just give it to you? There's no crime in learning more, is there?"

"It's not about crime, Mel. It never was. It's about control, and at the moment, The Association controls me, or at least they think they do. Anything I do that leads them to believe I'm not staying in my lane they regard as suspicious."

"They're such jerks."

"No lies detected. One last detail. I'm not going to send you home with the portable charger or tell you how to enable the spoofing program—at least not yet. There are things I want to work out first, and I need the extra battery when I go out again."

Melissa put her hands on her stomach. "No problem. I don't think I would have the intestinal fortitude to go out on my own anyway."

"Okay, cool. I may need you to summon up courage for other things, though."

"Oooooh, okay. Do tell."

I outlined the basic plan and asked her to poke holes in it. She showed keen interest and obliged and gave excellent feedback. Her overall impression, however, was that I was out of my mind and setting myself up for the greatest error in judgment I would ever make.

"So, you want no part of it?"

"I didn't say that."

"Well, you don't approve."

"I didn't say that, either."

"I can fix those issues you brought up."

"I know you can, and I know you will."

"Then, what is it?"

There was a long, pregnant pause and I regarded her with caution. It wasn't a staring contest or similar challenge, but I didn't know what else to say and it looked like she struggled with how to phrase her next sentence.

"You know I love you. You know I'd do anything for you. You know I think you're the smartest person I know."

"Thanks—"

"Let me finish, there's a 'but.'"

"I had a feeling there was."

"But if this doesn't work, it will mean disaster for the movement, which is gaining strength by the day, you know. The girls are sowing the seeds of discontent and it's working."

"But they need a catalyst to take it to the next level. If there isn't that opportunity, if they don't have an inside girl, as it were, then it'll be decades, maybe longer, before the needle moves as much as a hair in the right direction. The deck is stacked against us—all of us, not just the women." My voice hitched as I thought of my father sitting in confinement for a crime that I committed.

Melissa put her hand on my shoulder. "I know, but if this doesn't work, which as much as I want it to, I'm afraid it won't, and if it doesn't work then"— her voice hitched—"then we lose you. And then what? Where does that leave us?"

"It leaves you right where you are, doing the things you do. Trying to both improve the world and save it."

"We'll need a leader."

"I'm not a leader."

"Yes, you are. You're an inspiration to so many."

"Another will take my place."

"You're sure about that?"

"No, but I'm sure what I'm going to do is going to work, so it's a moot point." I flashed my million-watt smile.

Melissa shook her head and conceded. "You're impossible, you know that?"

"I'm beginning to think you might be right."

We shared a laugh and sat in silence for a minute except it wasn't an awkward silence. It had feelings of familiarity and comfort. A contemplative peace that you can only experience in the presence of people who understand and support each other to the highest degree. We made eye contact and nodded in near perfect synchronization. The conversation was over. If there had been what one considered an argument in all of that, I could claim victory—not that I kept track.

We walked back to the office, and I put my device back on my wrist, ended the program, removed the charger, and placed it on the wireless charging pad on the desk. Then, I did the same for Melissa's.

"It was nice sitting here in silence with you for a bit, Melissa. Comforting in a way I can't quite explain."

"My pleasure, friend. I feel the same way, though since it's been so long since we've hung out, we should probably have a proper conversation at some point and catch up on things."

"Oh, there's nothing to catch up on. Things have been pret-ty boring for me."

We both giggled, then, the giggles turned to chuckles, which turned to full-blown side-splitting laughter. We fell to the floor in a fit and howled, tears streaming down our cheeks, until we gasped for air.

After our private conversation in the bathroom, the milquetoast discussion in the office was entirely for the benefit of those listening. I had a brief moment of anxiety when I considered they might analyze our speech patterns and realize that we hadn't spoken with our usual cadence and inflections. Commander comprised the sum total of a billion people's knowledge combined with artificial intelligence working based on a formula that mathematically calculated the precise reaction to every determinable action in the known Universe. Knowing that, my anxiety was justified. On top of everything else I had going on, brushing up on my acting skills didn't need to go onto the pile.

Our conversation drew to a natural conclusion when we both realized the remaining topics would get me into a steaming pile of trouble with the authorities. Melissa left, hopped into her hover car, and glided away. I waved to her from the front stoop. In the recent past I'd tasted freedom, but it wasn't the type of freedom others enjoyed. In that moment, it struck me as rather sad that they thought they were free. Worse still, most of them either thought that was good enough or didn't realize The Association controlled them to the point where the slightest inclination toward individualism gave them the illusion of freedom. That didn't prevent a pang of jealousy as my friend left, off to go wherever she wanted. It required approval first, but she still got to go—most of the time. A denied request was for your own good, right? There were reasons and you didn't question them.

On my front steps, with my friend long gone, I stood in a semi-trance considering my options. In a typical eureka-type moment, the idea took me by surprise. It was an odd sensation. Your brain looked and looked for a solution to a problem, and when it found it, you still felt shocked, as if you weren't looking for anything specific but rather wandering around aimlessly and have it fall into your lap. I bypassed the wonderment of why that was, ran inside, sat down in front of my disconnected tablet, and started to code.

Assuming I got what I needed to work the way I wanted, my principal concern boiled down to size. As it was, my program took all but a couple seconds of the total PMID downtime to upload. If making the program any bigger put me at risk of going beyond the time constraint, I'd be in trouble. I filed it as a problem for Future Me to sort out and concentrated on getting the program to work. Once I had that in place, I'd worry about the other details like upload speed and testing it—though I already had an idea about how to tackle that part.

I ignored any schoolwork that day and coded instead. My younger brother and then my mother came home to find me huddled over my desk, fingers typing at a furious pace as my favorite music blared from the console. Thinking the loud music might bother my brother or mother, I turned around to give my back a stretch and shut the door to the office. I turned the volume down a notch as a general courtesy but otherwise went back to my work, closing my eyes and relishing the unique and spectacular feeling of achieving what experts in a field called "flow."

If only to keep up appearances, I needed to do a modicum of work for my classes. After a successful first campaign with evaluations in every class exceeding all expectations, I didn't want to deal with the onslaught of questions about why my performance dropped. It wasn't easy, but I if I attended all my virtual lectures, did all my assignments and labs, and at least put in the minimum required effort, I'd fly under the radar. The problem was that didn't leave a monstrous heap of time left over if I wanted to have downtime, eat regular meals, keep up my personal hygiene, and get a good night's sleep every night.

The time was there, though; it became a matter of prioritization. If all went according to plan, and even if it didn't, my future would be much different in a couple months. I sat down at my tablet and listed everything in my life that took up any reasonable measure of time. I meticulously documented my days in five-minute intervals for the entire twenty-four hours. Then, I made cuts. Right off the bat, I cut down my homework time by fifty percent for three of my classes. Those classes, while stimulating, did nothing to further my agenda. As such, they received the bare minimum required to avoid raising an eyebrow. I shaved fifteen minutes a day off of bathroom breaks and grooming. Not that I wanted to let myself go, but showers every other day, quick ones, keeping my hair in a ponytail, and not dilly-dallying helped. "Pee with purpose," I muttered as I typed it into my time tracking app. I took a similar approach for meals and ensured I split the prep time for dinner with Chadwick to ensure he wouldn't shoulder the full load. My breakfast and lunch remained simple, and I ate them at my desk while doing schoolwork. With all social interaction cut out, save time set aside to interact with Melissa or Terre, the last part of my day left to trim came out of sleep.

Advancements in sleep assistance over the last several decades led to, if nothing else, a well-rested society. It wasn't as if everyone lay around napping all the time or loafing around all casual about life, but if you didn't get your eight hours a night at least four or five nights a week, then you were the exception. My intent was to become an exception, and I set a sleep schedule of six hours a night. The exact time of night varied an hour here or there depending on my school schedule, but the total time didn't change. With the math done, I looked at my regimen, and while I wasn't jumping for joy over any of it, it would get the job done, and that's all that mattered. With the schedule set, I got to work.

I kept to my schedule every day, making sure to set alarms on my PMID to keep me on schedule. To my mom and brother, I looked every bit the part of a dedicated student, which suited me fine. The less they knew or suspected, the better. For three weeks, I kept to my time management system and it worked. I performed adequately in the classes less relevant to my purpose and above average in the ones that were. As for my extracurricular endeavors, I was ready to run a test. I needed to enlist the help of my favorite Zone Technician, Bryndolin, and on a beautiful Wednesday afternoon, I took time out of my programming schedule, opened the case of the 3D printer, and knocked the communications chip loose.

Ten minutes later, Bryndolin stood beside me in the office chatting idly about her growing frustrations with the damage I kept inflicting on the poor device. Of course, the conversation was a ruse designed to appease the ever-present Commander and whoever else the all-knowing supercomputer shared the information with.

While Bryn went through the motions, I directed my attention to my disconnected tablet. On it I wrote, *I have added a location spoofing algorithm to the program so I can keep the device on my wrist. I need you to help me test it.* She nodded to indicate she understood. I connected the charger to my tablet and then to my PMID. It took two seconds to tap the connectivity disabling code onto the screen, and the instant the countdown started, I tapped my tablet. I coded in more efficiency to help with the upload speed but had no idea if it was enough to counterbalance the additional functionality. Overall, the footprint of the program shrunk by a few kilobytes, and I thought of no reason for it to take any longer to get from the tablet to the wristband. One lesson I'd learned over the years, however, was that theory didn't always align with practice. Despite the ever-present Commander dictating what you could and could not do, an approved idea simply meant no foreseeable downstream repercussions. It wasn't a guarantee it would work out to your satisfaction.

The progress bar on the tablet ticked along at the same pace as before. I kept an eye on both, ready to jettison the cable attaching the two devices at the literal last second if need be. The upload appeared to pause right at the end, as it did before, but I stared at it with a newfound anxiety. As the countdown hit one second remaining, the upload completed, and I unplugged the charger from the tablet and disconnected it from my wrist.

Bryn typed on the screen. When I stepped back, I read it. *Does it require a special charger or will any charger do?* I tapped in my reply. *Any charger will do. I need this particular model to upload the program. After that the charger charges* ☺. Bryn tapped in another sentence. *Can you put the program on my device?* I smiled and entered my response onto the tablet. *I thought you'd never ask.*

I repeated the process for Bryn, and then I showed her how to enable the feature. We both stood in the center of the room, silent in the face of the ever-present Commander. Using hand gestures and mouthing words, I set the location information into the watch. This consisted of fixing the current GPS coordinates and then recording a route. At each point where I came to a stop, I told the program how long to wait. This way, I mimicked walking through the house, sitting on the toilet, or taking a nap. Since my ultimate use for the program was at nighttime, it was easy math, but in the daytime, I required a more realistic set of location data.

With that done, it was time to test it out. I mimed for Bryn to leave her technician's tablet on the desk and follow me into the bathroom. Once inside with the door closed and the tap in the sink running, we spoke freely.

"I need you to go back to your tech tablet and track my movements. I'm assuming you have the capability to do that."

"Yeah, I can track anything that has a signal. If you want, I can tap into the database and get your voice and image data too."

"You don't say? The Association lets you do that?"

She shrugged. "I may have extended my reach by a little."

"You're a bad influence, Bryndolin Cole."

She winked and left the bathroom, returning a minute later. "Okay, m'dear, we're all set. Now what?"

"Now we have a proper conversation and see what your tablet thinks is going on."

"Cool. I have to say, I don't know what your endgame is for all of this, but I still think it's fantastic."

"I appreciate you saying that. It means a lot coming from a person I have a lot of respect for."

Her cheeks flushed. "Do I get to know what the endgame is?"

"Not yet. Partly because I don't want you to try to talk me out of it, but partly because I have no idea if it's going to work. The less you know, the safer it is for you."

"I can handle myself, no matter what happens."

"I know you can, and I didn't mean to suggest otherwise, but for a little while longer I need to keep everything on the downlow." I took her hands and held them. "Do you trust me?"

"Of course. Do you trust me?"

"Explicitly."

She nodded. "We should get back. They're going to want me to replace your printer with a newer model since you keep buggering this one."

"What about my work on 3D printer hardware acceleration?"

"Oh, right. I thought that nothing but a sneaky diversion."

"It was, but I still want to work on it. Call it a side project."

"Gotcha. I'll put that into my work order as justification for keeping the old one."

We walked back to the office and stopped running the programs on our wrist devices. Bryn tapped her tablet screen a few times and then turned it to face me. It listed a detailed account of my whereabouts, which consisted of a bit of wandering around the house and a trip to the bathroom, but not much else.

"So, because of your project to turn your printer into a prototype for 3D printer hardware acceleration, I'm not going to recommend a new one." Before she'd finished her sentence, an audio file popped up on my screen. I was impressed with her ability to be clever with my maintenance, though it came as no surprise given what I knew about her.

"Thanks. I feel bad I keep forcing you to come out here to fix my blunders."

"Don't sweat it. I mean that. It's not only my job, but it's a job I quite enjoy."

"That's good. I endeavor to have a similar job someday."

"Well, from what I can see, that's not going to be a problem. We'll see you next time you screw up your printer." She smiled and gave me a wink.

"Thanks again. I should get back to it. Lots to do, you know?"

"Yeah, no worries. I'll see myself out."

Bryn left with a smile and a wave, and I sat down at the desk. Thus completed the first phase of my plan. Phase two culminated with a major challenge and involved a good amount of luck in order for it to work, but in the event it didn't, I had a Plan B. I wasn't too thrilled with it, but my options were limited. If Plan A failed, then it was either Plan B, or I, and everyone I loved, would spend the rest of our lives in solitary.

Phase two began with a lot of coding and preparation.

I needed to understand everything I could about the biological interface with artificial intelligence. In a nutshell, I wanted to put my knowledge of computers together with the groundbreaking work in the field of the Shared Subconscious and see if I could bio-hack Commander. If I could prove my assumption that The Association manipulated the all-knowing AI for their own personal gain no matter who suffered as a result, it would be a game changer. For a long time, I suspected The Known Order existed as nothing but a fraudulent and flawed concept used to keep the masses suppressed under the guise of safety and harmony.

The next new moon was due sooner than I wanted, so I needed to get to work. With my ability to spoof my location and otherwise use all the functions of my PMID, I wanted to push the limits for my next excursion. Further, I needed to get both Melissa and Bryn back to the house and find a way to have a conversation with Terre. If things went awry, she was the one person I trusted to pick up where I left off. I might not be able to take it as far as I planned, but small acts of defiance would add up over time, and Terre had leveled up to expert when it came to small acts of defiance. Death by a thousand cuts took time and patience, but given enough of both, it was still an effective strategy. I had Plan A, Plan B, and a contingency and it involved me and three other people, maximum. Knowing this provided me with enough comfort to still sleep well at night.

In the days approaching the new moon, my busyness increased. Schoolwork and keeping up appearances to my brother and mom were hard enough, but I added in the extra work of figuring out how to interface a Shared Subconscious headset with a PMID along with the research required for my Plan B. Perpetual exhaustion became the new normal.

I did manage to make time to bring Melissa over, showed her how to start the program on her device, and told her to get a portable charger like mine. In addition, I asked her for a favor—a big one—but Melissa trusted me and agreed to it without question. Borrowing a Shared Subconscious headset from her school lab proved difficult enough but lending it to a convicted criminal for the purpose of engaging in an act of sedition was a whole other situation. She assured me it would happen, though, and all I had to do was say when.

Making time to bring Terre up to speed took a bit of creativity. There was a lot I needed to update her on, and her natural inquisitiveness would bring a ton of questions. I decided the best way to handle it was to take an afternoon off one Saturday, load the program onto my device and hers, and spend it locked in the bathroom talking it through. That required both my mom and brother leaving the house. A problem for sure, but not an unsolvable one.

The time constraints I faced were real, but I experienced less anxiety over it than I did about asking my friend to steal a ridiculously expensive scientific device for the purposes of overthrowing The Known Order.

Bryn's job was straightforward and technically not illegal, which was the best kind of not illegal. Heck, I could run it past Commander, and it wouldn't ruffle as much as a single feather. In the age of constant connectivity and digital everything it was unusual, to be sure, but if anyone could pull off eccentricity it was Bryn. I needed analog transportation. Untethered from the grid with no GPS or any biometric trackers. It needed to carry three people and have enough range to get from wherever Bryn lived, to my house, to the outskirts of town by Old River Gorge.

When the new moon arrived, I caught an additional break with a rare cloudy night. My geographic location didn't lend itself to many cloudy days, and even fewer cloudy nights, but that evening promised to be overcast with little chance of changing. Commander predicted the weather with remarkable accuracy, as it did with everything else, and called for nothing but clouds until the crack of dawn.

I got dressed into my black outfit, and as I did before, I tied my hair into a tight pony. My black stretch pants didn't have pockets, but I found an old waist pouch that held my portable chargers. At half past two in the morning, setting my location on my device was easy. As far as any digital entity would know, I lay in bed sound asleep. My last update to the program allowed me to set heart rate and body temperature fluctuations as well as spoof speaking and other ambient sounds. I took great pride in the programming, but I felt a slight twinge of regret at the thought that my ultimate plan would fail, and all my work would go to waste.

I slid out my window and dropped to the ground. Before leaving, I grabbed a small gardening stool from the shed and placed it under the window. With my eyes adjusted to the dark, I made out a dark smudge on the pale siding—a remnant of my re-entry from my last outing. I wiped it off with my sleeve, turned, and made my way to the back of my property. I issued one last check of my PMID to ensure it worked. The screen's digital readout gave me the current time, *02:37*, and below the "0" a red dot flashed once every second. I was good to go.

I planned to traverse the backyards and get a feel for moving with both chargers in the pouch around my waist. This preparation could end up unnecessary, but the before The Wars expression "Luck is where preparation meets opportunity" stuck with me. When forging your own path in the world, a skill long lost since the dawn of The Known Order, it benefited one to plan for every possibility.

Fences or other barriers lined a few of the properties, but for the most part there were either small paths, culverts, or other drainage ditches separating each plot. We didn't get a lot of rain—it's hard to when you don't get a lot of clouds—but when we did, it came down in buckets, and every neighborhood had an intricate system of drainage and other exterior plumbing that ran separate from the household sewage. When I did encounter a fence or blocked-off path, I went about the perimeter and then continued in a more or less straight line through the neighborhood.

I went the opposite direction as before since my actual destination on that occasion was unknown and not at all relevant. I needed to get as far away from my house as I could, turn around, and get back before pre-dawn broke the darkness of the night sky. The first twenty minutes passed without incident and my confidence grew. I moved with reasonable agility and speed, trying to stay close to houses and ducking under windows. Motion sensors existed, but they were uncommon, and I couldn't predict with any accuracy if I'd run into any. Besides, small animals like raccoons still wandered about and were known to forage. That was way more likely than a human sneaking around without a PMID. It made me wonder about the man from the other direction down the street. He was adamant that a human lurked in his yard. He spoke to a human from his front steps, not a raccoon. Why did he jump to that conclusion? I didn't have the luxury of time to sort it out and made a mental note instead. I stayed balanced and on the balls of my feet, ready to bolt with as much speed as I could muster should trouble find me or if I found it.

I moved with less caution than I did a month earlier. My confidence grew with every stride, but my eyes scanned my near pitch-black surroundings. I was attentive and on high alert. Every sound, every shadow, every slight movement I caught in my periphery. The motion could be a breeze or a nocturnal bird. Small numbers of owls still existed, albeit in smaller numbers than the raccoons. As I made my way through the backyards of the row of houses on my street, I thought of myself as the owl, but a small seed of doubt in the back of my mind questioned whether that was true and if maybe I wasn't a tiny mouse instead. None of it helped me with the task at hand, and I tried to block out the thoughts to keep my focus on survival in the moment. The rest I would ponder at a safer time.

It was hard to compare the two outings since the first one didn't have a clock for me to track the time. Based on where I ended up, and the fact I was much quicker on the return journey, I knew I'd made significant strides. On this trip, I covered much more ground in a shorter time, even with the paranoia that one battery pack might have come disconnected and left me as far away from my house as possible resulting in the need to run farther and faster to get home before my PMID battery died. It was a silly notion that I tried to not give power to, but in my state of over-preparedness, it was unavoidable. I had to be aware of every potential possibility, no matter how far down the ladder of probability.

I checked the time and saw that I'd been gone for thirty-three minutes and felt more and more like the bird. Time flew and though I was without wings, it gave me the feeling of flight as well. I set a target of sixty minutes to travel out and sixty minutes to travel back along the same route. There wasn't a plan to move quicker in one direction or the other so when I turned around, I should've been at the halfway point. Twenty-six minutes later, I got my bearings. I stood approximately three miles from home, and I was as fresh and alert as I was more than an hour ago when I woke up. I leaned up against the wall of a nondescript house like my own and took stock of my situation. Not a single house along the way had a motion sensor. That surprised me but that was another gift horse I wasn't going to look in the mouth. I saw a raccoon, which was the first time I'd ever seen one in person. It was hard to tell who startled who more, but at least I didn't hiss and then pee myself like the raccoon did when I came around the corner of a fenced-in property.

I turned around to go back, making sure to prepare myself for the twists and turns around the way. There were eleven houses with fences, four with a stone patio and pergola, and more than I could count with additional gardens growing foods that don't need full sun. One house had a pond or water feature that smelled like the pump to circulate the water hadn't worked in a long time. The setup with the pouch holding my portable chargers worked like a charm, and I came up with an idea to secure the power cables next time to eliminate that portion of my anxiety.

With a deep inhale, I turned and at more of a jogging pace, started my way back. I jogged past a couple houses, sprinted for a couple houses, and then strolled for a couple houses, enjoying the freedom, the fresh air, and the fact that for the second time in my life I got to experience life outside my house without anyone or anything monitoring my every move. I didn't have to ask Commander for permission. As far as knew, my excursion from the previous month had zero impact on anyone else in the neighborhood, which added further credence to the idea The Girls and I held since I uncovered those pictures and the spare PMID key tucked away in the stone foundation of the pavilion in the community green space.

As I jogged and then sprinted past the next several houses, I got an idea. When I reduced my speed down to a stroll, I moved items around in the yard. I stacked the deck chairs and moved them to an inconvenient spot. I opened the door to the tool shed and took out a spade and hoe and left them leaning up against the house. Then, in a final act of defiance, I took mud from the garden, and smeared it against the back wall of the house. I wrote a single word: PERSIST.

I wiped my hands on my pants and continued my journey back home. Every few minutes, I stopped and took a short break. If my little stunt ended up causing my undoing, I wanted to at least enjoy one last breath of freedom. With everything at stake, I felt a twinge of guilt over giving into my impulse, but if it did cause my world to collapse, it was still worth it. Nothing terrible happened and nothing would, and I'd have proof. A mild inconvenience of having to rearrange chairs, put away gardening tools, and wipe mud off a wall hardly qualified as terrible. The world didn't end. There was no slippery slope from a mild inconvenience to becoming a neighborhood terror or violent criminal.

I kicked my butt into high gear and made the rest of my journey home well under the planned two hours. Thankful for the step stool I left underneath my window, I used it to hop through without leaving a mark on my house or making much of a sound. Once safely in my room, I ditched my clothes under the bed and lay under my covers until I felt my heart rate slow. I meditated, and when I'd calmed, with my body temperature back to normal and my breathing slow and steady, I disconnected the battery packs, and with as little movement as possible tapped the disable code for my program into my PMID. From

Commander's point of view, I'd shifted in my sleep and had otherwise been in bed since ten o'clock the night before.

I slept well into the next day and awoke to lots of commotion happening in what sounded like our living room. My heart missed a beat, and for a moment I held my breath as I half expected CCC Follis and a team of other Association henchmen to kick down my door and haul me away to confinement, back to the void for an extended period of time. I listened with rapt intent and realized after a moment that the ruckus came from my brother, and he didn't sound scared or upset, but rather excited. I rolled out of bed and tossed on random clothes from a pile in the corner of my room. With tentativeness in my gait, I shuffled my way down the hall, around the corner, and into the main living room of the house. My brother sat frozen in front of the holovision where two Media talking heads—literally two semi-sentient artificial intelligence holographs—spoke about "the grandest display of public disorder in half a century" and "a gross violation of The Known Order punishable by a year in solitary, if not longer."

Chadwick saw me walk into the room and waved me over. "Katie, come check this out." He shuffled over on the couch to give me room to sit down.

"What happened? Is there another war coming?"

"For one person, at least. Look! And it happened a couple miles from here. Practically around the corner. Mom says she knows the family that lives in that house."

The holovision displayed a family of four, the ever-popular mom, dad, girl, boy configuration not unlike my our own, standing in their backyard. The mother wept. The children stood with their arms folded looking like they'd rather be anywhere else. The father, perhaps after realizing that his wife was in no condition to give an interview, fumbled his way through what happened.

"… *as I said before, my wife came out to tend to the garden and needed my spade to turn over the soil to get a late crop into the ground. We had a bit of a failure with the carrots, and a portion of our garden needed attention. You know how it is, right? You do everything you're supposed to and nothing happens. Bad seeds, the wrong sunshine and water mix, whatever it is.*"

The interviewer looked as frustrated as the mother looked hysterical, but the man blundered on.

"Anyway, she goes around back and—Honey? It would be better if you could tell this part. Are you able?" She blew her nose into a handkerchief and shook her head. Her husband uttered a short *harrumph* in protest but continued on with the story as he knew it. *"She goes around back and notices the chairs stacked in a neat pile in the corner of the patio. We always keep the chairs out and facing each other in a sort of diamond pattern so people can sit face-to-face, you know? She thought maybe I'd done it in preparation for cleaning the patio or reorganizing of the backyard or whatever. Then, she looks over at the tool shed and sees the spade and rake sitting out leaning against the side wall. Another family member could have left it out, of course, and that possibility crossed her mind but when she turned around and saw how this deviant vandalized the back of our house, I knew all this was the work of a deranged lunatic, and probably related to that convicted criminal living a couple miles over. Should've kept her locked up is what I say."*

The camera panned to the left to show the crudely written word I put on the house six hours earlier. I could see why the woman was upset. In the daylight, even though I wrote it in mud, it looked vaguely like dried blood on the house siding. The word itself had more positive connotations than not, but when styled to look like it was written in a murderous rage, perception changed. It never occurred to me to consider font and kerning when performing my small act of rebellion. I looked down at my hands. There was dirt under my fingernails. It wasn't much, but if you were looking for it, it stood out like a sore thumb.

"Katie, they think you did it. But how's that possible? You're monitored twenty-four-seven and can't leave the property."

I broke my trance-like gaze from my hands and put them behind my back like a soldier standing at ease. "I—I—have no idea, Chaddy. Where's Mom?"

"She went out back to see if anything is missing from the shed or smeared on the house. Pretty sure every person within a five-mile radius of the Fratellis' is checking their sheds and houses this morning."

"Yeah, I bet." I gave my head a shake. "Are they saying anything else or is it the same loop of useless interviewing?"

"Same stuff. Talking head tells us about the atrocity, interview hysterical mom, confused dad, apathetic teenagers, show the vandalism which was written one-hundred-percent-no-doubt-about-it in a murderous rage, repeat."

"Figures." I patted my brother on the shoulder as I made my way toward the front door. As my hand reached out for the handle, it swung open, and missed whacking me in the head by a hair's breadth. I jumped back to avoid contact as well as to let my mother in.

"Oh, I…I didn't know you were there. Sorry about that."

"No harm done. Did you see anything out back?"

"Not that I could notice. Certainly nothing written on the siding, but I don't go back there much. Tending the garden and using the back patio for fresh air is more your activity, or at least was since we got you back."

"I'll go take a look." I squeezed past my mom and gave her a token peck on the cheek as I passed by.

To keep up the appearance, I gave the shed a cursory check and wandered aimlessly around the patio and property perimeter in case any of the neighbors had their eyes on me, which I was sure they did. On both sides, I saw the flutter of a curtain as I turned around. I walked along the edges of the property, careful to stay a foot inside the boundary so my device wouldn't think I was making a run for it. As I worked my way back to the house, I glanced under my bedroom window. The gardening stool wasn't there. I kept my walking pace casual and finished my reconnaissance of our yard and worked my way back to the shed. I examined the contents. A wheelbarrow full of dirt and several garden implements hung from hooks on the wall or thrown slipshod into a crate sat in the corner. Inside the door, to the right and on the floor, tucked into the corner, was the garden stool.

I closed the shed door and went back inside. My mother was in the kitchen preparing lunch. "Everything where it should be, honey?"

"Yeah, it's all squared away." I made eye contact and held it. My mother's eyes glistened with unshed tears.

While looking at me, she barked a command at my brother to turn off the holovision and get ready for lunch. He protested as only a pre-teen boy could and whined, "Why are we eating so early?"

"Because we're taking a trip today. Pack a bag, too. We'll be spending the night." I swallowed and I saw that she struggled to keep her emotions in check. "I" —her voice cracked. "I hope you understand, dear. We can't be here with all the commotion going on. It's not good for Chaddy."

A lump formed in my throat. "I know."

"I love you." She wrapped her arms around me and gave a tight squeeze.

"I love you too, Mom."

"Tell me it's going to be okay."

"It's going to be okay," I lied.

OOOO1111 [Fifteen]

My latest program wasn't finished. To do this, I wouldn't have time to test it, and I could have used my mother's expertise. I would have to try it on my own and see what happened. Failure was an option. I had a Plan B, but it was the backup plan for a reason, a massive reason, for if it failed as well, I had no Plan C.

When I last spoke to Melissa, we set up a code phrase. If I wanted her to bring me the device from the lab I would message: *"How long did it take to write your last exam?"* If she replied with a specific number of hours which represented the amount of time she needed to procure the items, I would then reply with the number of hours before I needed it with: *"I'm pretty sure my next one will take me eight hours. LOL!"* If Melissa found she couldn't get into the lab and borrow the equipment I needed then she'd write: *"Haven't written it yet but I have something due on—"* whatever date and time she thought worked best, and the plan changed from there. I sent my friend the first coded message and waited.

I didn't have to wait long. Melissa replied seconds after the message read indicator lit up. *Ugh, like, 2 hours. Maybe a bit longer.* My heart pounded in my chest. It would happen. Tonight. Sooner than I expected, but with the neighbors freaking out and casting blame, rightly but unknowingly so, and my mother giving me the green light and leaving the house with Chadwick, it was time. I replied to Melissa: *I'm pretty sure my next one will take me 16 hours. LOL!* Mel's responded with an *"LOL"* with a thumbs-up emoji.

Next, I needed to square away transportation with Bryn. Rather than kick the chip loose on my 3D printer, I straight up submitted an immediate service request. Half an hour later, she showed with her work tablet and her fix-it bag filled with every tool or repair part she would ever need. I didn't ask, but I assumed that there were more parts for various other devices out in the service vehicle.

Bryndolin didn't need to knock. I met her at the door and opened it wide for her to march through with her gear. I had a big smile on my face. "What's up, chicken butt?"

"Is today terrible rhyme day? No one told me."

"Why so serious? You're acting mysterious."

She shook her head and closed the door behind her. "You're weird, you know that?"

"Yup. I get told that on the regular."

"Okay, so at least you're self-aware."

I flashed a smile that I hoped indicated playfulness. "Suivez moi."

"Huh?"

"Follow me." I led her to the office where I had already removed the case from the printer. "I think the office console is flaky as well."

Bryn called out her service request authorization for the console and after receiving the go-ahead, unplugged it, opened the bottom, and slid out the backup battery. She gave me a slight nod of her head. We attached our portable power chargers to our PMIDs and tapped in the code to start the spoofing program. We each double-checked to make sure it worked before speaking and stood close together so we wouldn't have to converse too loudly. I broke the silence first.

"I need the off-the-grid vehicle tonight. Three in the morning. It needs to carry the two of us plus one more."

"Who's the third?"

"Melissa. She's bringing me the key hardware I'm going to need."

"You think it's going to work? I mean, has anyone tried this before?"

"I think it *could* work, but if it doesn't Plan B *should* work. As for anyone trying it before, no, as far as I could find out, no one's attempted it."

"And that doesn't concern you?"

I shrugged. "Not particularly. I learned a lot about how computers and AI work from my mom, researched more than I ever thought possible, and happen to have a natural knack for writing code. I think no one's tried it before because for however many hundreds of years no one thought they needed to, or if they did, they either didn't have the aptitude for trying or didn't have the access."

"And you have both."

"I do. Not to get too big a head about it or anything, but yeah, I do."

"So, it's happening. Tonight."

"Tonight. Can you help?"

"Of course, I can. Since you mentioned it to me last time, I've been working on it nonstop."

"Will it work?"

She put her hands on her hips and pursed her lips. "I'm not going to dignify that with a response."

"Geez, Louise, calm your tits. I'm more than a little paranoid. One mistake and we're all screwed."

"I know." She stepped forward and wrapped her arms around me and gave a big squeeze. "It'll be okay. You got this."

I squeezed her back and held her there in silence for a moment. "We should get back online and let you out of here to not raise any suspicions."

Bryn broke the embrace and put her hands on my shoulders. "One last question."

"Sure."

"Was that you who did the graffiti a couple miles over?" She pointed in the direction of the house I vandalized. "I mean, I have no idea who else it could be, unless it was one of their idiot kids looking for attention."

"Yeah, that was me."

"Why'd you do it?"

"I was testing a theory."

"And?"

"I was right to a degree but underestimated how much it would upset that lady. I suspect had the husband found it he would have washed it off and that would have been that, but his wife—" I whistled and then in my best Southern accent finished with, "Boy howdy, I do declare she had a serious case of the vapors."

Bryn laughed. "Without a doubt, my dear. Without a doubt."

I stepped back and huddled over the 3D printer, turned my head to look at her again, and raised my finger to my device screen. I nodded and we punched in the program disabling codes in sync. "Okay, I've studied your design, and it looks like if you bypass the subroutine transistor and introduce a weak magnetic field to the calibration arm, you'll be good to go."

"Thanks, Technician Cole. What about my console?"

"It looks fine. I'll get it back working for you in a second." She reassembled the printer and then the console. "I'll see myself out. Good work on the printer program, I have every confidence it will work." She winked.

"Thanks, me too."

I watched Bryn leave and sat back down at my disconnected tablet to crunch numbers and upload one more program to my PMID. I knew how to integrate the device to accept external input and pass it through the interface to Commander, but it was untested code and came with a good amount of risk. The simulator I got from Melissa and that my mother helped me configure a while back worked, but it wasn't the same as a physical apparatus. Before the sun rose the next morning I'd know, but until then it was out of my hands.

With the program uploaded to my device and everything otherwise squared away, I checked the time and determined that rest was in order. I lay down on my bed, set an alarm for three hours later, and much to my surprise fell asleep without any problem at all.

I was out cold when the alarm chimed with the song I composed in isolation, and I let out an audible gasp when it jarred me awake. I lay in bed, put my knees up, and wiggled my fingers and toes while staring at the ceiling and blinked. I learned this trick from my online holovision yoga instructor, Mike Chapman, and it worked to bring myself back to the land of the living. There were still several hours to kill before I had to make my way out my bedroom window and to my driveway and I needed to eat, so I got up and went into the kitchen to prepare a meal.

It was delectable, gourmet eating. A vegetarian burger with greens picked fresh from the garden and a cob of corn right off the stalk. With everything cleaned up, I sat on the couch and turned on the holovision to watch mind-numbing shows while I charged up my portable power packs and PMID.

Time passed at a glacial pace. I felt like it stopped altogether. If it wasn't for the seconds ticking away in the bottom corner of my wrist device, I would have sworn it hadn't changed in minutes. Restlessness set in. I got up and paced around the living room, and then the rest of the house, and then the perimeter of our property. The anxiety bubbled up from my stomach into my chest and gripped me like a fall into a bathtub of ice water. I went back inside and turned off the holovision. With a couch cushion in the center of the floor, I sat down, crossed my legs into the lotus position, closed my eyes, and took long, slow, deep breaths.

I inhaled for a count of six, saying out loud, "Be better, not perfect." I exhaled for another count of six and spoke the words again, "Be better, not perfect." After more than two hours of meditation, I managed to reach an acceptable level of calm though my internal clock told me the hour of three inched closer and closer. I opened my eyes and checked the time. Two forty-five in the morning. The pillow bounced off the couch after I removed it from under my butt and chucked it across the room. I left it there and went to the bedroom to get dressed. As I pulled on my shirt, I heard *"psst"* coming from outside under my window.

I poked my head out, and Melissa stood with her arms outstretched to the side, her body forming the letter "T" with a tiny smiling head on top. In each of her hands, she held a headband. The bands looked metallic blue in color, but the poor lighting made it hard to tell. About an inch wide and a quarter of an inch thick, they weren't full circles but instead had a gap at the front, stopping at the temples. Each end had on it a circular light, which from pictures and holovision presentations, I'd seen illuminated yellow during the preparation phase, then red when transfer occurred, and then green when transfer completed.

I looked down at my smiling friend, standing tall and proud after committing no fewer than half a dozen violations of The Known Order. She wasn't wearing her PMID.

"Mel, where's your PMID?"

"I didn't want it to track my location, so I left it at home plugged into a portable charger which I got at your recommendation."

"I had a way to solve that problem, but no matter, this'll work too, provided we don't take more than a couple hours to make this happen."

"You sure? I can go back."

"No, that's fine. It's not out of the question this all goes to hell, and we're screwed regardless. It'll work, though." I paused and cocked my head to one side. "Wait, how'd you get here then? Any vehicle you have access to has a tracker in it."

"I walked."

"You walked?"

"Yup."

"With two of the most expensive pieces of stolen lab equipment in the Zone?"

"Yup."

"And you weren't followed? No one saw you?"

"Nope." She flashed me a big toothy grin.

"You've got guts, girl, I'll give you that much. I'm finishing up getting dressed. I'll be out in a second."

I finished all my preparations insomuch as my clothing was concerned. I put on my waist pouch and dropped the two portable chargers inside, connected together to provide maximum charge. I tapped my PMID screen a few times and fixed the end of the charging cable to the underside of my wrist device. As far as Commander, CCC Follis, Hadewijch, and The Association were concerned, I was in my bed fast asleep, same as Melissa, and if all went as planned, same as Bryndolin. With everything prepared, I turned out my bedroom light and hopped out the window.

Hanging off the sill by one hand, I slid the window closed. I wasn't sure why that was important to me, but I did it anyway and then let go and dropped to the ground. I exchanged a hug with Mel, and we walked around to the front of the house and sat on the front stoop to wait for Bryn.

At three o'clock on the dot, a small black vehicle rolled into the driveway barely making a sound. It looked like an old model hover car, but there was no top and it had wheels. We got up off the stoop and stood beside the car. Melissa's mouth looked like it tried to form words, but nothing came out. I shared her shocked feeling but managed to speak.

"It doesn't hover."

Bryn smiled. "Nope."

"It doesn't drive itself either."

"Nope. I have to steer it and control the speed and stop it and everything."

"What makes it go?"

Melissa walked around the car and ran her fingers along the sleek, practically seamless exterior. There were no doors, and nothing gave any indication how it worked.

"Battery. A big one. It's buried under the front of the car. It powers an axle that connects to this steering column as well as the wheels. There are two pedals on the floor. One makes it go faster and one makes it slow down. It's a before The Wars design. It's virtually silent except for a soft hum of the wheels when you bring it to a certain speed."

"And you built this?"

"Yup, in my garage. Let me tell you, the wheels were a challenge, but I got them."

"Where?"

"Probably best if you don't know."

"I'm not sure it's going to matter in an hour."

"Fair enough, but I'd prefer to leave them out of it, you know?"

"Seems reasonable."

"Okay, you and your silent partner here hop in the back and lay low. I'll cover you with this blanket. There's not a lot of room, so don't be shy. I can have us out to the gorge in no time."

We hopped in and crouched down in the back. It was tight, but we fit, and Bryn draped a blanket over top of us. We each grabbed onto a corner so it wouldn't blow away. A few seconds later we were moving.

The ride out to the gorge took about half an hour and it wasn't smooth. We were accustomed to floating on air or in a magnetic field, not bumbling along on roads designed for hover craft. When they arrived at the destination, Bryn stopped the car, and everyone hopped out. It took a few seconds for me and Mel to stretch out, but otherwise we were no worse for wear from the journey.

Bryn spoke first, "So, now what?"

"Now, my dear Bryndolin, I put these lovely headbands to work. I should let you know that if it doesn't work, I'm only going to have a short amount of time to revert to Plan B."

"What's Plan B?"

"I'll let you know if you need to know, but not sooner."

Bryn folded her arms across her chest and muttered unintelligibly.

"Mel, the headbands please." She handed them to me.

I put the one on my head, ends on the temples and the rear at the base of the back of my head. I tapped the power button and winced as the band tightened against my head. I uttered a faint "ouch" as the electrodes broke the skin.

"Here's the fun part, my friends. I need to interface the other headband with my PMID. To do this, I need to break the connection with the power charger to hardwire the band to the wrist device. I can still run my location spoofing program, but with it and the new program I loaded to interface with the band, I don't have much time before the wristband battery dwindles."

Mel spoke for the first time since Bryn pulled into the driveway with her weird-looking car. "Then what?"

"That all depends on if this works or not."

"What are the chances of that happening? Give me the odds."

"I never give odds. It's either going to work or it isn't." I turned on the other headband and plugged one portable charger into it. The other end tucked under my wristband which operated under its own power now. The charger worked exclusively as a conduit between the headband and my PMID. I tapped the screen a couple times and took a deep breath. My head hurt from the band attached to it, and my heart pounded in my chest. My breathing was shallow. I pressed the temple part of the headband and winced again as I felt the electrodes surge to life. Out of my peripheral vision, I saw a yellow glow. I pressed the temple pieces of the other headband attached to my wrist device, and they glowed yellow as well.

"Here we go."

The lights on the bands turned red, and my head snapped back like I'd been hit with an uppercut. Both Bryn and Melissa stepped forward, but I held my arms out, one hand holding the band and the other clutched into a white-knuckled fist. I tried to close my eyes, but I couldn't, and I fought to keep them from rolling back. My subconscious accessed Commander, but it wouldn't let me in. Not completely at least. Overwhelmed with information, I fought to get my bearings. Bits and pieces of data stood out from the rest, but there was no rhyme or reason to it. No organization.

"I can't find it."

Melissa held my free hand. "Find what?"

"Commander's operating instructions. I know it's not pure AI, and I can get that much from what I see, but it won't let me see the parts that aren't its own."

"If it's preventing you from seeing it, then it knows you're trying to access forbidden files. The Association is on its way."

"It's on its way to where it thinks I am, which is about as far across town the opposite direction from here." I winced again.

"How long before they figure it out?"

"Any second now."

"So, now what?"

"Plan B." I tapped the temple lights and they shut off. The lights on the one in my hand turned from red to yellow.

"For the last time, what's Plan B?"

I looked over at Bryn and then back to Melissa who started to cry.

"I go all the way in and don't come back."

"No." Melissa screamed and tried to grab the headband out of my hand, but Bryn held her back. Melissa struggled but was no match for her. "No. I won't let you do it. What if that doesn't work? You'll be gone in every sense of the word, and it'll all be for nothing."

I put my hands on her cheeks and looked her in the eyes. "It won't be for nothing, I promise. Terre has everything needed to continue on."

"No. I won't let you—"

"You have no choice. Clock's ticking, my friend. If you don't want to watch, go back to the car, or whatever that deathtrap of a vehicle is and hide under the blanket."

She sniffled, turned, and ran back to the car.

Bryn stepped in front of me and wiped a tear off my cheek. "You're warm."

"I'm scared."

"What do you need me to do?"

"Make sure I hit the ground."

"I don't want to do that."

"You don't have a choice. Why do you think I picked the gorge? It's a long way down. Reanimation exists, but only if there's a shadow of consciousness left in the brain, and after this, there won't be. They will reanimate me for the sole purpose of making an example. You know this. I know this. We need to make sure that doesn't happen. Would you rather bludgeon my head with a rock?"

"Not particularly."

"Then make sure I hit the ground."

"How will we know if it worked?"

"You won't go to confinement."

"What about your family, all your friends?"

"I'm either going to be right, or it's not going to be my problem anymore."

"Harsh."

I shrugged and tapped the lights on the temples of my headband. The yellow glow illuminated Bryn's face with a sickly jaundiced glow. I tapped my PMID a few times. "This has a better chance of working. Inherited Consciousness is less experimental than anything involving the Shared Subconscious."

"I know."

"I know you know." I paused. "Once the lights go red, hold me to keep me from falling. Once the lights on the band go green, I'll be gone, and you can let go. Tell Melissa I'm sorry she won't get the bands back."

"I'll tell her." She looked at me with tears in her eyes and cupped my cheeks with her hands. "I'm so glad you were the one who found my pictures."

Her words echoed in what was left of my mind, bouncing around like a rubber ball in a closed box. "I'm sorry, what?"

"I'm glad you were the one who found the pictures I drew and the key I hid."

I weakened, physically and mentally, but clung to my few remaining faculties. "That was you? How? Why?"

She let out a soft chuckle. "I don't have near enough time to explain. Let's just say that the world needed to burn. I had the fuel but not the spark."

"It might not be enough."

"It's enough. You are enough."

The yellowish reflection on her face turned a fiery shade of red. I closed my eyes and Bryn put her hands under my arms. The last memory of my short time walking the Earth was the soft touch of her lips on mine.

It was my first, and last, kiss.

0001000 0
[Sixteen]

"Okay, class, settle down." Ms. Nowak didn't possess a commanding presence, but the small collection of sixth graders respected her, and they all settled quickly and without incident. "Today, we are going to continue our march backward in history." Most of the kids sat up in their chairs and a couple of groans emanated from the back row. "Who would like to provide a summary of the most recent era?"

Duncan, a goofball of a kid, with a serious case of prosopagnosia and a knack for never realizing he was usually the smartest kid in the room, shot up his hand. "The modern era is also known as the time of Exceptional Growth."

"And what does that mean?"

"It means we have moved beyond the era that came before it, the time of home—homeio—homeostatics."

"Homeostasis."

"Yeah, that. It means society is on its way to a new destination. Innovation is back and driving us forward. We've gone past the 'new normal' and work to build a bigger, better normal for those that will come after us."

"Excellent summary, Duncan. Thank you. Who wants to summarize the era that preceded Exceptional Growth?"

Know-it-all Serena sat ramrod straight and raised her hand with near military precision. "The era that preceded Exceptional Growth was Homeostasis." She perfectly annunciated the last word and made sure to add some emphasis as she glanced over her shoulder at Duncan.

He rolled his eyes and discretely showed her his middle finger.

She continued, "Homeostasis is where humanity reached and maintained a prolonged period of stability. Confusion no longer reigned. Life was adequate, comfortable, and people were free. The world had healed, but the scars still remained."

"Thank you, Serena. Now apologize to Duncan for your sass."

She turned around to face him. "Sorry, Duncan."

"Now, Duncan, your turn."

"What?"

"You know what."

"You saw that?"

"PMIDs and active listening consoles may be an intrusion of the past, but teachers still see and hear *everything*."

He sighed. "Sorry, Serena."

"Good. Now, who would like to summarize the era preceding Homeostasis?"

Andie, a quiet girl, pale as a ghost with jet-black hair that hung in front of her face, spoke without raising her hand. "That was the period of the Known Disorder. Chaos and confusion ruled the world like the great dinosaurs of the Time Before Humanity."

Ms. Nowak liked Andie but always wondered if she didn't enjoy dark subjects a little too much. "And why was there such chaos and confusion?"

She paused. "Everyone was used to everything being known, orderly, and approved and in an instant that changed. Katherine Webb short-circuited Commander, only she didn't just short-circuit it, she completely redesigned it from the inside out. People didn't know what to do. Like, imagine a bunch of kids who were used to having their meals made for them by an adult or a replicator suddenly having to make their own. It would be a mess."

Ms. Nowak let out a soft chuckle. "Yeah, that's one way to put it. Thank you. Now that we're all caught up, we're going to learn about what precipitated the change from The Known Order to the Known Disorder. Andie touched on it when she mentioned Katherine Webb and Commander. I had a lesson planned, but maybe this story is best heard straight from the source. Do you want me to change the lesson plan?"

The class cheered, "Yes!" More or less in unison.

"Okay then, let's do it. Mercury, tell us the story of how you came to be."

A soft voice floated out of the console sitting on the front edge of the teacher's desk.

It would be an honor, Ms. Nowak.

My name was Katherine Webb.

THE END

00010001
[Hidden Figures]

Several Easter eggs or other goodies appear in the book you just finished. Some might be more obvious than others, and for some, you'd have no way of knowing but might have been curious about anyway. With that in mind, here are some behind-the-scenes tidbits you might enjoy.

The idea for this book came to me while watching my children play in the lobby of the Great Wolf Lodge in Niagara, Ontario. Fitbits were all the rage then. As I checked my steps, I heard a staff member start barking orders to people so they could make room for children to sit in front of the creepy animatronic tree and woodland creatures for story time. My daughter, Avery, who was four years older than her brother, AJ, explained to him what was going on. "Should we do what he says?" he asked her. "No, we're not in the way. We can keep coloring." Katherine and Chadwick's personalities were modeled (at least a bit) on my daughter and son, to whom this book is dedicated.

Katherine Webb's name is a combination of Katherine Johnson (NASA mathematician) and James Webb (NASA administrator for whom the telescope is named).

Carlton Sedgwick is the last names of my favorite high school teachers, Mr. Carlton (calculus) and Mr. Sedgwick (physics), put together to make one name. Mr. Sedgwick is the reason I went on to study applied physics at the University of Waterloo.

Chadwick was named after Chadwick Boseman.

Terre was named after a friend of mine who's super tech savvy, super resourceful, super feminist, super activist, and a super loyal friend. Naturally, she needed to be Katherine's bestie in the book.

Eunice and Bryn are my daughter's friends.

Melissa is named after my dearly departed friend Alex's wife.

Caillou is so named because no one likes that whiny cartoon character, and I wanted an unlikable name for her character in the book.

Oswald Webb, Katherine's father, is named for my daughter's friend

Ozzy.

CCC Aalto's name was taken from writer A.J. Aalto. You should read her books.

Hadewijch is the name of a former colleague of mine. I liked the name so much I had to use it in a book.

CCC Follis's name is taken from a friend of mine from university. His first name, Elwood, was taken from the character in The Blues Brothers, played by Canadian actor Dan Aykroyd.

In the book, Katherine reads *The Scattering Winds* by Gordon Bonnet. Gordon is a very close and dear friend of mine, and he references *Known Order Girls* in *The Scattering Winds*. I also mention another one of his books. You should check out his stuff. It's really good.

"Nevertheless, she persisted" refers to the incident in 2017 where Senator Elizabeth Warren was silenced during a confirmation hearing in an alleged violation of a Senate rule. After the vote, Senator Mitch McConnell said, "Senator Warren was giving a lengthy speech. She had appeared to violate the rule. She was warned. She was given an explanation. Nevertheless, she persisted." The phrase was immediately adopted by the feminist movement along with hashtags #Shepersisted and #LetLizspeak.

The figurine and the phrase "I dissent" directly reference former U.S. Supreme Court Justice Ruth Bader Ginsberg.

I took the micrography idea from Carol Bloomgarden's work as an artist, from whom I bought a t-shirt with Ruth Bader Ginsberg's silhouette done in micrography.

OOOIOOIO
[Acknowledgements]

Thank you to my children for inspiring the opening scene of Chapter One and continuing to question authority and carve their path in the world.

I also want to thank my wife for her endless patience and support. She's smart as hell and tolerates me even when I'm at my most annoying. Sharing time and space with her is a true joy.

I owe my invaluable writing colleagues and beta readers a debt of gratitude. This book would not be the same without your keen eyes and objective criticism. I will rest easy if reading this book brought you even a fraction of my enjoyment when writing it. Yes, a sequel is in the works. No, I don't know when I will finish it. Yes, there will be a third book to close out the trilogy. No, I don't know when that will happen either. See the previous paragraph about endless patience.

Gari Strawn edited what can only be described as a grammarless hellscape and made it into something readable. If you need an editor, I can't recommend her highly enough. Any problems you found along the way rest squarely on my shoulders.

Robert Chazz Chute has a keen eye for cover design and was the catalyst for switching from the original cover to this one, and my designer, Linda Ryan, worked her magic, as she always does.

This book wouldn't exist without my brudder from another mudder, Gordon Bonnet. He read the first draft, with all its warts, and saw that it was good. His annoying, relentless demands that I get this book out into the world eventually paid dividends. It took a couple of years, but here we are. Thank you, Gordon, for believing in me and not letting me put this book in a drawer and forget about it.

Lastly, it's with profound sadness that I remember Alex Kimmell. When, at the insistence of Gordon, I blew the dust off Known Order Girls, I opened my book bible for the project. Under the heading "Beta Readers" was Alex's name. Before I'd even finished the first draft, he told me he wanted to be one of the first to read it. Alas, he shuffled off this mortal coil before I could make that happen. I am sure he would have loved it. His memory is not just a blessing; it is a treasure I hold dear.

00010011
[About The Author]

Andrew Butters is a married father of two living in New Brunswick, Canada and he will tell you that his first published work was *Losing Vern* as part of the *Orange Karen: A Tribute to a Warrior* anthology. In reality, it was a 500-word anecdote about the time he lit himself on fire. That story made it into the third installment of the *Darwin Awards* books.

Not all his distinctions are as dubious as appearing in a Darwin Awards book. There was the time he participated in a trick on stage with Penn & Teller. He had a solid minute of screen time on the Super Dave Osborne Show. He scored a game-winning goal at Maple Leaf Gardens and even "sold" music to filmmaker Kevin Smith. He was also given a whole three seconds of non-speaking airtime in a TV commercial, and don't forget when he appeared as a fighting homeless man in a rap video.

He writes, creates, snacks, blogs, toils over his next book, makes videos, is a huge fan of golf, science, equality, and the Oxford comma. Andrew sometimes lets his love of attention override common sense. You can find evidence of this pretty much anywhere you find Andrew.

Website: potatochipmath.com

Facebook: AuthorAndrewButters

Bluesky: andrewbutters.bsky.social

Substack: authorandrewbutters.substack.com